DARK THINGS II

A HORROR ANTHOLOGY

Edited by Ty Schwamberger

ISBN: 978-1-61706-044-1

Printed in the USA by
Pill Hill Press
Cover design by Jessy Marie Roberts
First Printing October 2010

1 2 3 4 5 6 7 8 9 10

DARK THINGS II

A HORROR ANTHOLOGY

Edited by Ty Schwamberger

Pill Hill Press

Chadron, Nebraska

TABLE OF CONTENTS

YOU'RE GONNA DIE
by Derek Muk

MARY BETH sat on the bed and looked at the clock on the nightstand: 4:10PM.

She watched as the seconds quickly ticked by, watched as the minute hand moved forward another notch. She sat there staring at the precise, steady motions of the clock hands until her eyes started to blur and grow tired, until the rhythm of the ticking and her heartbeat were one.

She then got up and started pacing the small room anxiously, clasping her hands together. She stopped for a second and studied a cross that hung on the wall, a hopeful look on her brown-skinned face. Her big brown eyes next gazed at a sculpture of Jesus on her dresser bureau.

She knelt before the cross and prayed for a moment before walking over to the window. Outside, a light rain was falling gently from the gray skies. The streets below were quiet and deserted on this late October afternoon. Across the street was an empty parking lot and next to that was a drug store that displayed Halloween masks and plastic jack-o'-lanterns behind its windows. Further down the block was another run-down hotel, and beyond that were some boarded up storefronts.

Turning away from the window, she studied the small hotel room once more, looking at the walls of peeling white paint, at the cheesy painting of a hobo sitting on a train that came with the unit and at the cheap, plastic dining table and chairs.

Her dark eyes then moved to the open suitcase lying next to the bed and at the few pieces of clothing that hung from the closet rack. The suitcase and two bags had carried her entire existence for the past couple of weeks and now she was hoping to settle down and find some meaning and purpose to her life. But something was holding her back. She didn't feel at home quite yet: there was still

1

that feeling of being at a 'temporary' spot or lost in limbo, as she often liked to describe it.

She looked at the suitcase again, sighing. *Let's worry about that later*, she thought. She shrugged into her matching black sweater and skirt, black stockings, polished black shoes, and her nun's black and white veil. Lastly, she grabbed an umbrella and left.

***

She walked the quiet, rain-slicked streets of downtown Reno; a young, slender woman of twenty-four years of age. She was a woman that felt that she didn't have any purpose in her life, who wanted to be challenged, and who wanted to make a difference in the lives of others. The light rain was getting her stockings a little wet but she kept walking. When she had the right of way at the crosswalk and a motorist cut her off and sped away, she didn't look at the driver. She kept walking. When an aggressive panhandler cursed at her and called her a racial slur for not giving him change, she kept walking.

Walking past some of the casinos, she peeked through the windows, but showed no interest. She heard the sound of coins clanging down into a tray from a slot machine as she strolled past Harrah's. Crossing the street, she went down a block to the bus station. As the rain got heavier, she sat down on a bench inside the sparsely populated station. It reminded her of the Greyhound bus depot not too far away, with its few snack and soda machines, bus schedules posted behind glass, and the usual assortment of drifters and transients loitering around.

A man with disheveled, greasy hair wearing a camouflage jacket and ragged jeans approached her and asked for change, but she politely told the man she didn't have any. He mumbled something incoherent, and then limped away. A woman pushing a shopping cart full of bags of aluminum cans kept talking to herself as passed by Mary Beth.

Mary Beth noticed that a skinny Latino man with a thin mustache and a pockmarked face kept looking at her. He stood leaning against the wall near the door. She pulled her skirt down more, covering her knees. When the man didn't stop looking, she moved to another bench on the other side of the room. A few minutes later, she looked over her shoulder and saw that the man was still watching her.

Her bus arrived momentarily and she boarded it. As she was sitting in a seat in the middle, she saw the skinny Latino man step on board and proceed to the back. As he passed her, he gave her a look, and she turned away immediately.

About thirty-five minutes later, she got off on Belvedere Avenue, noticing that the man hadn't followed her. She felt immense relief as she walked the two blocks to St. Michael's Catholic Church. The skies above were already dark.

Upon arriving at the church, she went straight to the business office. She shook her umbrella free of water and glanced at her watch before knocking on the wooden door. Ten minutes before six.

Several seconds later, the door opened slowly to reveal an elderly man with snow white hair and wearing a pair of glasses. He was dressed all in black and had a white collar around his neck.

He smiled pleasantly at her and said, "Sister Mary Beth?"

She nodded. "Father Andrews?"

"Yes, that's me. Did you find the church okay?"

"I did."

"Good," he said, leading her to his office. He sat behind a large oak desk, while she situated herself in one of the guest chairs before the desk. He poured her a cup of hot peppermint tea. "Basically, the job description you saw on the Internet sums up the position pretty well. You'd be teaching two classes three days a week, an English class and a history class. The position is part-time with the possibility of becoming full-time in the future. Both classes are comprised of sixth graders and they're well-behaved kids," he said, smiling a little. "You'll also be teaching here in the church classroom."

She sipped some of her tea, nodding.

"Any questions?"

3

DARK THINGS II

"Uhm, no. Sounds very interesting and challenging."

Father Andrews smiled again. "I'm glad you think so." He looked over a sheet of paper. "Seems like you have a fair amount of experience teaching, Sister Mary Beth. What subjects have you taught?"

"English, math, art, and history."

"What do you think you can bring to our school that would make it a better place?"

She put down her cup, thinking a moment. "I think my love of working with kids is one of them. If you talk to my previous employers, they'll tell you that I'm very committed and dedicated to children. I've been a teacher, a mentor, an advocate, a counselor…I have three nieces and one nephew who I have mentored and provided much inspiration and guidance to as well. I also thrive on challenges and new situations." *Did I answer his question?* She said to herself. *Hope that sounded okay.*

He nodded with a smile, looking at the piece of paper once more before putting it down. "Well, we'll be making a decision in the next couple of days, and will let you know the outcome either way. Thanks very much for coming."

***

As was expected, she experienced much anxiety and tension in the following two days about whether she would get the job or not. Much of the time was spent in her room at the Traveler's Hotel, sitting on her bed and staring at the phone and the clock, studying the seconds hand tick by. Stared until her eyes began to blur and grow tired. Sometimes she looked at the phone and wished it would ring, but it didn't. She alternated the gazing with pacing around the room, clasping her hands together. She would stop at the window periodically and watch the empty, vacant streets, seeing transients and drifters pass by every so often. Occasionally, she'd hear a drunken man yelling in the hallway outside.

She prayed often in front of the cross and also finished

4

hanging up the rest of her clothes in the closet. From time to time, she looked at the framed pictures of her nieces and nephew on her dresser bureau, smiling. Walking over to the tiny kitchenette with its yellowing, curling linoleum, she poured herself a glass of water from a bottle and drank it slowly. From the corner of her eyes, she saw a large cockroach crawl quickly across the kitchen countertop. She grabbed a wad of tissue paper and smashed her hand down on the bug, balled up the Kleenex, and tossed it into the garbage can.

It wasn't until the next afternoon that she received the phone call from Father Andrews. She felt her heartbeat grow faster as she waited in suspense about the news.

"Sorry I haven't called you earlier, Sister Mary Beth...we'd like to offer you the position," he said.

"*Yes*," she replied, trying to suppress her excitement. "Thank you so much, Father. Thank you."

"You're quite welcome." She heard him flipping some pages over the phone. "Can you start this coming Monday?"

"Sure."

***

On her way to the bus station, she passed by a group of kids dressed up in Halloween costumes, watching them walk up the steps of a house to ring the doorbell. When she arrived at the station, she saw the same skinny Latino man watching her, leaning against the wall. She immediately moved to another bench.

From her peripheral vision, she noticed him approach slowly. She turned to him when he was about five feet away.

He gave her a hostile look and said something quietly in Spanish.

"I'm sorry," she said.

"You're gonna die," he said in the same low tone of voice.

"What," she asked, her mouth dropping open.

"You heard me," he said, and walked away.

Throughout work that day, she was constantly preoccupied

with thoughts of the man. Who was he? And how dare he have the gall to say something like that to her! Thinking about it more just made her turn red with anger. She told herself to just forget about the whole incident. Heck, she didn't know him; he was an *absolute* nobody to her. But as much as she tried to block him out of her mind, those three words kept echoing eerily in her head: *You're gonna die.*

After her last class that day, she passed by Father Andrews' office and saw him going over some papers inside. She wanted to go in and tell him what had happened, wanted to be consoled through their shared faith. But for some reason, something held her back and she simply left the church.

A few days passed. She didn't see the man again. Breathing a sigh of relief, she was able to teach her classes that morning and afternoon without much anxiety or tension. Maybe it was a just a rare, freak incident, and she would never see the man again. She hoped that was the case.

After her English course, a student named Morris stuck around for some tutorial assistance on an assignment. He was a quiet, soft-spoken dark haired kid who had problems being assertive, but he was well-mannered.

After going over the homework assignment with him in her office, they left the church and walked to the bus stop together. The rain had finally stopped and the streets were starting to dry up.

Sitting on the bus later, Morris turned to her and said, "Sister Mary Beth…thanks for helping me. You're the first person that's done that, and I really appreciate it."

"What about your parents? Do they help you?"

He shook his head, looking away. "No, they're always too busy, or not around. I asked my father to help me with an essay once but he went gambling with his friends instead." He shrugged. "My mom works three jobs and by the time she comes home, she's exhausted."

She nodded solemnly. "Do you have any friends?"

He shook his head again. "Not really. I mean, I talk to some of the other kids in class sometimes, but we don't hang out on the weekend or anything."

"What about brothers or sisters?"

"I don't have any."

"So you're by yourself a lot."

"Yeah."

"Would you like to be more social?"

"I don't know…maybe it would be nice, but I like being alone. I guess I'm used to it."

"What are some of your hobbies?"

He looked out the window for a second. "I like drawing, writing, collecting comic books and *National Geographic*."

"Oh, that's a good magazine. I used to buy it from time to time."

"I like looking at the pictures of different countries and places because I'd like to travel around the world someday and learn about different cultures. I daydream a lot about the places I see in the magazine, about visiting those areas…'cause I don't want to be stuck in Reno for the rest of my life. I feel sorry for my mother. She was born and raised here and has never been outside of Nevada." He looked out the window again. "I think that's sad. All my life I've seen her do nothing but work, work, work. Working at her jobs and working at home. I tell her to take it easy sometimes but she doesn't listen; she says it's all for me. To support me and to have money for me for college…I'll say, 'Mom, slow down. Remember what the doctor said about your back and leg pain.' Sometimes my mother and I will sit together and look through an issue of *National Geographic* and I'd point to her the countries I'd like to go to. I want to show my mom the world but I know she'll never leave this place."

Mary Beth thought for a moment. "I hope you'll be able to achieve your dreams of traveling."

Morris pulled the stop request string and said, "I do, too. Well, see you tomorrow."

***

DARK THINGS II

That night, she called her brother in California, checked in with him briefly, and then spoke with her nephew and nieces. After saying goodbye to her five-year-old nephew, she put the receiver back on the cradle with a smile on her face.

After correcting some essays and papers, she checked her refrigerator and noticed she hardly had any food inside. Frowning, she shrugged into her black sweater and put on her veil before heading out the door.

She went to Gina's Diner, which was located a block away from the hotel, and sat at a booth near the window. There were two couples inside, but the place was mostly frequented by drifter types.

As she tried to enjoy her omelet, she heard an old man sitting at the counter talk to himself all evening. About twenty minutes later, the skinny Latino man with the pockmarked face stepped in and grabbed a stool a few spots down from the old man. Mary Beth felt her heart skip a beat as she looked at the man, moving closer to the window and lowering her head close to her food, hoping he wouldn't be able to see her. So far, he didn't see her yet. He looked around the diner before studying the menu.

She quickly ate the rest of her meal, left some bills on the table, and quietly left the booth. Before she reached the door, the man turned on his stool and gave her a look.

"You're gonna die," he said. "The devil's gonna get you."

Who was he? What did he want?!

She ran back to her room, slammed the deadbolt and chained the door, before jumping into bed and pulling the blanket up over her head.

"Why won't you leave me alone," she said to herself in the darkness.

***

During her lunch break at the church, she saw Father Andrews sitting inside his office again reviewing papers, and wanted to go in

8

and tell him about the man. But once more, she hesitated. Was she afraid of what he would think of her if she told him? I'm not crazy, she thought. *It happened.* Yet her muscles froze and she didn't go in.

She taught her afternoon English class as scheduled, but was terribly preoccupied and anxious with thoughts of the skinny man. Some of her students, including Morris, noticed the change in her behavior, looking at her with concern. She asked Morris to read some passages aloud from one of their textbooks, then gave them their homework assignment and ended class fifteen minutes early.

"Are you okay," Morris asked, after everyone else had left.

She looked at him briefly. "Huh? Uhh…yes."

"You can be honest with me, Sister Mary Beth. What's bothering you?"

She looked at him sympathetically. "I'd rather not talk about it now. But thanks anyway."

He paused for a moment, before asking bluntly, "Do you believe in the devil?"

"Why are you asking me that, Morris?"

"'Cause I can tell he's the one that's probably bugging you. You see, he's been harassing me, too, and following me. I've seen him on the bus, at the mall, in my neighborhood."

Her look became more serious. "What does he look like?"

"He's a thin guy with a mustache."

Mary Beth felt her heart sink, stepping backwards a little.

"Are you all right?"

She didn't respond. Her big brown eyes stared off into space instead. A few moments later, she looked back at him and asked, "What do you know about this man?"

"Well, first of all, he's not a man," Morris explained. "He's *Satan.*"

Mary Beth handed him a cup of hot chocolate and he took a sip of it. She brought a tray of cookies over to where he sat on the love seat in her hotel room. She sat next to him, lacing her fingers around a cup of tea.

"When you say he's the devil, you mean that literally," she

DARK THINGS II

asked.

"Oh, yes. I've seen him shape shift into other people, into animals, even a half goat, half man type creature with horns and hoofs. It definitely sent chills up my spine."

She shook her head. "It just seems so hard to believe...I mean, I thought these are the kind of things one sees in a movie or reads about in a book."

"No, it's very real, Sister Mary Beth."

"Have you told your parents or anyone else?"

He shook his head, sipping some more hot chocolate. "They would've thought I was nuts. And I guess I wouldn't blame them. I don't want them to get involved, especially my mother, 'cause I don't want anything bad to happen to her."

She nodded. "Why has he been bothering *you*?"

"'Cause I know his secret."

"And what's that?"

Morris looked at her for a moment, and then said, "He used to be a part of our church."

She frowned a little. "In what way?"

"Maybe I shouldn't tell you. I don't want him to harm you, too."

She told him about the incidents involving her and the man. "See, I'm in it as well. So you might as well tell me."

"That's because you're new to the school, and he probably thinks you're a threat of some kind. . .no, I'm sorry, Sister Mary Beth, I better not tell you. For your own safety." He took a cookie, nibbling on it.

She looked at him silently, but didn't say anything.

On Saturday afternoon, Mary Beth headed back to St. Michael's. She was off on the weekends but her curiosity got the best of her and she followed her heart. The church was quiet and empty except for Jorge, the janitor, and Father Andrews. She smiled and waved at Jorge, who was dumping a pumpkin into a dumpster, then went inside. Standing five feet from Father Andrews' open office door, she could see him sitting behind his large oak desk,

10

writing on a legal pad. He didn't see her, his ruddy face serious with intent as he kept scribbling notes.

Again, she considered going in and telling him about the skinny man with the mustache but found herself hesitating once more. She felt terribly conflicted about what to do and frustrated at herself for not making a decision. She thought for a moment, then finally came to a verdict and waited outside Father Andrews' office until he was done.

About fifteen minutes passed before he switched off his desk lamp, closing his office door and locking it. He left the church with a briefcase in his hand.

She took out a paper clip and inserted it into the door's keyhole, jiggling it around. Thinking she had it a couple of times, she shook her head when the doorknob wouldn't turn. She was at it for another ten minutes before the tumblers finally aligned themselves and she was able to open the door.

After closing it behind her, she went straight to Andrews's desk and began looking through the drawers. *What was he always writing?* It seemed important. She didn't find the legal pad he wrote on but did come across a black leather journal with a locked clasp on it. She tried to open it with the paper clip but was unsuccessful.

After searching through the other drawers and cabinets and finding nothing unusual, she left quietly with the journal.

***

Sitting on her bed Indian style, she smoothed out her black stockings before attempting to unlock the clasp with another key at first, then a pair of tweezers, then the paper clip again. When all three methods proved fruitless, she cut the clasp's leather band off with a serrated knife.

She flipped through the journal and some loose photos fell into her lap. Some were of Father Andrews by himself, while a few others were of him and the church's staff. Her face froze when she saw the remaining two: they showed the thin man who Morris had called 'the devil.' In one yellowing picture, the man appeared much younger, maybe in his mid to late teens, and without the mustache. He had a big smile on his face, and was dressed in an altar boy's uniform. In the second photo, he was closer to the age she had seen him while at the bus station, that of his mid-thirties. His dark hair was short and neatly trimmed, his mustache like pencil lines.

Mary Beth kept flipping pages quickly until she reached the most recent journal entry, dated yesterday:

I've been thinking about Daniel a lot. I see him in my sleep sometimes. I keep thinking about the sad day his sister discovered his body in his apartment with the bullet in his head. Suicide, the police said. I never meant to hurt him, despite what he claimed. It was all a terrible misunderstanding. . .also, I noticed that I've been followed on a number of occasions, by different people. Once by a street person on my way home, once by a young woman going to St. Michael's, a couple of times by a businessman, and a few times, strangely enough, by a dog. It's odd. I don't know what to make of it.

Mary Beth turned to an older entry, dated May 19, 2000:

It's all a horrible misunderstanding. The media are having a field day with this stuff: priest sexually molested a man when he was a young altar boy. I won't lie. It did happen. But the way Daniel and the press are telling it is wrong. I never forced him into it, he consented. He was young and curious, at an age where boys are adventurous. So we went back to my apartment. There was no violence or physical abuse as they claim. It's scary how they want to rip me apart and throw me to the wolves, anything to sell papers or entertain the public. I'm so sick of it! Maybe I was a little rough with him at certain times, but I had flaws, too. I'm human.

She shook her head disturbingly, taking a deep breath. She flipped back to another early entry, dated June 9, 1983:

I keep thinking about Daniel. Maybe I was wrong in forcing him to do what we did. I've been thinking about it a lot and feeling guilty. Maybe I shouldn't have pushed him too hard. But he didn't resist and seemed interested. It all seems confusing when I look back at it. I can't remember all the details, it was so long ago. Maybe it's

12

better to just forget it.

And one dated July 18, 2000:

Did I drive him to commit suicide? Did all the memories push him over the edge? He needed help. I told him to see that therapist but he wouldn't listen. I feel like it was my fault, I don't know. I don't know.

Mary Beth studied the photos of Daniel again, frowning. She looked at his big smile and her frown got deeper. She looked at the pictures of Father Andrews, shaking her head. Then she closed her eyes to pray for a moment.

***

When class ended, she saw Morris still sitting in the back of the classroom by himself, reading something. She approached him quietly, sitting at a nearby desk.

"What are you reading," she asked.

He flipped the pages of the magazine back to show her the cover. It was an issue of National Geographic. Then he returned to the photos of the skyline of New York City.

"What's your dream vacation?"

He looked up from the magazine, thinking. "That's a tough one…it's going to be a toss-up between Africa, Australia, and England. Where would you like to go?"

"Back to the Philippines, my native country. I miss my relatives."

"Did you grow up there?"

She nodded. "There and the U.S. My family and I moved here when I was fifteen…Morris, have you seen Father Andrews, today?"

"I saw him early this morning and then he left in a hurry. He was upset because someone broke into his office and stole his journal. I saw him questioning the other teachers and Jorge. The police came, too."

"They did," she asked, feeling some butterflies in her

stomach.

"Yeah. Talked to some people." He shrugged. "And that was it."

"Did Father Andrews say where he was going?"

Morris shook his head. "But I overheard him telling one of the police officers that someone had been following him for the past couple of days."

***

She learned from Morris that Father Andrews lived on Collinswood Avenue, about four miles from the church. She got off the bus and walked the three blocks to the small stucco house, buttoning up her black sweater as a cold wind blew past her.

Looking through a window, she saw a reading lamp turned on inside, next to a brown leather recliner. Resting face down on one of the arms of the chair was an open book. A fireplace was near the recliner, with a poker resting on some ashes. She walked to the front door slowly and rang the doorbell. When there was no answer, she pushed the button again, hearing the bell ring from inside.

Silence except for the sound of crickets in the early evening.

She walked up to the window and looked inside but didn't see Father Andrews, or anyone else, for that matter. She started to worry, a frown forming across her brown-skinned face. She tried the doorknob but it was locked. Then she went down the side alleyway of the house to the yard, testing the backdoor knob. It was also locked.

Grabbing a nearby shovel, she gently shattered the glass of the door, reaching in past the shards carefully to unlock it. She wrinkled her nose a few times after stepping in, sniffing the air. Something was burning. She proceeded to the kitchen. Nothing. All the burners on the stove were off. The toaster was unplugged. *Then what was that awful smell?* She covered her nose and mouth with her hands. It sort of smelled like…like burning meat or flesh. Of course, she never smelled human flesh burning, but imagined the odor to be that way. It was a putrid, rotting smell.

She walked further into the house, into the empty living room. Silence. She looked at the book lying on the arm of the recliner, at the stillness of her surroundings. Something definitely didn't *feel* right. She felt around her neck for the chain holding her cross, and when she finally touched the object's sharp points, she breathed a sigh of relief.

"Father Andrews," she queried. When there was no response, she called out his name again.

Suddenly, there was a scream coming from one of the bedrooms. She approached the door cautiously, peering inside. Her jaw dropped open wide when she saw Father Andrews nailed to the wall in a Christ like pose, crucified. Blood ran from the palms of his hands, as well as from his mouth, and parts of his skin had been burned. His snow white hair was matted with blood, his glasses smashed. The black clothes he wore were stained with blood and tattered.

He raised his head and saw Mary Beth at the doorway. He shook his head and said hoarsely, "Get away from here, Sister! Go now! He's here. Go!"

"Who," she asked naively.

The room was dimly lit, and she had a hard time seeing what else was inside. But then she heard something else from within, something that didn't sound or smell human. It smelled like an animal.

When she heard the growl again, she switched on the lights. Jumping back a little, she said, "Oh, my Lord."

It was part man, part goat. Tall, hairy, with horns and hoofs. Its dark eyes were evil and menacing. Instead of having two hands, it had two claws, both of them sharp and bloodstained. It turned and looked at Mary Beth for a moment, before advancing slowly towards helpless Father Andrews.

Andrews shook his head. "No, no, please don't hurt me... please..."

Mary Beth quickly grabbed a folding chair from another

room and said, "Hey, over here!"

The creature turned to her again.

"Yeah, you, you ugly thing. C'mon, get me!"

The beast's dark, evil eyes stared at her for a second, then it growled angrily before coming in her direction. She threw the chair at it but the thing deflected it with its hairy arm like it was a piece of paper. She picked up a nearby lamp and threw it with all her might at the goat-creature but the thing knocked it down and kept moving towards her. It started lashing out at her with its claws, ripping the fabric of her sweater. Blood began oozing from cuts on her arms. Another swing knocked the black and white veil from her head. She yanked the chain free from around her neck and pointed the cross at the creature, reciting a passage from the Bible.

The beast growled again. The growl sounded like mocking laughter this time.

She kept saying the passage aloud, undaunted. The beast swung its claw at her again, tearing the right arm sleeve off of her sweater. She had closed her eyes for a brief moment, clenching her teeth tightly together, expecting her arm to get ripped off. Resuming the recitation of the Biblical passage, she continued stepping backwards until the half-goat, half-man creature was five feet from her

She watched it raise its muscular, hairy arm high in the air for one final swing. *This is it*, she said to herself, forcing to keep her eyes open this time. *Here I come, Heaven. Oh, Lord, please forgive all my sins.*

As the creature's long arm came down, she heard Father Andrews yell in the background: "Leave her alone! Come over here! It's me you want, not her."

The creature stopped its swing in mid-air, looking at her for a second before turning around and heading back to the bedroom.

"Come take me, you fool," Andrews screamed. Blood continued to drip from the nail puncture wounds in his palms, his body sagging more from the crucified position. "C'mon!"

The creature stepped forward and lashed out viciously at

him, severing Andrews's head from his body, like it was a ragged doll. Blood spurted quickly from the wound.

She felt like throwing up but forced herself to remain strong, running to the fireplace to grab the poker. When she got back to the bedroom, she rammed the poker into the back of the creature and it immediately screamed in pain, trying to remove the metal rod. She jammed it deeper into its body, causing the creature to fall down on its knees into a slumped position. Within several seconds, it stopped breathing, and its body began to spark up into flames.

The fire started spreading quickly, engulfing the whole room shortly in wild orange flames. Mary Beth looked at the burning bodies of Father Andrews and the creature once more before taking off.

***

She sat on her bed, looking at the clock on the nightstand. Studying the minute and second hands move forward. It was a quarter after ten in the morning. After watching the minute hand move up another notch, she got up, not wanting her eyes to blur or grow tired from staring too much. She looked out the window at the sunny November skies. The parking lot across the street was still empty and the Halloween merchandise and decorations were gone from the drug store window.

She looked inside the closet that was full of clothes, at the suitcase sitting on the floor, then closed the door. She put on her veil and black coat, said a brief prayer before the cross on the wall, and then left.

She saw Morris sitting by himself on a bench outside of St. Michael's.

Even though it wasn't a school day, he was dressed in his dark school uniform and a black overcoat. In his hands was an open comic book. He looked up as she approached the bench.

"Good morning, Morris," she said.

"Morning, Sister Mary Beth," he replied, closing the comic.

DARK THINGS II

"How are you?"

She looked down at the ground, thinking for a moment. "Fine." She looked at him. "I found out about the church secret... I'm glad you didn't tell me. It was better that I discovered it on my own." She shook her head. "What Father Andrews did was horrible. I'm sorry you had to know about this at such a young age. It sets a terrible example."

"You don't have to be sorry. What happened happened. Now we have to move on."

She looked at him again, nodding. She opened her purse and took out an item that was wrapped in brown parcel paper, and handed it to him.

"What's this?"

"Open it," she replied, smiling a little.

He slowly undid the tape along the edges, then removed the brown paper, looking at the small stack of National Geographic magazines in his lap. A wide grin formed across his face. "Thank you."

"You're very welcome. I had them tucked away in my suitcase and forgot they were there."

"Hey, you want to go to the mall and get some ice cream? It beats going by myself."

"Sure, that sounds fun."

They got up and headed for the bus stop.

About the author:

Derek Muk is a writer and social worker from California whose short stories have appeared in various small press magazines. He's had three chapbooks published and one collection of short stories. http:// theoccultfilesofalberttaylor.wordpress.com/

DEATH TWITCHES
by Indy McDaniel

"**FUCKING** spiders…" Sara Fielding muttered as she stomped on the scampering arachnid. Its smaller form flattening under the heel of her boot left her with a feeling of satisfaction and safety. One down…a few trillion to go.

Hell, I'm young, she thought, flicking her dyed-black hair away from her forehead. *If I really work at it, I might be able to do it.* She twisted her foot from side to side a couple times to make sure the spider was good and squished then scrapped the bottom along the sidewalk to get the majority of the bug guts off. With her job finished, she continued on her way, keeping her eyes open for any more of the little bastards out for a nighttime stroll.

"Dude," Sara's friend, Pinkie Gardner, spoke up from beside her. "What's your deal with spiders? Every time you see one you go totally ape-shit on its ass."

Sara lit up a cigarette and took a long drag, blowing the smoke out into the night air. "I had a bad experience." Which was her attempt at avoiding having to dredge up traumatizing past experiences. Sara wasn't in the damn mood. It was already bad enough that over the past week there seemed to be a rapid increase in the spider population around the city. *And I swear to fuck, the little bastards are getting bigger*, she thought.

"Man, don't gimme that shit," Pinkie prodded. "You're like super, tough chick. Mega-bitch on roller-skates. Wonder Woman if she went all Gothy. Yet, anytime you see a spider, I swear it looks like you're about to shit your pants and run screaming into the night. Little shit trail to show where you're going." Pinkie laughed at her own joke and kicked a glass bottle out into the street where a passing cyclist swerved to avoid it and wound up colliding with a parked car.

Normally, a scene like that would have both of the Goth girls cracking up and tossing choice insults at the fallen bike-rider.

DARK THINGS II

This time around, Sara hardly noticed the incident and Pinkie was too pre-occupied in her attempt to goad her friend into spilling her embarrassing reasons behind her arachnophobia.

Sighing, Sara decided it'd be easier to just get the story out there so she could go back to trying to repress it. "Fine, you miserable little bitch. I was thirteen. Deciding that I was far too anti-social for a young lady, my parents figured a summer camp was the best idea. And they wonder why I hate them so much. Anyway, for the most part the shit was just boring as hell. Spent most of the time boycotting the activities and staying in the cabin. Somehow, though, I got talked into participating in this game of team tag. I donno, I guess I figured it might be fun to chase down the other dorks there and punch em' in the arm. But of course, I wound up on the team that was 'it'. Fuck it, I figure. I'll do some running and if anybody comes near me, I'll kick em in the shin."

"What nobody told me, though, was that the woods around the camp were chock full of spiders. Big ones. They'd have their webs strung between trees and just sit right in the middle, waiting for some idiot to disturb them." Sara took another long drag off her cigarette, holding the smoke inside for as long as she could take it. The nicotine was helping to calm her nerves but not much.

"Don't tell me," Pinkie cut in. "You were that idiot."

Sara nodded. The memories were coming back now. No way to avoid it. Running through the woods, heading between two trees about three feet apart. Just before she passed between them, she saw the web. No time to stop or change direction. Then there was the familiar feeling of spider web on her skin. A heavy thud against her chest. She'd looked down into the face off a clearly pissed off arachnid. And while her terrified memory may have exaggerated the actual size of the thing over the years, it had still been pretty damn big.

The spider rested between her partially developed breasts for a mere heartbeat before it went on the offensive. Eight legs moving rapidly as it climbed Sara like a mountain. Sara's wide, horror-filled eyes locked onto the numerous, black eyes of the spider and in a purely instinctual reaction she let out a scream of terror and began slapping at herself. She felt the spider's legs against her throat before she knocked the monster away to land in a pile of leaves several feet to her left.

Not giving a shit about whose team she was on or whether or not she got tagged out, Sara ran back towards the cabins. It felt as though the spider was still on her. Not just on her neck, but everywhere. Her entire body was tingling. Bursting into her assigned cabin, she ran for the bathroom, flung the door open and made a dash for the shower, already tugging her shirt over her head.

It was only when she glanced towards the mirror above the sink that she noticed something was off. She turned and moved towards it, wondering why her skin was apparently rippling. When she got closer, she saw that it wasn't her skin rippling; it was what was covering it. Hundreds of baby spiders were crawling through her hair and down her face. They were on her shoulders and spilling down over her chest, getting tangled up in the cups of her bra.

She felt a scream working its way up from her lungs but she didn't dare open her mouth for fear that the spiders would make a dive for the dark hole of her throat. Instead, she let out a whimper and hurled her spider-infested shirt into the sink before tugging the rest of her clothes off and diving into the shower. The ice-cold water blasted against her skin, making her shiver but she didn't care. She just looked down and watched the multitude of spider babies washing towards the drain, stomping her bare foot at them as they went.

Sara shuddered and realized her cigarette had burnt down to the butt. Flinging it aside, she pulled out a fresh one and lit it up. "Happy now," she asked, turning to Pinkie. "Can we get on with our night, or do you want me to tell you about the almost as traumatizing event that was the losing of my virginity?"

"Dude, I was just curious," Pinkie shot back. "Don't gotta bite my frickin' head off. Geez."

"Whatever." Sara shook her head. "Let's just hurry up and get to the bar already. I need to get drunk, get stupid and, hopefully,

DARK THINGS II

get laid."

***

Sara let out a groan. It felt like someone had cracked open her skull, stuffed a bunch of cotton balls inside and stapled it shut again. In a word, she felt like shit. Which wasn't all that uncommon a feeling after a night of boozing with Pinkie. Still, this didn't feel like the average hangover from hell. She kept her eyes shut—she didn't think her aching head could take the added sensory input—and tried to remember the events of the previous night.

They'd wandered into a real dive. One quick survey of the limited clientele was enough to convince Sara that she wouldn't be getting laid. At least, not without a whole lot of alcohol in her first. So Pinkie and she had taken up seats at the bar and started ordering drinks. Things began to get hazy from that point forward but she definitely remembered at one point Pinkie crawling her fingers up her back and claiming that, "The spiders are coming to get you, *Sara*," in an entirely not funny voice.

The next thing she remembered was being in the alley behind the bar, vomiting up a good portion of the cheap but potent booze she'd guzzled down. Pinkie had been there, too. And there had been…a sound… Some kind of scuttling…

Then…nothing.

The pain in her head was starting to subside, which allowed her to become aware of certain other strange things. Like the fact that she didn't feel like she was lying prone. Instead, it felt like she was being suspended from something. *Goddammit*, she thought. *I must've hooked up with one of the freaks in that bar and he's got some kinda bondage fetish.* Not that Sara was anti-bondage; she just didn't take too kindly to the fact that she'd apparently been tied up and left for the night.

Deciding to chance a look around, Sara pried her eyes open. The first thing she realized was that she definitely wasn't in some perverts' basement-turned-home-made-dungeon. It looked more

22

like a warehouse. The second thing she realized, she was suspended about ten-feet off the ground. But that wasn't the worst thing. Hell, she had no problem with heights and she'd made ten-foot jumps to the ground before.

No, the worst thing wasn't that she was suspended; it was what was suspending her. From her neck down, her body had been encased in what looked like silky strands. Turning her head, she could see that she had been placed near the outer edge of a massive web. The lines flowed out from around her and disappeared into the darkness of the warehouse.

"Okay," she said, trying to keep her voice steady but already feeling the panic working its way through her body. "Pink, if this is some kinda elaborate practical joke, it is most definitely not fucking funny. Okay?" There was no response. "Pinkie!" she yelled.

To her left, there was a pained groan from a familiar voice. Sara turned her head and spotted a second human-sized silk-bundle. This one also had a head protruding from it. Pinkie had been suspended upside down, her long black hair dangling below her. Her eyes fluttered open and she took in her surroundings, clearly as confused as Sara had been a few moments earlier.

So, I guess that means she's not in on this joke, Sara thought. *Which means this probably isn't a joke.* The panic was skyrocketing out of control. Already, images of a giant spider crawling out of the darkness were flashing through her mind. The years she'd spent building up her tough chick persona were about to go right out the window as she felt hot tears welling up in her eyes.

It's a bad dream, she thought. *Just a bad, horrible, terrible fucking dream and I'm gonna wake up now. I'll wake up and I'll be tied to some loser's bed and he'll probably be sucking on my toes or something. And as gross as I think foot play is, I will be so thankful to be having some random asshole licking my feet.*

But it wasn't a dream.

And somewhere in the darkness, Sara heard the scuttling sound again. She started to squirm as best she could in an attempt to get free of the fucked-up cocoon she was in. She could barely move her legs and her arms were stuck firmly at her sides.

"Sara," Pinkie called, her voice groggy. "What the hell's going on?"

Sara looked back to her friend and responded with a scream of pure terror.

Just beyond Pinkie's feet was the monstrous spider. Ten feet long and maybe twice that wide with long, boney legs stretching across the web. It was brownish black in color and its head was twice the size of Pinkie's, which was currently tilting forward to see what Sara was screaming about. Her blue eyes went wide with shock. "What the fuck, man!"

Sara stared in horror as the massive spider crawled over her friend. It lowered its head and plunged its fangs through the silken sack and into Pinkie's abdomen. She cried out as the two sharp points of the spider's fangs punctured her stomach and injected its venom into her. Her body was quickly engulfed in a burning pain. Sara watched as Pinkie began to go into spasms. Her eyes rolled back into her head as bloody foam spilled from her gaping mouth.

As Pinkie's thrashing subdued into more sporadic death twitches, the spider turned and scampered back into the darkness. Sara had managed to get her screaming under control but the tears were still flowing freely down her cheeks. She was breathing heavily, on the verge of hyperventilating, and staring into the pain-racked face of her dead friend.

Then her fingers brushed against something hard. It took her a moment to realize what it was. Her switchblade, the one she kept tucked into the hem of her waistband. Feeling a glimmer of hope, Sara worked her fingers around the handle of the knife and pulled it free. She positioned it as best she could to avoid stabbing herself and hit the release mechanism.

The razor sharp blade sliced cleanly through the silk. Sara began to work it back and forth, slicing through the sack she was encased in. Little by little, it became easier to move her body. She'd nearly worked the blade up to her head when the sound of the spider's movements returned.

INDY MCDANIEL

Sara froze as the monster arachnid came back into view. For a terrifying instant, she thought it was coming to bite her as well. But it stopped at Pinkie's bundled corpse instead. Her fellow Goth's face looked sunken in; deflated in a way. The bloody foam that spilled from her lips had dried but there was now blackish sludge oozing out of her mouth and nose.

Once again, the spider plunged its fangs into Pinkie's body and began to slurp up her liquefied innards. Sara felt fresh tears spring from her eyes as she watched the spider feed. She began to work the knife at the silk again, moving slowly and keeping her eyes focused on the spider to see if it took notice of her escape attempt.

With a final slice, the sack split up the middle. Sara didn't bother to think twice. She pushed the sack apart and leapt out. She hit the ground hard and felt something snap in her right ankle. She cried out and immediately regretted it as she turned her head and saw that the spider's attention was now solely focused on her. Pushing herself up, she limped as quickly as she was able away from the web and its horrifying occupant.

Stumbling, Sara went down. The pain in her ankle was radiating up her leg, making it hard to move let alone put any weight on it. She glanced back just long enough to confirm her worst fear was giving chase. Then as she looked forward again she felt salvation flood through her.

Just in front of her, covered in a thick layer of dust, was a large can of kerosene. Already, Sara's hand was fishing into her pocket and pulling her lighter free. She forced herself back to her feet and closed the distance between herself and the can. Gripping the cap, she twisted hard. The rusted metal cut into her but she kept twisting. With a pop, the cap came off and she hurled it aside.

Flicking her Zippo open, she lit it and dropped the flaming lighter into the open can. Grabbing the handle, she rose to her feet, turned and hurled the kerosene with all her might at the approaching behemoth arachnid. Elation filled her as the can struck the spider in the center of its head and exploded in an impressive fireball.

The creature let out an inhuman screech and immediately

25

DARK THINGS II

began to backpedal but it was too late. The flames were engulfing it rapidly and as the spider reached its web again, the silk strands quickly went up in smoke. Sara leaned heavily against her uninjured leg and watched the giant spider's demise for another minute before turning and looking for a way out of the warehouse.

Already the fire was spreading, filling the warehouse with thick smoke. Sara coughed, covering her mouth and nose as she limped onward. She spotted a door and headed for it. She grabbed the handle, twisted it and pushed forward, exiting the warehouse and falling to the ground in a coughing, sobbing heap. She managed to crawl forward a few more feet before collapsing completely.

Sara wasn't sure how long she lay there. It felt like an eternity. Slowly, she became aware of what sounded like crackling. At first, she thought it was the warehouse burning. The sound grew louder and she realized it wasn't coming from behind her but in front of her. Lifting her head, she blinked her bloodshot eyes, forcing them to focus, and immediately regretted it.

Surging into the opening of the alleyway was an army of spiders. Wolf spiders and crab spiders and black widows and tarantulas. They were all rushing forward, drawn together by the death screams of their queen. Sara let out a scream of her own and pushed herself onto her back and crawled as quickly as she could away from the mass of arachnids.

As if sensing they'd discovered the one responsible for killing their queen, the horde of spiders rushed towards Sara. She continued to scream as they drew nearer, ignoring the rough cement scrapping at the palms of her hands. Her right ankle was twisted at an awkward angle and each time it bounced against the ground a sharp streak of pain shot up her leg. Even that didn't get her to slow down.

"*No*," she screamed as her back hit the wall at the end of the alley. She looked around frantically for an escape route and came up empty. Then the spiders were on her. She began to kick at them as they started crawling over her legs. Dozens were crushed under her booted feet but she couldn't stop the onslaught.

INDY MCDANIEL

Sara could feel them slipping under her jeans and crawling up her legs; the sharp sting of their fangs latching into her. Still more rushed over the outside of her pants and began to climb her torso. Slapping hastily at herself, Sara's eyes stared in horror and she continued to scream, shredding her vocal chords.

Then the spiders were on her face and in her hair. She felt them start to squeeze down her throat, biting at her along the way. Her throat swelled up, cutting off her screams. Her vision grew dark as her entire face was covered in angry arachnids out for vengeance.

About the author:

Indy McDaniel lives in Florida and has been writing stories since he figured out how to scrawl letters onto dead trees. Besides writing, he's also an aspiring filmmaker with a desire to one day have a booth at a horror convention between Bruce Campbell and Reggie Bannister.

THE WEEPER
by Tim Lewis

THAT night they took the old Sea Road, which ran through the evacuated part of town. Garbage was piled high on the sidewalks and plastic sheeting hung from burned-out buildings. Away to their left was the empty darkness of the ocean.

They turned into an abandoned parking lot and Creadle shut off the engine, but left the high beams on to illuminate the empty office block in front of them. They looked up at its dark windows for a moment, and then Newman reached for the door handle.

"Well, let's get it done," he said.

"Hold on," said Creadle. "Quick briefing for the rookie first."

He turned to look at Lemack in the back seat.

"You sure you're okay for this?"

"Sure," Lemack shrugged, catching Newman's smirk in the side mirror.

"As you know, we had a call from someone who claims he saw a Weeper in there. Most likely a false alarm but we've got to check it out. As this is your first time, I want to explain a couple of things."

Lemack glanced at Newman who was studying his 10-gauge, acting bored.

"According to the plans, there are three separate stairwells. So we take one each, work it from the bottom up. Once we get to the top, there's nowhere left for it to go, right?"

"I bet the bitch is on my watch," said Newman.

"Like I said, there probably isn't one," Creadle went on. "This whole area was eradicated years ago. However, just in case, there are a few things you need to remember. First and foremost, never ever, look a Weeper in the eyes. You know what happens if you do, don't you?"

Of course, Lemack had heard the stories as a kid. If a Weeper

28

could hold your stare for long enough, she would hypnotize you and freeze you to the spot.

"What if I do accidentally catch her eye?" Lemack asked.

"Brief eye contact is okay. But then look past her, over her shoulder."

"And then let her have it," Newman said.

"She'll try and lock you in, get your sympathy," Creadle said. "That's how they work. You can't let her do that. Also, Weepers don't like the light, so shine your torch right in her face. It won't blind her though, so keep your eyes averted."

"And don't take any notice of her crying," added Newman. "When you hit her, be ruthless. Because if she gets just one chance… she will kill you. Without hesitation *and* without remorse."

He studied Lemack's face in the glow of the dash lights.

"You scared?"

"Nah. I just need to know what to do, that's all."

"Right," Newman grinned again. "I hope I get her. I'll fry the bitch."

Fact was, Lemack wasn't as scared as Newman might have thought. Since they'd left the station earlier, he'd had a strong suspicion that this was all just a test. It was well known that the Academy liked to do this kind of thing, putting trainees into fake real-world situations to see how they reacted.

Even though he'd heard all about Weepers, no-one he knew had ever seen one. They were supposed to have been wiped out. To his generation, they were nothing more than a scary bedtime story. How they would hang on the ceiling making that odd high pitched cry that gave them their name. And how they liked to devour the softest parts of your body while you were still alive.

He was about to ask if either of them had actually come face to face with one, when Creadle said, "Well that's it. When we get inside, we split up. Be sure to maintain radio contact at all times. There's no electricity, so make sure your lights are working. Let's do this. I don't want us to be in there any longer than we have to."

They got out of the vehicle and headed towards the building, a sea breeze whipping across the lot.

Creadle unlocked the door and they went inside, waving their flashlights around the lobby. There was plenty of trash and broken furniture all over, and it smelled of dust and stale urine.

"Check your radios," Creadle said quietly. "And keep me posted each time you clear a floor."

Newman took the left stairwell and Creadle the right. Lemack waited until their lights had flickered out of sight and stood listening to the wind upstairs. Then he headed up, slowly moving his light around the ceiling and flicking the safety off the Remington. One shot should be enough, he thought. Just shine the light, she freezes, you kill her. Piece of cake.

He reached the landing, kicking through a pile of old newspapers. The door to the first office was off its hinges and it was pitch black inside.

He hesitated then, thinking, shit, what if this isn't a test? What if there is something in there? Fighting the urge to go back downstairs, he made himself go inside. He shone his light quickly around, saw nothing, and stepped back out into the passageway.

Then he heard Creadle's voice over the radio.

"Lemack. How you going?"

"Still on the first floor," he whispered.

"First? Get a move on, will you? We're on the second already. You'll have us here all night!"

He could hear Newman laughing, meaning their radios were linked. He felt stupid, realized he hadn't checked the first room properly because he was acting like a frightened little kid.

Angry with himself, he stepped inside the next room without pausing and waved the beam across the ceiling and walls. He was about to leave when something caught his eye. He swung the beam back, holding it steady over what looked like several deep scratches in the plaster.

"Come on then, you crying bitch," he whispered.

The rest of the floor was clear so he started up to the second, the wind whistling through the broken windows at the end of the passageway.

"First floor complete," he reported.

"Roger that," said Creadle. "Pick up the pace a bit, rookie."

He started working his way through the rooms, getting a rhythm going. Pausing, going in, waving the flashlight, aiming the scatter gun. He was armed, he was the law, this was his building, and there was nothing here to be afraid of. Right?

After a while, as he made his way up through the empty offices, he started to relax a little, becoming ever more convinced that this really was just a dumb test.

Even so, each time he reached a new floor and shined his light down the hall, he half expected to see something. Like, maybe the Academy had stuck a dummy on the ceiling.

Just then, as Lemack reached the sixth floor, Newman's voice exploded over the radio.

"Holy shit! I've found her!"

"Which floor?" he heard Creadle yell.

"Seventh! Shit, she's ugly!"

"Look away from her eyes, Newman," Creadle shouted. "You hear me? I'm on my way."

Lemack listened to the sound of heavy boots on the stairs, Creadle breathing hard. Then a single gunshot. He heard it over the radio and he heard it echoing through the walls.

"Sergeant," he called into the handset.

There was a pause, and then Creadle said, "That is one repulsive creature. Good work, Newman."

"Sergeant," Lemack repeated. "Did you get it?"

"Don't worry, Lemack. Newman hit it."

Lemack was sweating and his mouth was dry. So there really had been a Weeper and it could just as easily have been in his part of the building.

But then he had a second thought, and asked, "Can I come see it?"

There was another pause, before Creadle said, "We have the Weeper, patrolman. Finish your sweep first. Let's do it by the book.

DARK THINGS II

Which floor are you on?"

"Sixth."

"Okay. We'll regroup downstairs."

Lemack started moving down the passageway, thinking now, that there was something in Creadle's voice, the way he answered, and thinking about Newman's blasé attitude, that maybe he really was being set up to be the big joke back at the station house. Well, fuck them. Rookie or not, he would insist upon seeing it.

He went up to the top floor, worked his way quickly to the last room and poked his head inside. There were a lot of stacked up desks, bundles of paper and storage crates. He eased his way in and looked around. Then he crouched on the floor and peered underneath the tables. Nothing there but trash.

He called into the radio. "All floors secure."

"Okay, Lemack, get down here and we'll show you what a dead Weeper looks like."

He put his weapon on safety and stepped out into the passageway. Secure or not, he'd had just about enough of this place.

He had taken just two steps when he heard the noise. A high-pitched whining, faint at first, then gradually getting louder.

It sounded more bestial than human and the hairs lifted on his neck. Very slowly, he looked up, pointed the light and there she was, hanging from the ceiling, just above his head.

She clung to the gypsum with her white, gristly fingers, face up, so all he could see was her black cape and knotted hair.

He could feel his heart thumping, realizing that in his haste to finish the job, he must have walked straight under her. She cried again and a shudder ran down his spine.

"Sergeant," he hissed into the radio. "I have one too."

"Repeat that, Lemack!"

"I have a Weeper, sir. Seventh floor."

In the background he heard Newman say, "Another one? They told us there was only one."

But now Creadle was shouting. "Remember what I told you, Lemack! Don't stare into her eyes. We're coming!"

TIM LEWIS

Lemack stayed still, raised the Remington, and the Weeper's head slowly began to turn, her neck creaking around a full half-circle until her bony face was looking straight into his.

Her eyes were black holes, trying to probe the beam of his light, but as he looked into them, he sensed that she was actually afraid of him, as if she knew he meant to harm her.

But how could he? She hadn't done anything to him. His panic briefly evaporated and feeling almost sorry for her, he moved the light to one side and lowered the gun.

That was when she smiled.

It was a most awful smile, stretching across her thin lips. If she had snarled or screamed, it would have been less terrifying than that smile.

Lemack could hear Newman and Creadle racing up the stairwell, Creadle shouting, "Lemack, for God's sake, shoot it!"

Really, he wanted to shoot her. He wanted to move. But he just stood there as the Weeper's smile spread wider, revealing a sharp set of yellow teeth.

And then she dropped from the ceiling.

About the author:

Tim Lewis has spent the past thirty years getting ready to be a writer. Now he's doing it. He lives in sunny Thailand where he spends most of his time sitting in bars, watching people, and thinking up stories.

THE DEVIL'S FOOTPRINTS
by Jack Horne

"**GOD** save us!" John's father slammed the door shut, and began hurriedly bolting it, his hands trembling. "The Devil's been walking abroad during the night, Mary," he told his wife, crossing himself several times and repeating the Lord's Prayer.

"What nonsense are you talking, George," John's mother snapped.

"I'm not going out anymore today."

"It's only six o'clock in the morning. Snow or not, the farmer's animals will still need tending to." She took her husband's heavy woolen coat and made to open the door.

"No!" John watched his father's terrified expression as he barred his wife's access to the door. "No, you can't go out there."

"Well, if you're not going to work today," she argued, "I have to shake the snow from your coat before it all melts in here." She glared pugnaciously. "And take off your boots!"

"A little wet on the floor won't hurt us." He still stood between his wife and the door. "But who can say what harm Satan would do to us."

She studied him angrily. "Have you been drinking? We can't afford for you to take time off like this. It's hard enough paying the rent and feeding the five of us on your wages as it is."

"There are footprints outside," he stammered. "Footprints everywhere."

"Well, what of it?" She scowled, and added sourly, "Honest folk on their way to work, probably."

"No, you don't understand." His eyes were still staring horribly. "They're the Devil's hoof prints."

John's mother snorted. "You're the only devil. A *lazy* devil."

The younger children began to cry, and John, who had been listening keenly, called his brother and sister to him. "Don't be

34

JACK HORNE

scared," he whispered. "We're safe in here."

***

As his parents and twin siblings warmed themselves by the crackling fire, John crept to the window and peered out expectantly, but the twelve year old was disappointed to discover that the thick panes were opaque with a coating of ice. *I wonder if I could creep outside without them knowing,* he thought. *I've got to see the Devil's footprints for myself.* He slowly unbolted the door. He waited, hardly daring to breathe. They hadn't heard him. He opened the heavy door as quietly as he could. *Please don't creak.* A blast of icy air engulfed him as he stood, mesmerized, in the doorway.

He no longer felt the customary irresistible childish urges to rush outside to make a snowman or to throw snowballs. He wasn't dazzled by the brilliance and beauty of the snow. Instead, he marveled at the seemingly endless trail of hoof marks leading away from their garden; his father's footprints clearly visible in the deep snow approaching the gate.

His father broke the spell by roughly dragging him into the cottage. "Do you want the Devil to get us all, boy," he raged, slamming the door and shooting the bolts home once more. "He'll drag you to Hell by your braces."

Little Joe and Anne began to cry again, and John's mother shouted, "What nonsense you're frightening the children with! I wish you'd go to the Devil, George Tailor!" She cradled the twins to her ample bosom, whispering, "It's all right, my dears. Daddy saw a horse's hoof marks, that's all."

"It wasn't a horse's hooves! Not unless a horse can walk on two feet for miles." He stubbornly relit his pipe and sat by the fire once more, a bottle of brandy in his hand. "John, come and sit here. I want to know exactly where you are."

Sulkily, John obeyed his father, and for an hour or more he quietly sat remembering the footprints zigzagging across the virgin snow, wondering, *What could have made them? Could it have really*

DARK THINGS II

been the Devil?

"If you don't think it was the Devil, what do you think it was," he asked his mother in a whisper, afraid of disturbing the peacefully sleeping four year olds and his snoring father, who held the emptied brandy bottle in a vice-like grip. "They weren't caused by a horse"—he drew the peculiar U-shape in the air with his finger—"they were like that."

"Oh, it was a donkey with a damaged shoe."

A sudden thought occurred to him: *Mother would let me go out.* "A donkey with a damaged shoe? Yes, that sounds about right," he said brightly. "Please could I go out to play, then? I want to make a snowman."

***

John triumphantly stood at the gate, light snowflakes brushing his face, his boots sinking in inches of snow as he scanned the pure white landscape. He pondered, *If it's the Devil, will he really drag me down to Hell? I wonder if he's dragged any of our neighbors or any of the boys at school away already. I hope he's taken Nathan Collier.*

He ran to the nearest hoof prints and looked back at the imprints left by his own boots and by his father earlier that day. The human footprints were clearly different to the ones which had so alarmed his father. *I think a lot of the men were frightened, too,* he thought, looking about the deserted walkway. *It must be about 8 o'clock by now but it's like I'm the only person in the whole village.* He imagined the school bully Nathan Collier trembling, his eyes wide with terror at his father's reports of the Devil's footprints and he laughed scornfully, knowing that he would never fear him half as much again. *Mother always said he was just a coward,* he thought.

The prints could be the Devil's, but I want to rule out anything ordinary first, he thought. *They definitely weren't made by a horse or a donkey with a damaged shoe.*

Using his hands as rough guides, he measured the length and

breadth of the hoof prints; and the distance between several. His mind fully concentrating on the unscientific method, he estimated, *They're around 4 inches long and just under 3 inches wide; and they're always 8 inches apart.*

His mother broke his concentration by shouting from the door, "John! Your meal is ready." She didn't comment on the nonexistent snowman.

He hadn't realized how cold he was and huddled with the twins by the hearth, wallowing in the comforting wood smoke smells.

"I think you were definitely right about it being a donkey," he told his mother as she ladled broth from the well-used pot suspended over the fire.

After they'd eaten, John asked, "Ma, could I go out to play in the snow again please?"

"No," his father slurred. "It's not safe, son."

John's mother snapped, "And since when has a donkey been a threat to anyone?" She winked at John. "You go out and build your snowman."

I hope the footprints aren't covered by fresh snow, he thought, running to the door.

The prints were still there; but so were dozens of people, their footprints adjacent to, and crossing, the mystery ones. The watery afternoon sun had emboldened John's neighbors, curiosity having finally got the better of them. Each had heard rumors and little groups were engaged in gossiping.

I suppose that talking about it makes them less afraid, John analyzed. *I hope they won't exaggerate anything they've heard or seen.*

He decided to make his snowman a little distance away from them so that he could listen without being seen to eavesdrop.

They won't ask my opinion as "children should be seen and not heard", he thought. *I don't want anyone asking what my father makes of all this and guessing that he's scared half to death.*

As he half-heartedly made a snowman, his back to them, he

could hear their voices quite clearly, but, on the whole, he couldn't tell whose opinion he was listening to.

"Bless the child! Look at him innocently playing in this terrible snow," he heard a woman say. "Anyway, I heard that the River Exe froze over in the night, and the Devil's footprints continued on the other side of it."

"I've been told that Old Nick must have walked through a 6 inch drainpipe," a man said. "His prints were on either end of it."

A third speaker added her story, "His hooves walked across the rooftops of houses. His prints carried on after my twelve-foot wall, too."

"Satan must have walked right up to my door," a second male voice added. "My Nathan nearly wet himself with fear."

John suppressed his laughter. Nathan Collier would never scare him again!

He turned his attention to a second group: each had his or her pet theory on the origin of the prints.

"They're not footprints," one man informed all and sundry. "A mouse or a rat has been out in the snow."

"I've heard that a bloke in Sidmouth has a kangaroo," another said with a confidential tone. "The kangaroo might have escaped. It could probably jump over walls and onto rooftops."

"It was the Devil!" John recognized the shrill voice of Miss Parsons. "I've heard that he walked a hundred miles last night."

More people joined in the conversation and John gave up trying to identify each speaker.

"You'll find it's nothing more sinister than a crane or a swan."

"It was a badger. They put their hind feet into the marks of their forefeet, you know."

"I've been told by a very reliable source that it's a balloon from Devonport Dockyard."

"I think it's just someone having a joke."

"Well, he went to a lot of trouble! I've heard that the footprints are in Topsham, Lymphstone, Exmouth, Dawlish and Teignmouth."

"It was probably Spring-heeled Jack. He used to leap over

JACK HORNE

cemetery walls."

"Maybe it was Pan. I remember from school that he had the hind legs of a goat."

"My dogs were terrified of something last night." John's ears pricked up as he overheard the unmistakable tones of Sam Bewes the poacher. "They yelped like pups and refused to go into a thicket."

"It was a cat and I intend to tell my congregation that this Sunday." The Reverend Fusden always had the final word and no one dared to openly contradict his theory.

John eyed his snowman without enthusiasm. *That will do*, he thought. *I don't think I'll learn anything more from the neighbors.*

It was late afternoon and John noticed that, whatever their personal theories, the villagers all began to vanish, to retreat to the safety of their cottages on the approach of the dark, as though all their courage had died with the weak winter's sun.

Taking one last look at the hoof prints, which still stood out among the scores of villagers" footmarks, John decided, *I'll creep out tonight and see if he comes again.*

***

After the family had eaten Mother's hearty stew, they sat around the fire, amusing themselves by looking for vaguely recognizable shapes in the flickering flames. Happy talk, such as "There's a dog" and "It's a boot", turned to uneasy silence as John laughed, "It's the Devil!"

Why did I say that? Father's getting nervous again, he thought.

He then sat in contemplative silence, recalling the villagers" stories and theories. Did they really believe the explanation lay with various animals? *No*, he thought. *If they believed it was an animal, the men would be in the Inn, as usual.* He longed to open the door and see the footprints once more.

***

DARK THINGS II

That night, he was too restless to sleep, his excited mind still racing with ideas, wondering, *What if I see the Devil? What will happen?*

After midnight, he listened outside his parent's room, hoping for reassuring snores. Smiling, he then tiptoed down the narrow flight of wooden stairs, cautiously avoiding the two creaky ones in the middle, half expecting at every step to hear, "John, is that you?" He slowly unbolted the door and cringed at the resultant noises, sounding not unlike gunshots in the still cottage.

Please don't let Father hear me.

After waiting for a few seconds, he finally opened the door and stood looking out onto the shadowy deserted world beyond their gate. He muffled his freezing face in his scarf, and, a million butterflies fluttering in his stomach, he stepped outside. Before walking resolutely in the crunchy snow, he studied the humble cottage, the only home he'd ever known, wondering if he'd ever see it and his family again.

Ignoring the human tracks, he decided to simply follow the hoof marks.

What if the Devil is out tonight? No one will be able to save me, he thought.

Suddenly, he sensed a presence behind him. Afraid to turn around, he stood rooted to the spot. He felt someone touch his shoulder. His heart almost stopped beating.

The Devil is here, he thought. *And I will face him.*

A deep voice spoke into his ear, "I knew you'd come to me, John. You don't belong with these fools."

Slowly, John turned around.

***

In the morning, John's frozen footprints were discovered in the snow, alongside hoof prints. Both tracks suddenly disappeared, as though the boy and the unknown entity had stepped into a different world.

"Old Nick came and got him," his mother sobbed. "All we

can do is pray for my poor boy to come back."

***

The Devil never returned to the region again. And neither did his latest recruit.

About the author:
Jack is married and lives in Plymouth, England. He's had quite a few short stories, poems and articles printed in UK, USA and Australia.

POLARITY
by David W. Landrum

I had established a pretty steady cliental when Blake Philips contacted my cousin Staci and said he wanted someone to be in his "ceremonies." Staci sent me to his house. Men want you to do weird things sometimes, and I'm wary of that because the guys who go for the bizarre stuff are usually the ones who do you harm, so you have to be careful.

When I got there, I expected to be shown the bedroom, but he took me to a small room all hung with black cloth and with a table in the middle. Two black candles sat on the table.

He told me to take everything off. I was wary, like I said, but I did what he told me, since he had already paid. I waited. After a moment he brought in someone else—a girl who had to be a teenager. I thought for a minute he wanted us to have sex while he watched (I don't have sex with women, though I have occasionally faked it, smooched and hugged and put on a show for customers who get off on that kind of thing). He pointed to a spot.

"Stand there," he told me. He looked over at the girl. "Carrie." She walked to a place opposite me as if she knew the drill.

I glanced over at her. She had blonde hair and was slender with small but well-shaped breasts and a strong, flat stomach that curved nicely down to the tuft of light brown hair between her long legs. She looked athletic. She did not acknowledge my being there. She only looked straight ahead, her face impassive.

Philips stepped up to the table. Carrie and I stood, one on each side of him. He lit the two black candles, walked back, and hit the light switch so the room went dark.

It looked spooky. The three of us cast big shadows on the wall. Blake had dressed all in black: pants, boots and a turtleneck. He opened a bin the bottom of the table, took out a hooded robe, also black, and pulled it over his head.

He raised his hands like a priest and began to chant—Latin, I think—some language I did not understand. His voice got loud and gravely and a little scary. I felt something like static electricity go through the place. As he chanted, I stole glances at Carrie, wondering who she was and what she was doing here—if he had also hired her (she seemed way too young to be in the business). I could tell what we were doing disgusted her.

The "ceremony" took some forty-five minutes. Philips chanted and raised his hands. My legs got numb from standing so long. Finally he stopped. The candles went out. I did not see him snuff them or blow on them, but he must have. We stood in total darkness. I heard his footsteps. The lights came on.

The girl turned and left the room. Blake looked over at me and smiled.

"Okay, Millie, that's it. You can get dressed."

He held the door for me when I exited. I got my clothes on. Outside, in the living room, bright with reflected snow, he asked, "Are you okay with this?"

His question struck me as odd, though I recovered from my surprise and answered.

"Sure. Do you want me to do anything else?"

"Just what you did today."

I almost asked him who the girl was but decided it was none of my business. If he wanted me to stand naked in a room while he did some kind of magical mumbo-jumbo that was fine. It was three-hundred bucks and I didn't have to put out. Being there with a girl who looked underage bothered me a little—but he had not touched her, just as he had not touched me, so I decided not to ask questions.

He said I could come back next week.

***

Wednesday is a busy day. I live in a small town in Vermont and share a house with my cousin, Staci, who is also in the business. Staci is pretty and has rich clients—men from business and government. She goes to the capital in Montpelier a lot. Me—well, I'm a little more plain and I get the blue-collar crowd she doesn't want to deal with—the day-laborers, truck drivers, high school boys coming for

43

their first shot, casuals who are passing through or who drive fifty or sixty miles here so they won't be seen, an occasional hiker from the Appalachian Trail. I also do "house calls" for guys who live alone. I charge a hundred more for a house call, but I like doing them. Over the year I've been in town I've got to know a couple of these guys fairly well, and the deal usually involves spending time talking with them, having a drink, and then going to bed. I'd finished a trick with a guy named Lonnie, and that was all for the day. I'd had five johns that morning then my two house calls. I'd made $1600.00. Staci would be happy about that, but I was really worn out.

I went to Arni's, an old-fashion diner with fifties décor—round stools, flip-page juke boxes, waitresses in white blouses, pink miniskirts, and little white paper hats. I'd gotten to be friends with a couple of the waitresses. They knew what I did for a living but seemed friendly and not snooty. I ordered a BLT and a soda, which they make in old-fashioned glasses with fluted sides and a stem bottom. I had finished eating ordered a coffee when I saw Carrie come into the place.

Beside her stood a boy her age, blond and good-looking. They talked at the door, he left, and she came on in. She wore jeans, a sweatshirt, and a dark purple and lavender North Face jacket. Snow had settled on her hair and shoulders. The backpack she carried made her look very much the typical high school girl.

She saw me. I smiled, thinking she would not want to acknowledge me given the situation that had brought us together. To my surprised, she came over.

"Can I sit with you," she asked.

Clara brought my coffee.

"Would you like a cup?"

She nodded. I told Clara to make it two.

The girl seemed awkward. Of course, when you've met someone standing buck naked at some sort of occult ceremony, it is a little hard to break the ice. Clara brought her coffee.

"I just wanted to introduce myself," the girl said, "since my Dad didn't bother to do that yesterday. I'm Carrie…Carrie Philips."

DAVID W. LANDRUM

"I'm Millie…not Millie Cyrus, Millie Ramer."

"You're not Millie Cyrus, I'm not Carrie White."

I gave her a puzzled look.

"You know…from the movie *Carrie*…the one from the book by Stephen King."

"Oh yeah."

"I feel like her sometimes. She had a weird Mom. I have a weird Dad."

I could see she wanted to talk, so I decided I would not beat around the bush but get right to what I was wondering.

"How old are you," I asked.

"Seventeen."

"What your Dad had you do the other day," I said, making sure no one was near enough to hear, "is illegal. You're underage."

"I know it's illegal. I don't want to talk about it here, but it would be nice to tell someone what's going on." She glanced around to make doubly certain no one was listening. "My Dad doesn't molest me," she whispered. "It isn't that at all. In fact, I'm a virgin. I really am, I'm not just saying that to cover something up. Can you meet me at the public library tomorrow morning?"

I thought of my schedule. I had a couple of customers that morning.

"What time?"

"I can get a pass from school to go there at eleven. I can stay there till one."

"That will work. I'll be there at eleven thirty."

We sipped our coffee in silence. After a while I asked about the boy I'd seen her with.

"I like him. He's a cool guy. He's on the wrestling team. He really likes me." Glancing around again she added, "That's part of why I want to talk to you."

I nodded. She finished her coffee, said good-bye, picked up her backpack, and headed out into the snow.

***

45

DARK THINGS II

The next morning I had a guy who is pretty average then a guy who comes every other week and has me do the "blind virgin" act. I pretend I'm a blind virgin and he goes through the spiel about how his wonderful love can give me my sight. He starts screwing me and I say, amazed and bewildered, how something strange is happening and at the end I say I can see. He always gets off at that point. The whole thing is so pathetic and ridiculous I can hardly keep from laughing while it's going on. But he pays me an extra hundred bucks to do it, so I play along. Staci says he got the whole thing from a movie about whores.

After he left, I went upstairs where Staci and I live (all business is done on the lower level). She was home that morning, sitting at the computer and dressed in a tennis outfit. She played tennis in college and is pretty good. She has lots of clients who play and often will go sets with them before her dates. In winter she plays on indoor courts at a country club.

"Finished," she asked.

I nodded.

"I got three new inquiries. You want to do them?"

We advertise on the internet. Prostitution is illegal in Vermont, like it is most places in the US, but we're careful to advertise ourselves as caregivers and to state that men are paying for our time and companionship—the sex, we say, is incidental and our personal choice. The loophole works. We've never been arrested, though the authorities know all about us. Staci has politicians who are clients. I have cops on my list of customers.

"Set them up for this afternoon. Say, two o'clock."

"You want to do all three?"

"Sure."

Staci and I both got started at this about the same time. We knew we were both in the business but only started working together last year after she got out of jail. She got busted with four other high-class call girls and got a two-year sentence of which she served fourteen months. After that she decided to start her own service and is careful to watch the legal side of things. She said she would arrange for the johns to be here at two, three, and four. I said I was going out to get something to eat and would be back in time to do them.

A bright film of snow had covered my car, but the sky was clearing, the clouds blowing past the mountains that surround our town and sun showing through. Winters are long and cold here, so you always smile when the sun comes out even on chilly days. I drove over to the public library.

I was early so I logged on to one of the internet stations and started to browse. I looked for things on occult worship and found some pretty creepy sites but stumbled on to one set up by a church that described Satanic worship. A line of the script read, *The celebrant stands between two women who are always naked ("clothed with the wind" is the term they use); one woman must be a virgin and one must be a prostitute.* I sat still and read the line over and over, now understanding what I was doing in Philips' occult ceremony and what Carrie was doing there as well. I read a little more, heard the door open, and saw her walk in.

She stomped the snow off her boots and looked around, smiling when she spotted me. She came over to my table, sat down, and wiggled out of her coat.

"How are you," she asked.

"Okay. You?"

"Pretty good." She glanced at the computer screen. "I see you've been doing research."

I had forgot to exit the page. I didn't know what to say to her.

"That's what my Daddy does for a living."

"Worships the Devil?"

"Not exactly. He curses people with the Devil's power. That's why he hires you and forces me to be there. Did the website say anything about virgins and prostitutes?"

"It did."

"Then you know why we're there. I told you I'm a virgin. That's my part of the deal."

DARK THINGS II

"Your boyfriend is good-looking. What's his name?"

"Curtis."

"Well, if you don't like doing what your Dad makes you do, and if you have to be a virgin to do it, and you have a boyfriend you like…all of that suggests a pretty easy way out of the whole mess."

"I'd do it in a minute, Millie. I want to, but if I lose it he'll kill Curtis. He has a lot of evil power. Once I just flat out refused to stand. He got some Satanist girl who's a virgin…some of them take vows like nuns do so they can be in the ceremonies…and put a curse on my Mom."

"Is you Mom here," I asked.

"She lives up in Burlington. She used to live here but got born again and left my Dad. He threatened to kill me if she claimed custody for me. She got my sister and brother but I stayed with Daddy. When I did what I just told you…refused to be the ceremony…he put a spell on my Mom. She almost died. I agreed to start doing it again. He lifted the curse and she got better. He'll do the same thing to Curtis if I go against him."

Silence fell. Carrie glanced up at the clock.

"But there is something we can do," she said, her eyes full of fear.

I lowered my voice. I was afraid too, even though I had no idea what she would suggest.

"What?"

"We can both go negative. We represent good and evil." Then she blushed. She reached over and took my hand. "Millie, I didn't mean that. Don't take it wrong."

I did not say anything.

"Look, I know you aren't evil. I know girls at my school who would never give it up to their boyfriends and they're the most selfish, destructive, hateful bitches in the world. Please don't take what I said wrong."

"Go on," I replied.

"It's something like polarity. When my Dad curses someone, he stands in the presence of evil…demons, I guess, or the Devil

48

himself. When the air gets all thick and electric, that's what you're sensing. They're evil and would tear him apart except that he creates a zone of safety for himself. He stands between what people think is pure good, me; and what people think of as really bad…but I know that isn't true of you…"

I waved my hand. "Keep talking," I said.

"If I could lose my virginity and you could stop being a working girl, that would…like reverse the polarity. He would be positive and not negative. He would not be protected. The demons would drag him down to hell."

She paused and licked her lips.

"But it has to be both of us. It can't just be me. It has to be you too. I can give up to Curtis…and I want to anyway. But you would have to stop doing what you do too. Otherwise, it won't work. He'll kill me and my family if I'm not a virgin. And he'll know immediately. But if we both do it…if we pull a reversal on him…he won't detect it until it's too late."

I sat there. I did not know what to say. How do you stop being a prostitute?

I supposed I could tell Staci I was finished. She would be angry and insult me—a thing I dreaded she got so vicious and said such cruel things when she even thought I was considering leaving the business. I heard Carrie put her coat back on.

"Leaving?"

"I need to get back to school," she said, a bit of an edge on her voice.

"Carrie, let me think about it."

"If you don't want to…"

"It isn't that. I've thought about leaving what I do several times. It's just…"

I didn't finish. She stood there, her coat half-on, half-off.

"Just what?"

I clouded up. I don't cry a lot. If you do what I do for a living you learn to distance yourself from your feelings. You have to. It's part of the job. But for some reason I was overwhelmed. My emotions got the best of me for once.

Carrie quickly slid into her coat. She sat back down and took my hands.

"What, Millie," she asked, her voice full of innocent concern and love that maybe only a virgin can express. This made me cry even harder.

"I don't know if I can do anything else."

Carrie gripped my hands.

"No. That's *not* true. You could do anything. You could get a job. You could go to school. You're smart. And you're good. Whatever my psycho Dad and all his wacko friends think about good and evil, I can tell you're good. You're kind. You cared about me. I could see when we were at the ceremony that you were concerned about me. I know you can do something else. I know it."

I managed to stop crying. People were staring at us.

"Let me think of how I might go about this," I said when I got things under control. "I'll do it, Carrie. Somehow I'll think of a way."

"Remember: he has powers. He's dangerous. He can harm you with his magic. You've got to make sure it's a real switch...that you're really, truly stopping what you do for a living."

She looked up the clock on the wall behind the circulation desk.

"I have to go. If I'm late and the school calls him he'll get suspicious and start asking questions. So I'm leaving."

Then she leaned down and kissed me on the lips. I stared as she turned and hurried out the front door.

It was 12:15. I had to go back and get ready for the new customers. I went out into the freezing cold and drove back home.

After I finished with the four afternoon contacts, I took the money up to Staci. She had come back from a date with a tennis-playing executive—and probably a thousand dollars richer.

"Nice," she said when I handed her the cash. "We did well today."

Then she noticed the expression on my face.

"What's wrong," she asked. "Were they weird?"

I decided I had to tell her now.

"Staci, I'm finished. I want my share of the money. I'm moving on."

She stared at me, her mouth open in amazement. She looked pretty: reddish hair cut short, a pretty face with bowed lips and big eyes; slender with strong arms and legs. She filled out the little white tennis dress admirably.

"Are you in a blue funk again?"

"No."

"Okay, I know you were busy this morning. Maybe I shouldn't have had those guys come in this afternoon."

"I agreed to it. It isn't that."

"Then what is it?" Her patience had started to wear thin.

"I've had it. I'm quitting. I want to get a job."

She grinned maliciously.

"You've got a job."

"You know what I mean. And don't' start in. Don't start saying I'm too stupid to get a job or make it on my own. I don't want to hear it."

I threw her a curve here. She had a standard lecture she gave me when I said I might want to leave the business. She twisted her mouth into something between a smirk and a sneer.

"Okay. But you'll be back in a week."

"No, I won't.

"When are you planning to leave?"

"Right now. I'm getting a place in town…a place of my own."

"You can't do that! You've got regular customers."

"You have lots of contacts. I know you do from when I got sick those two times. You can get someone to replace me."

"That never works out. The guys are used to and they like you. They won't be happy about having someone else."

"I'm leaving."

Now she looked vicious. She put her hands on her hips.

51

DARK THINGS II

"Listen to me, you stupid…"

"Don't call me that," I shouted. "Just give me my share of the money so I can go."

"You're not getting a cent from me."

"You said it was fifty-fifty."

"The bank account is in my name," she leered. "I'll give you something, but not half."

"You said it was half. You said we split everything evenly."

"I guess I did. I've changed my mind. You'd better not get mouthy or I may not give you a goddamned cent."

"Maybe I have to threaten to tell the wives of some of those rich guys you date about the cute little bimbo they got tucked away at the country club."

Fear flashed through her eyes for a just a second. She tried to look contemptuous but I could see I had shaken her.

"Millie, don't. If you try to blackmail my customers, you'll end up dead. They'll take you out. They can hire hit men and they will. I've seen it happen."

"You're probably right. But I imagine they would not want to leave any loose ends and so they'd get rid of you too. You'd end up strangled like that woman on *Bullitt.*"

She shuddered. Once he had watched *Bullitt,* the old movie with Steve McQueen, and the scene where they show a woman strangled by the Mafia gave Staci nightmares for months afterwards. Her composure started to go. I've know her long enough to know that once you get by her standard strategies of control, she folds up.

"I want my half."

She stood there, not knowing what to do. Then she drooped, deflated.

"All right, you stupid bitch."

"*Don't call me that!*"

My anger and vehemence startled her.

"All right, all right. We need to get this done so I can start calling to find someone to take your place."

I pointed to her computer. "Bring up the account. I want to

see exactly how much we have in the bank."

She brought up the bank account. We had quite a bit of money. She wrote me a check for half of it.

"Here. No tricks. I promise."

I took it and put it in my purse. She gathered up the cash lying on her desk—what we had both made today that had not yet been deposited.

"Take this."

"Part of it is yours."

"Take it. Let's call it severance pay."

I stuffed it in my purse. I wanted to thank her or even give her a hug but she had gone cold and aloof. She sat down and started to surf the internet. I decided I would not say good-bye. I turned and left.

I cashed the check right away. I had more than enough money to set myself up and live for a long while even if I didn't find a job. I swung by the house, piled all I own in the car, and then went to a motel and rented a room.

I showered and lay down. I had done it. I had repudiated the business. But I still didn't feel like I had shaken it off. Something more seemed in order, but what?

***

I woke up in the morning and knew. I waited until ten and called. The pastor said he could see me right away.

I don't believe in God—well, only sort of. I guess there must be someone out there. Otherwise, where did ideas of good and evil come from?

I drove to the church. The sky shone blue and clear, the sun a white, weak light that gave no warmth. I trudged through the snow and went into the church. The pastor was there to greet me.

We went into his office. He asked how he could help me. It was embarrassing telling him I had been a whore. I guess priests and pastors seem more holy or close to God and so I didn't like saying the w-word. He took it in stride, though. He's probably heard it all and is not easy to shock. He listened as I told my story, though I didn't say anything about the Satanic stuff. I said I wanted to do something decisive, something that would serve as a marker that would signify a clean break with the past.

He sat in thought a moment and then looked at me.

"You could pray and tell God you want to start new."

"I don't know how," I said.

"I'll pray with you."

We knelt by his desk. He prayed. He told God about me—as if God needed to know. But I realized what he said was a much for me as for God. He made me feel comfortable. When he fell silent I told God I was sorry and I would never sell myself again. I asked him to help me get a job and make a new life. I did the best I could at praying. When I got quiet the pastor closed us off.

We talked a little more. He invited me to their regular church service. I said I would come.

I left the church. It was freezing cold. I went back to motel, bought a paper, and started checking want ads. I wondered what I could do. Not many jobs were listed. The motel room seemed big and empty. I didn't know what to do with my time. By now I would have been welcoming my first customers of the day.

Rather than hanging out at the motel, I went to Arni's. At least there I would have the waitresses to talk with.

I was only there then minutes when Carrie called. I told her what I'd done. She seemed surprised.

"Praying…that's a good idea."

"You?"

"Chad's coming over in an hour. My Dad is gone and we both have excuses. We're going to do it."

"Be careful."

"I will."

I bought coffee. Clara came in and we talked. I told her I was looking for a job. Clara knew what I did but she studied my face when I said I wanted to work somewhere here in town.

"There's an opening here," she said. "You want to fill out an application?"

I filled it out. Clara got busy. I watched the sun on the snow. Carrie, I thought, was probably getting it now for the first time. I remembered my first time and wondered how I got going down the path I took. Clara brought over the manager. She said I could start on Saturday.

Everything seemed to have fallen into place, but I worried all the same. I have not had a lot of experience with occultism. I know, though, there is reality behind it, and that is what makes it scary. I'd felt the air get thick and full of bad energy at Blake's place. Carrie said her plan would work, but how could she be certain? Her Dad might have tricks up his sleeve she knew nothing about. I sat by the front window of my little motel room and watched the snow shine in the sunlight and the icy blue sky arch over the mountains. I had bet all my chips on one turn of the wheel. My fate was in other hands so I just accepted it as best I could.

Time rolled around to go to his place. It had begun to snow again. I arrived and went in, slipped into a bedroom and took off my clothes. Three hundred-dollar bills lay on the bed. I stuck them in my purse.

This would be the last money I made as a working girl whichever way things turned out.

I went into the room. Carrie stood in her place on the right side of the altar. She looked at me. Her eyes told me she had done it—though, of course, she was cautious because her Dad might suspect something. After the quick look, she turned her eyes straight ahead. Blake prepared for the ceremony. I tried not to look nervous but when he glanced at me and smiled I saw green like I do when I'm about to faint, but I recovered and smiled back. He turned to his altar and started the ceremony.

He chanted, put his hands over the candles, and went on like nothing was different from before. I waited. My legs got tired.

Probably twenty minutes into the ceremony, it started.

DARK THINGS II

The air in the room pulsated with energy—like before, like a lot of static electricity was in the air, though somehow this energy felt aggressive. It rose to a certain level, like other time, but then it got thicker and felt more evil. The room went murky, like it had filled with smoke, but it wasn't smoke. What it was I'm not sure but I was certain it was not good. The sense of evil, fear, and danger grew at an alarming rate.

Philips seemed annoyed at this. His raised his arms, fingers shaped like claws, and yelled something in that language—Latin, I guess. It sounded like he was barking orders. Then it happened, all at once.

The candles on the altar melted. The altar itself split in half.

I felt something—like a hard puff of air, though if I say that I'd have to add it was an *evil* puff of air—the only way I can describe it. it knocked me down, picked Philips up, and threw him to the ground. He began to convulse but then shouted some foreign words and staggered to his feet.

I got to my hands and knees. I looked up and saw him glaring at me, his eyes filled with an intense hatred—hatred like I had never seen, ever in my life. I would not have thought a human being could look so evil.

"You worthless whore," he spat. His spittle landed on my shoulder burned like acid. I cried out in pain. "What did you do?"

Fear and pain kept me from answering.

He opened his mouth—I guess to curse me, but a young voice from behind him called.

"It's not her, Daddy, it's me—both of us!"

He looked back at Carrie. I could see his mind working.

"I'll kill you both," he growled. "I'll send both your souls to the deepest pit of hell." I write "hell," but he used some other word for it—a frightening word I had never heard before. The very sound it made me numb with terror. He pointed a finger at me.

I felt—how can I describe it? It was as if suddenly my body stopped working. I could see, hear, and think, but my breath and heartbeat were gone. My body—the body we know so well, with its noises, urges, shifts of fluid, rhythm and heat—had gone still. I sank down. He had pulled the life from me. All my strength went and I collapsed, hitting my face against the floor.

Noises started. I thought maybe he had sent me to hell and I could hear the screams of the damned, but I realized after a moment it was him. I also felt my body again. My chest pounded wildly as my heart started up, but I could breathe and I felt life had returned to me. My nose was bleeding.

I raised myself and opened my eyes. Blake Philips lay face up on the floor, eyes wide, mouth open, his skin convulsing with moving lumps like you see on horror movies when some kind of parasite gets under someone's skin. Carrie stood, watching with horror. The lumps moved all over him. We heard what sounded like his bones crunching, a scream—and then silence.

The room felt normal again. The evil in the air had gone.

Carrie rushed over and knelt by her father. She touched him. It looked like he was alive.

"I'll call 911," she said. "Let's get dressed."

I got my clothes on. A small red scar burned on my skin where he had spit on me. The police arrived in ten minutes. EMTs took Blake to the emergency room. He was alive but died an hour later. Doctors said he suffered what they could only describe as a "massive epileptic seizure" that had caused his bones to break, starting internal bleeding. After only an hour his corpse began to decay to such an extent that Carrie arranged for on-site cremation.

***

Carrie stayed with her Mom until she turned eighteen. After graduating from high school she enrolled in Bennington College, not far from where I live. She can see Eric that way. At least twice a week she comes to visit me. She is studying to be a writer.

I still work at Arni's. Staci has found a couple of new girls to work for her and she and I are back on speaking terms. I date Lonnie, the guy I used to do house calls for, and I think he's going to ask me to marry him. Working as a waitress tires me out, and I sure don't make as much money as I did at my old job, but I get by. Carrie tells me I should go to school and train to be a nurse or computer clerk. I'm thinking about it. I do still go to the church. I don't buy the born-again stuff, but the people are nice. They seem to care about me, and I can't say anything against that.

Some nights I wonder if the evil will return. I wonder if Philips' friends want to avenge him—or if, because I was in the same room with demons, they'll come for me. Sometimes the scar on my shoulder aches. There are doors that should never be opened. I'd seen past those doors, even if only for a few seconds and not by my own choice. I hope for the best. I know now hope is the most important thing.

About the author:

David's horror/supernatural fiction has appeared widely. He's had stories in Sinister Tales, Dark Distortions, And Now the Nightmare Begins, Horror Through the Ages, The Horror Zine, and many others. His novella, The Gallery, is available from Eternal Press through Amazon.

R.F.

by Mel Clayton

YOU can see the mill clearly from the ferry. It sits there in the distance, gleaming through mossy oaks and dead pines like a twisted car wreck. To get to it, you have to cut through the swamps on the mainland and you'd have to know which of the narrow dirt roads through the woods would take you to the gates and onto the grounds. Scratched onto the back of an envelope were my directions and the name R.F.

R.F was the groundskeeper, a friendly old guy with a lame leg. He let me through the gates and rode back with me down the rutty, overgrown, path to the mill. Along the way he puffed his cigarette and told me how he was the one to find the body.

"Body?"

"Down on the river side of the mill. I thought maybe that was why you came. Drew a lot of attention to the mill at the time. "Was me and Todd Barron. He was helping me out around here at the time. Started our work as usual, walking the grounds, bagging litter, rocks, things that might choke the lawnmower. He resigned that day.

"I stood out there for hours with the police," he said, fidgeting with his lighter, "watching them mark things with yellow ribbon. Damn ferry drifted by once, coming through the fog long enough for tourist in straw hats to snap pictures. On account of it being a crime scene, we didn't clean for a while.

"Always had my work cut out for me cause of teenagers coming here on Friday nights to get drunk and break things for shits and giggles. But about six years ago they stopped coming. How come you want pictures of it? It's an eye sore."

"I guess I have a thing for eye sores," I said.

He chuckled and flipped his cigarette out the window. As we came around a bend in the road, I could see the mill ahead. It looked capable of grinding people to bits like some giant polluted paper shredder. I parked next to a rusted pickup I assumed belonged to R.F since there were no other vehicles around.

"That cabbage fart smell you smellin' is the marshes. You get used to it over time."

He got out and lit another cigarette as I got my camera equipment out of the back seat. He told me to go wherever I wanted, just take care around areas marked with orange tape and if I was planning on going inside, let him know first so he could go along with his flashlight since there was no electricity.

"Where was the body," I asked, taking a quick picture of the rusted pick up and a shot of the mill.

"You see that big twisted dead tree out there," he said pointing towards the river. "Was right there near it. Guy was shot in the head." He leaned in a bit and said in a lower tone, "Some people say the Sheriff did him in. Was too close to a couple of truths that Winslow didn't want to get out."

I snapped a picture of the tree, zooming in as close as I could. "Who was the guy?"

"Some ex con. Nobody gives a shit about ex cons, let me tell you. I don't think they tried too hard to solve it."

R.F went on to say that it was never the same after the corpse; always felt like eyes were watching him and it made him kind of jumpy when the mower was making so much noise that you couldn't hear if somebody came up behind you. "Can't share thoughts like that with most people. They'll just say you're crazy. Hell. Maybe I am crazy."

R.F walked over to the rusted pick up and started putting on his work gloves and goggles so I headed down to the river for some pictures. On my way back to my car I heard a phone ringing from inside the plant. R.F was nowhere in sight. I called out but there was no answer. A light moved across a window on the second floor.

Through a collapsed door on the side of the mill I called for R.F. The phone kept ringing, echoing through the metal catwalks and rusted pipes in the darkness, and I could hear music. I stepped

MEL CLAYTON

inside.

The place was pitch black in corners and only had light in spots where the sun shot through holes in the exterior. Before my eyes adjusted to the dark, I bumped my legs on steps and machines and once banged my head on a low hanging beam. Occasionally calling out for R.F., I followed the sound of the ringing phone, which was inside of a small office, encased in glass. It was on a metal desk and behind the desk was the jukebox, rotating in a rainbow of color. I tried to open the door but it was locked.

"He knows we know," a female voice whispered. The voice came from behind me, somewhere in the dark.

"Hello," I shouted.

I heard clicking heels along the catwalk overhead and figured maybe R.F was having a rendezvous with some woman crazy enough to play hide and seek in an old mill.

I was heading for the door when the phone and music stopped. Through the door I caught a glimpse of a blond in a red dress, long legs running through the grass towards the river. She was waving her arms.

Outside, I couldn't see anyone at first. Then I noticed someone on the ground by the river, at the oak tree where R.F said he'd found a body years ago. It had the same faded navy t-shirt R.F was wearing and the same white pants. The blonde in the red dress was floating face down in the river.

Frantically I searched my pockets for my cell phone as I ran down to the river, tripping over stumps and rocks and nearly falling several times. I realized my phone was probably still in my car but figured it would be better to get to R.F, see if he's ok before going for the phone.

R.F was far from ok. He had a bullet hole in his forehead and was badly decomposed. The lady in the water had drifted away from the shoreline, well out of reach. As I ran to my car, I wondered what the hell happened? When? How could I explain it to authorities?

"He's been shot dead," I shouted to the 9-1-1 operator. She said emergency agents were on the way, sit tight. I explained that the

61

shooter was still at large and I didn't think sitting there was a good idea.

I hauled ass back down the rutty dirt path, branches and leaves pounding my car. I swung the gate open and drove to the main highway. I could still see the main gate from where I sat. For thirty-five minutes I sat in my car, shaking and terrified that whoever killed R.F would come for me.

When a deputy Sheriff and an ambulance arrived, they said they used to get these calls all the time, usually from stoned teenagers. They seemed to speak to me in that way mother's do to scared children. I reluctantly rode with the ambulance down to the mill to show them what they already suspected. Nothing. R.F was not by the river. There was no groundskeeper. Not since Todd Barron quit six years ago when he found his friend's body by the river.

"Well whose truck is that?"

"Belonged to Farrow."

I spent a few days at the hospital suffering from shock. Over time, once I felt I could handle it, I drove back to the steel mill gate. R.F showed up, same as he had the first Saturday and the same way he would every Saturday after that. On each ride with R.F to the mill, I tried to get more information on the Sheriff and what he knew that would lead to his murder. But each time he always said the same things, no matter what I said in return.

About the author:

Mel Clayton is a member of the Horror Writer's Association and a graduate of the University of North Carolina at Wilmington. Her most recent story, "Life Without Forelegs," appears in the anthology XX Eccentric: Stories About the Eccentricities of Women, available at www.mainstreetrag.com. You can follow her blog at www.melclayton.wordpress.com.

THE OLD MAN OF WEEVIL CREEK
by Adrian Ludens

THE Deegan brothers emptied two whiskey bottles the night they decided to kill The Old Man. He lived all alone in a decrepit shack in the swamp known to locals as Weevil Creek.

"The Old Man went to grammar school with Moses," Joe, the oldest and marginally wisest brother said. "He won't even hear us creeping around."

"Yeah but what if he does?" Charlie asked after a bouquet-wilting belch.

"Then we beat his ass and pitch him into the swamp," Howard volunteered.

"Hell yeah! Food for the gators." Joe clinked his nearly empty glass against that of his youngest brothers' in agreement.

Charlie leaned closer and lowered his voice. "I hear he has thirteen mason jars filled with gold coins or some shit."

Joe nodded his head. "Buried pirate treasure. All his life he kept it. That right there proves he's crazy. Money's made for spendin'."

The residents of Weevil Creek say and think a lot of things about The Old Man that generally keep him safe from hell raisers with a mind for stirring up trouble. Despite the almost certain fact that he hides a fortune somewhere in the vicinity of his shack no one has ever made a serious attempt at robbing him. The Old Man was a very strange person, that's for sure. He's believed to have been a World War II veteran; but he's so old that no one can remember when he was young. Perhaps he'd served in World War I instead.

Among the gnarled Cypress trees in the front yard of his aged and neglected residence, The Old Man maintains a strange collection preserved animals, oddly grouped and posed. It is whispered about town that the animals have not received the benefits of taxidermy but have been preserved through darker and more blasphemous means.

DARK THINGS II

This collection frightens away most of the younger delinquents who muster up enough courage to travel deep enough into the swamp to find his shack. Only a select few have actually laid eyes on The Old Man. His long white hair and beard are said to resemble that old Irving character Rip Van Winkle. He is said to hobble about on a shriveled stick of a left leg. The general belief is that the bite of a hungry but inefficient gator made him a cripple but no one knows for sure. It simply adds to the mystery of The Old Man.

But there are other things that scare the older and braver folks who sometimes steal up to his shack to peer in through the cracked and grimy panes. These folk say that on certain nights beneath a waning full moon, the Old Man will dump out the treasure-filled mason jars onto his bare earth floor. They also say that he strips off his rags and writhes around naked in the pile of coins. They say he pisses on the treasure, pleasures himself on it and cuts his arms and drips his blood on them. He utters strange chants that no one can make heads or tails of. Those who have watched The Old Man in these dark rituals do not care to watch him again.

But the Deegan brothers didn't believe all that claptrap. The general impression of the trio in Carver's Creek was that they were all 'meaner than water moccasins, sneakier than wildcats and coarser than wild boars'.

Joe, Charlie and Howard Deegan saw in The Old Man merely a tottering, helpless and pitiful wreck. He couldn't even walk without the aid of his knotted cane. They imagined his thin, weak hands shaking as he cowered in fear.

The Deegan brothers didn't give a rip about the old fellow, nor did they think to fear him. They didn't believe the stories. The lure of a decrepit geezer who pays for his few necessities at the general store with Spanish gold coins minted over two centuries ago proved to be impossible for the brothers to resist. Suffice to say they talked late into the night and when they left the roadhouse, they had murder and money on their minds.

The moonlit night made it easy to find the turnoff to The Old Man's shack. Joe killed the headlights a mile from their destination and let the moonlight guide them the rest of the way. He navigated the rusty pickup to within a quarter mile of The Old Man's shack in Weevil Creek and then steered it into the wet ditch and killed the engine.

"I don't much care for the moon tonight," Charlie hissed. "Too bright. If someone drives by they'll notice the truck."

"Nobody's gonna drive by 'cause nobody has any reason to," Joe murmured back.

The trio made their way stealthily down the trail toward The Old Man's shack. Joe carried a tire iron while Charlie held a baseball bat and Howard cradled a two by four. The moon did indeed seem strangely bright, as if the swamp had been lit up like a big Hollywood sound stage. The cypress trees pointed accusatory branches at the brothers as they rounded the bend. Then the night sounds took center stage, but only for a brief moment.

After what happened next, a legend was born.

***

Little things can cause considerable excitement in tiny towns. That is probably the reason that folks in Weevil Creek talked all that summer and fall about the three Deegan brothers who disappeared that night. And some of the more inquisitive folk stopped by the Deegan house to pry for clues from the boys' haggard parents. Legends sprang up almost immediately about ghosts and murders and such. But no one except me has ever gone far enough into that part of the swamp to confirm the fates of Joe, Charlie and Howard Deegan; my brothers.

A girl with no tongue can't go around telling her side of the story and nobody asked me to anyhow. But after the state came and took me away when I was fifteen, I learned to read and write really good. Now I can finally tell my story.

I was there in the bar when my brothers hatched their idiot plan. I rode along in the back of the truck when they drove out to The Old Man's shack. But as usual my brothers were caught up in the excitement of the moment and forgot all about me. Most everyone did back there in Weevil Creek. My daddy called me 'Runt' and Mama acted like I wasn't even real. I'm not bitter; that's just the way things were. Sometimes I think my being a mute dwarf, and 'just a girl' at that, saved my life that night.

I heard Joe shouting directions as my brothers surprised The Old Man as he dug up his treasure. I heard the old man's cries of pain as my brothers beat him down. I heard them chuck him into the water and listened to them laughing it up as they watched the gators fighting over their scrawny meal. I closed my eyes and heard the money being divided, hefted and redistributed. Then my brothers came thundering and staggering through the swamp like wild boars, weighted down with their ill-gotten gains. Something went wrong almost immediately. Their screams scared me so bad I cowered in absolute terror. I couldn't have moved if my life depended on it. But like I said before, maybe that was for the best.

The legends talk about 'drowning in quicksand'. Others take it a step further and swear that you can hear the brothers screaming on certain nights. It's also a badge of honor to claim to have heard the ghost of the old man laughing.

Bullshit; all of it.

Truth is stranger and more terrible than fiction every time.

***

Only one person has ever been brave enough to walk right up to The Old Man's gate since that night. You see, I had to know. I wish I hadn't, but there are some things you just have to find out for yourself.

The moon was bright in the sky; just like the night it happened. I took my time, making my way down the overgrown dirt road real quiet-like. I saw the strange collection of preserved animals up close. Wild boars stood upright. Snakes were split open, turned inside-out and sewn back together. A massive owl hung upside down like a bat, wings outstretched in a five foot arc. Every creature looked horrid and unnatural. A light flickered dimly from within the shack. I tiptoed toward the closest window and scanned the yard for something that I could climb up on in order to see inside. My breath caught like the muggy swamp air had suddenly turned to sludge in my throat. My brother Joe crouched near the corner of the shack.

His eyes were milky white and stared at nothing. His skin was waxy gray. Joe's clothing hung about his frame in shredded tatters. One arm bent back behind his head at such a sharp angle that I could see his shoulder blade bulging out against his skin. My brother looked like a statue draped in rotting party streamers. His mouth was open so far I almost felt afraid of tottering into the darkness within.

Around the side of the shack I found Charlie. He had the same horrible gaze, the same waxy shade of a preserved corpse. His arms were still crooked in a way that led me to believe he didn't let go of the jars of coins even after all hell had broken loose. Now instead of mason jars, Charlie's arms were crooked around pots holding climbing hydrangea vines. The green tendrils had already begun to wind around my brother's arms and neck.

I could hear chanting coming from inside the shack. I heard the coins jingling and clattering as the ritual was performed. I had lost all desire to see inside, but would not flee until I had learned the fates of all three of my brothers. Part of me wondered if The Old Man had perished after all. I imagined my youngest brother capering around like a lunatic inside the shack and didn't like how plausible it seemed.

I navigated lightly across The Old Man's property by the light cast by the moon. I avoided a large suspicious-looking wet area. It looked at first like quicksand but something about how it seemed to bubble and froth got me wondering about its purpose. I stood like a statue and listened to the muffled chanting coming from inside the shack and the frogs singing all around me in the swamp. I already said I had a knack for being invisible and after ten or fifteen minutes my patience was rewarded. A young raccoon came wandering right past my foot. I gave it a good hard kick and sent the poor critter through the air and right into the bubbling puddle.

DARK THINGS II

My hair stood on end as the raccoon squealed and thrashed in the muddy mess. The animal struggled to get to safety but instead got sucked into the ground as if unseen hands had grabbed it and dragged it down. I stared at the quicksand until all movement ceased. Then I heard a sound coming from the shack and quickly pressed myself up into a crevice in the massive trunk of the closest cypress tree. The entire action took no more than a second, and a second was all I had. I gazed in awe and horror as The Old Man shambled from the back door of his shack toward the bubbling pits.

The Old Man still lived. He lacked a right hand, and his left leg ended at the knee; but he still tottered forward. The moonlight showed me enough to see True Evil glittering in his crazed eyes. I could hear the air of each labored breath whistling through at least one hole somewhere in that wretched frame.

The Old Man paused and stooped over the spot where the raccoon had gone under. He muttered a word that I could not quite hear and a slime-covered travesty emerged from the muddy pit and handed over the dead animal. The figure was hunched and twisted, as if every bone in its body had been broken and mended at painful angles. The bubbling quicksand dripped from the figure as it stood silently watching its master.

The Old Man hobbled to a shallow pool of swamp water and quickly cleaned the fur of the dead animal. Then he set about posing the newest addition to his collection. When he'd finished he cackled and held the critter up for examination. The Old Man had bent the raccoon backwards until its spine had snapped. Then he'd twisted all four paws together and trussed them up with the tail. The poor animal looked like a fluffy bag of trash ready for pickup, except for the sad bandit face hanging limply to one side.

I trembled in horror as The Old Man placed his new creation on the ground and began shambling back toward his shack. Seeing what he'd done to the raccoon made me feel pity for the poor creature. Seeing what had become of Joe and Charlie made me feel worse. But when The Old Man stopped at his doorstep, turned and croaked out another indecipherable word of instruction meant for the slime-covered travesty that had assisted him, that's when the tears began to freely fall down my sunken cheeks.

The twisted and gnarled figure that turned toward me and slowly immersed itself in the muddy bubbling quicksand was that of my youngest brother. Howard stared right at me huddled there against the cypress tree. Our eyes locked in the moonlight, and as he sank beneath the muck Howard's eyes didn't even blink.

About the author:

Adrian Ludens is a member of the Horror Writers Association. Visit his author page on Amazon for other books and magazines he has contributed to, including two previous Pill Hill Press anthologies. Become his friend on Facebook for updates and links. Adrian lives with his family in the Black Hills of South Dakota where he runs a classic rock radio station.

DOLL'S HOUSE
by Lisa J. Marcado

THE old house gave her the creeps. Ashley Fairfield stared at the splintering wood and peeling paint. Eerie willow trees flanked both ends, their tendrils of Spanish moss dripped from brittle branches like cobwebs. "Why did Aunt Mary have to leave us her ugly house? It looks like it hasn't been cleaned in years."

"That's the funny thing about wills; they can bring about unexpected surprises to the next of kin." Elizabeth shook her head, tossing back her dark ponytail. "Let's get this over with."

"Wow, talk about in dire need of maid service." Ashley wrinkled her nose in disgust following her sister inside. "There's got to be at least ten layers of dust on everything. How gross!"

"I'm sure your dorm room is in worse shape."

She snorted at her sister's comment, but said nothing. Despite the dust, the living room was rather homey in a strange outdated sort of way. Graying doilies covered old wooden furniture that at first glance seemed to be well cared for. Pale pink pillows were placed in a tidy fashion on what was once white sofa covers. Everything seemed to have an almost romantic feminine style to it. Lots of pink and lace, both of which neither she nor her sister cared much for.

"It's almost like some sort of a Victorian dollhouse." Ashley remarked tucking an auburn strand of hair behind an ear. "Way too girly though. No wonder she never married. No guy would ever want to live here."

"Ashley!" Elizabeth scolded in almost outrage.

"What? She's dead. It's not like she's going to come back and haunt me."

"It's rude and disrespectful."

Ashley narrowed her eyes in annoyance. Her older sister could be bossy, but nothing like this. She however was too stubborn to put any real thought into it. "She was just a crazy old bat who died

70

in her sleep. Like anyone is going to give a rat's-"

"That's enough!" Elizabeth cut her sister off. "You don't know anything about her therefore you have no right to insult her."

She drew back as though slapped. "What's your problem? You didn't know her either and now you're defending her like she was your best friend."

"I... Sorry." She touched her head then sighed. "Let's look at the rest of the house."

They wandered in each room, unimpressed with anything in particular. Elizabeth guessed that the furniture might go for a pretty penny at an antiques dealer, but like everything else it would need to be cleaned. Ashley suggested dumping everything on one of their other relatives until her sister reminded her that the money they would make if they were to sell everything off would not only pay for the rest of her education, but also finance the boutique and café they wanted to open. Nowhere on Ashley's life plan was 'starting a minimum wage job immediately after college.' She also knew that Elizabeth didn't want to work at the tiny diner forever.

Just when they decided that the house couldn't be any spookier, they encountered the stairs to the attic.

Ashley shivered. There was just something about attics, especially in old houses that gave her the heebie-jeebies. A flash of lightning appeared through the lone grimy window followed by an angry roar of thunder. "Great. Now it's storming."

Elizabeth said nothing. She brushed past her sister as though in a trance, her footsteps making loud creaks as she walked deeper into the room.

"Be careful, Lizzy. You don't want to fall through the floor." She let out a shriek when another loud boom shook the house and then scampered after her sibling.

If she thought the downstairs was dirty, compared to the attic, it was clean enough to do surgery in. Ashley coughed, trying not to choke on the musty odor as she stumbled past old lamps, broken toys, and battered books. A bright flash filled everything with light before plunging it into pitch black. Ashley swore, cursing their luck

DARK THINGS II

to be in the attic of all places when the power decided to go out. Now she would really have to watch where she stepped or else risk breaking something; possibly her own neck. "Lizzy, we should go back downstairs. It's way too dark in here."

Ashley cried out as she tripped over something, barely catching herself before she crashed into some boxes. "Lizzy? Are you okay?"

Lightning struck again, illuminating her sister's back as she knelt over something that Ashley couldn't see. "What did you find?" She stepped closer, her curiosity overruled her fear.

Elizabeth didn't react. She remained crouched in the corner of the cramped room.

Ashley angled herself to the other side then froze. Leaned against a tarnished mirror was a porcelain doll. Her golden curls framed a face painted with a rosy blush and petal pink lips. Her dress, also in a shade of pink was covered with a lacy apron that was once white. Matching stockings and shoes covered her feet. What took Ashley's breath away were the doll's eyes. Framed with dark lashes, the big blue eyes seemed to see right through her.

She dropped her hand on her sister's shoulder. "We should go."

"Why?"

The question was lifeless and empty. Ashley grabbed Elizabeth's hand trying to pull her to her feet, fear quickly creeping up her spine. "Please, come on, Lizzy. I want to go home."

The door slammed shut, the house groaned as though it were alive. Ashley bit her lip, struggling against tears. Her sister only continued to stare at the doll as though it were the only thing that existed. Her anxiety continued to build as the storm outside worsened.

She didn't even want to go to the spooky old house to begin with. It was all Elizabeth's idea. Now, she was trapped there because her older sister thought a stupid old doll was more important than she was. Enraged, she bent over to grab it so she could smash it to pieces when Elizabeth screamed like a banshee, striking her little sister across the face.

Stunned, Ashley backed away. She brought her hand up to her stinging cheek; drew back in shock as her fingertips smeared against something warm and slick. "Liz-"

"Don't touch."

The words came out in an almost unearthly hiss. The single light bulb in the room blazed to blinding life. Ashley covered her eyes in pain then gaped at her sister.

Elizabeth's raven locks had become golden ringlets. "How-"

"Run," a cool breeze seemed to whisper.

She screamed more in fear of the phantom voice than her own sister as she bolted to the door.

"Foolish, sister. You think you can stop me? You kept me imprisoned for twenty-five years," Elizabeth sneered. The temperature of the room continued to drop; her eyes seemed to glow an arctic sapphire; as hot as a flame. Loose papers flew around the room as books fell off the shelves.

"I…I don't know what you are talking about… Please don't hurt me!"

Her only response was a cruel laugh.

Ashley whimpered, slowly backing away. Just as she took another step, a loud groan erased all thoughts as she fell through the floor.

***

"Wake up."

Green eyes fluttered open as Ashley moaned in pain. What happened? Where was she? Was she still dreaming?

"You must get up," someone urged.

"Lizzy? Is that you?" She rolled over, biting back a cry as a sharp pain stabbed into her left shoulder. There was dust and debris all around her. Her head was pounding to the point that she could almost see stars. A sick sensation stirred in her stomach. Fighting not to vomit, she rolled over, narrowly missing the plunging blade.

DARK THINGS II

Head screaming, she pushed herself to her knees in time to dodge another slash of the butcher's knife clenched in Elizabeth's hand.

Windows shattered, the air around them shrieked. Books and knick knacks flew from the shelves pummeling the murderous sibling as though trying to save the other one.

"Stop trying to meddle, you worthless ingrate!" Elizabeth bared her teeth like a savage animal as she growled at the wind.

Ashley used the distraction to make her escape. Her mind struggled to comprehend what was going on. Her sister had never tried to harm her before so why now? She wished they sold the house as it was rather than set foot inside.

"Through the kitchen."

"Where other sharp objects that can be used to kill me are? Forget it!"

"If you value your life, you must listen to me." The voice warned in an urgent yet impatient tone. *"There is no time to argue."*

"Just who the hell are you?"

"Your crazy old bat of an aunt."

"You..."

"I should have known she would have latched onto your elder sister. She was named after her despite your mother's better judgment."

Ashley found herself at a loss. "I don't understand."

"Go into the pantry. Quickly. Then I'll explain."

"If you say so." She grabbed a kitchen knife for protection, even though she didn't think she'd have the heart to use it against her older sister. Reluctantly, she did as the ghost bid. The pantry, she realized was a small closet with a tiny door in the back. Without any further arguments she crawled through the threshold.

Her shoulder throbbed in protest, but she ignored it. Her mind was too distracted with unanswered questions to allow the pain to hinder her descent. One in particular seemed to haunt her; why was Lizzy trying to kill her?

Ashley froze at the sight of another small door. With a deep

74

breath she pushed it open. She frowned at the tiny cavernous room. Something felt very off about it. Along the wall rickety wooden shelves held what looked like ancient books covered in grime. In the corner was a large equally dirty mirror. On the opposite side of the wall, several other shelves held bottles of multiple shapes and sizes. In the center of the room sat a large rusted over kettle; cauldron her mind corrected.

"You were a witch. You cursed Lizzy!" She spun around, anger radiating off her like rays of the sun. The only thing that kept her from pummeling the ghost was the fact that she couldn't see her.

"Not precisely, child. Though, I do have to inquire...how badly do you wish to save your sister? Could you end her life?"

Ashley choked, her fury melting into complete horror at the concept. "How could you even ask such a thing? I could never kill Lizzy."

"Then you will die."

The reply was said in such a matter of fact tone that she felt as though she had been punched. "You can't be serious..."

"History is repeating. Part of it is my fault. Part is destiny."

"Destiny is for fantasy novels."

"You are here for a reason; to put an end to what had begun twenty-five years ago." The ghost paused as though collecting her thoughts. *"My sister dabbled in witchcraft. During her careless adventures she unleashed a vengeful spirit that took over her soul. I was less practiced but managed to seal her into a doll; the doll that your sister was drawn to. My sister's name was also Elizabeth."*

"But if you're Aunt Mary...I never heard about her...I mean you having a sister..."

"Hazel to be exact. I had a strong dislike to my first name, but that's beside the point. After her disappearance it was decided that she was dead. Because of what happened I asked that she never be mentioned. Not everyone heeded my wishes however."

"Why did you leave this place to us in your will? Did you know this was going to happen?"

"I was not certain how long the spell would last."

DARK THINGS II

Ashley rubbed her shoulder. "Now what?"

"Now…you die."

Ashley turned reflexively, then gasped more in terror than agony as the blade of her elder sister's knife sank into her left arm. Blood seeped from the wound in a light drizzle then gushed like a geyser as the weapon was ripped away.

"Binding me to that pathetic doll only delayed your suffering, sister. If only I could have found a spell to prolong your miserable life so I could torture you for eternity." Elizabeth smirked. She licked the blood from the knife and snorted. "You taste foul, but will have to do. Perhaps bleeding you out like a sacrificial goat would be the most enjoyable method of revenge."

"Lizzy," Ashley cringed, clutching at the cut, her arm screaming in pain. There had to be some way to reach her sister. "Listen to me. I know you're still in there somewhere. Fight her off! I know you can do it. You have to."

Elizabeth only laughed. "Fool. That poor excuse of a girl is dead. She will never hear your voice ever again."

"I told you. You must kill her."

"Shut up!" Ashley rushed to the shelves of books, tore them down in a heated rage. Elizabeth shouted at her, but she ignored her words. Instead Ashley picked up one of the boards then smashed it into the bottles and the mirror. Glass shattered, fire erupted as smoke filled the air.

"You whore," Elizabeth shrieked, racing to plunge the butcher's knife into her sister.

Ashley merely stood there, then at the last second, threw herself to the floor, rolled, and scrambled to her feet, bolting to the door that would lead her back through the pantry.

Just as the door began to close, she dove inside, crawling like her life depended on it.

She didn't know what she was doing. She only knew that she didn't want to kill her sister despite how much her mind tried to convince her it was the only way. Her only other option was to go back to the attic.

76

"What are you doing? You have to kill her."

"I told you to shut up. Leave me alone. I don't want to hear anymore. If something has to be finished then I'm doing it my own way." Ashley hissed, bursting out of the pantry. She raced up the stairs, the ghost still trailing behind.

"But…"

"You're already dead," she snapped, sprinting up the stairs. "Go away."

Ashley shoved her way into the attic. Everything in the room seemed to come to life as though they were some sort of guardians of their queen's chambers. That confirmed her suspicions; the doll had to be destroyed.

Books launched themselves at her head. Wires snaked out, lashing towards her limbs. She nearly got yanked back down through the hole in the floor that had formed when Elizabeth had attacked her the first time, but managed to escape from the attacking fan by smashing her foot into it.

She gasped for breath as a lamp cord wrapped itself around her throat. She wrenched her hand in between it then sliced her knife through nicking her neck in the process. Once she freed herself, what felt like an entire box of toys, rained down upon her. Ashley grabbed at them, tearing them off her clothes and hair. She could feel the bite of several cuts as sharp pieces scraped against her skin, but wouldn't let that prevent her from continuing her mission.

"Stop!"

Ashley swore under her breath at the sound of her sister's voice. Apparently trashing the secret room was not enough to keep her at bay for too long. She narrowed her eyes. "I'm bleeding, my shoulder is probably dislocated. Do you really think I'm going to listen to you? Think again."

She drew a breath and leapt over a pile of books, clothes, and other junk stacked up like a barricade. Her foot caught on a shirt sleeve, causing her to trip, landing hard on the odds and ends. The breath knocked out of her, she pushed herself up, and over the rest of the barrier.

DARK THINGS II

Limping, she reached for the doll, them screamed as a large amore fell over, attempting to crush her. In a flash, her sister was on top of her. Ashley blinked pondering how Elizabeth could have moved so fast as the blade plunged into her chest.

"I told you, you shouldn't meddle, little sister."

"Go…to hell." Ashley threw her fist into Elizabeth's face, kicked her off, then with all her strength dove for the doll.

Elizabeth and the ghost yelled as Ashley crashed into the mirror, shards rained down upon her, slicing her skin and clothes. Just as she felt the blade pierce into her back, she smashed the doll's fragile body into the floor. She glared at the broken porcelain littering the wooden floor as she struggled for breath. Gritting her teeth, fighting against the pain, she slammed it repeatedly until the remains were too small to piece back together.

It was then she could smell smoke. It seemed that Elizabeth was too bent on murder to bother putting out the flames which were probably going to swallow them whole. A chill crept over her body but she ignored it.

Pushing herself to her knees she turned around then cried out. Sprawled under the amore was her sister. A large puddle of blood surrounded her from a gash in her head. Her body looked lifeless.

"Lizzy?"

There was no answer. Ashley collapsed to the floor as she coughed several times, grimacing at the blood then everything went black.

***

Nancy Fairfield stared in disbelief at the still smoking remains of her ex-husband's great aunt's house; the last known whereabouts of her daughters. Her eyes filled as they fell upon the scorched license plate of her eldest's car. They were just supposed to look at the house, not disappear. Where could they have gone? Were they dead or by some miracle still alive somewhere?

78

LISA J. MARCADO

A firefighter approached her, wiping sweat from his brow. "Sorry Ma'am. There's still no sign of your daughters. Did they or the late Miss Fairfield by any chance collect dolls?"

"Not that I know of, why do you ask?"

He signaled for her to wait a moment then walked off. He appeared a minute later with a slightly burnt metal box containing two porcelain dolls. One had long dark hair pulled back into a ponytail, while the other had shoulder length auburn hair and striking green eyes. Both were clad in white dresses. "The crazy thing is, they kind of resemble the pictures of your daughters."

About the author:

Lisa J. Marcado, a graduate of the University of Central Florida, is one of three authors for the website, "TrinityGateways. net" where she has two stories posted; A Chance in Time and Stolen Secrets. This is her first short horror story to be published in an anthology.

A STRANGE TURN OF EVENTS
by John Grover

KEVIN zipped up his jeans and turned back to Tim, who was still in bed. "Do you know where my shirt is?"

"You mean I don't get to keep it as a souvenir," Tim joked, slipping the thermal Henley out of the twisted mass of sheets and throwing it to Kevin.

"Very funny." Kevin slipped it over his head and checked his jeans for his keys.

"Do you have to go?'

"You ask me this every time."

"I'd just like you to spend the night just once."

"I will sometime. When I catch up with my life. Work is insane and my dad is still in the hospital." He walked back to Tim and sat on the edge of the bed. He traced Tim's face with his hand. "One day I will, promise."

Tim smiled and took Kevin's hand into his own. "Well in the meantime, I really want you to meet my friend Sarah."

"Tim, you know I don't do the friend thing. Not yet."

"Why do you keep putting off meeting her?"

"Why do you keep pushing it?"

"Because she's my best friend in the whole world. Don't you have any girl friends, you know, that you gossip with or shop for?"

"Not really. Sometimes I think they can be a little annoying."

"That's terrible." Tim laughed and attempted to tickle Kevin but he pulled away.

"I really have to go," he told Tim again.

"Kev, I think I love you."

Silence swallowed the room. Kevin felt as if a blanket had been thrown over him. He couldn't see or hear anything. Tim's words repeated in his head.

Finally he mustered a smile, one of the fakest of his life.

"That's sweet, Tim. I really care for you but I'm not there yet."

Tim said nothing and looked down at his bed.

"I'll give you a call."

Kevin waved goodbye from the doorway and left the house quickly. *Christ! That was a strange turn of events. Didn't see that coming.*

The moon lit a path to his jeep sitting quietly at the end of the gravel driveway. He glanced up at the twinkling stars that dusted the night and turned on his cell phone. A voicemail message beeped at him.

The forest roads were long, winding and dark, and streetlights were scarce. Tim would have to live in the boonies. Every bend was darker than the last. Thick, towering trees crowded him on both sides. Not another car passed him for miles. Kevin smiled as he finished listening to his voice mail, switched on his high beams, and returned the call.

"Hey Gary," Kevin beamed. "I'm good how are…" The jeep rocked as it hit a bump. *Damn country roads.* "Sorry, just a bump. How are you? Good. I can't wait to see you either. I'm sorry I'm running a little late, work was brutal. See you soo…" The signal dropped.

"You gotta be shitting." He snapped the cell shut. *Out in the middle of nowhere again. I'm getting tired of this. Time to cut Tim loose.* He tried the cell again but there was no use. Finally he gave up and set his eyes back on the road, a passing cloud temporarily swallowed the moon.

He rounded another bend, a sharp curve in the road caught him off guard and he realized he was going too fast. As the jeep skidded, its high beams picked up a massive shape blocking the road.

Kevin slammed on his brakes and the jeep spun, lurching like a wild animal and nearly made a 180 before it stopped inches away from what was now clearly an SUV. Kevin slammed against the side of the jeep, his head bouncing off the window.

Silence settled on the scene. Kevin checked his head. Just

a bump. No bleeding. He looked around then opened his door. He broke the quiet with a cough and stepped out into the street. A crunch reverberated beneath his feet. He looked down. Something glinted in his headlights. It was broken glass. Everywhere.

He turned to look at the SUV and noticed the smashed windshield and the splintered driver's side window. *What the hell?* The front tires were flat. He approached the vehicle, strewn diagonally across the road, slowly.

"Hello? Does anyone need help?" There was no response. Kevin peered into the SUV and found it empty. The moonlight streamed from behind the clouds and illuminated the inside of the truck. He noticed what appeared to be blood glistening on the door in front of him.

"Hello," he called again, backing away from the SUV.

Something rustled in the trees to his right. Kevin stopped. His breathing paused. His heart thumped in his ears.

"Help me!" A woman's voice called from the black. "Oh God help me!"

Seconds later a pair of blood-soaked arms reached from the brush. A face, covered in scratches and twisted into an expression of terror, followed. Kevin sprang into action and rushed to the woman's aid.

He grabbed hold of both her arms and pulled until the curved blade of a serrated hunting knife swung inches away from his face. Kevin fell backwards as a tall, gangly man draped in a coat of animal skins and long hair matted to his gaunt face, emerged from the woods and snarled.

Speechless, Kevin watched in horrific disbelief as the man snatched a handful of the woman's hair and dragged her back into the darkness.

Kevin's legs trembled, threatening to pull out from under him, but he managed to climb to his feet. The woman's screams echoed throughout the forest. He started back towards his jeep for his cell phone but remembered there was no signal. He ran his shaking hands through his hair and groaned.

JOHN GROVER

Jesus Christ what am I doing? He rushed into the woods after the two strangers. *She's dead if I don't do this. I'm crazy... freaking nuts!*

Shafts of moonlight streamed into the woods as Kevin followed the sounds of a struggle ahead of him. He spotted a downed tree branch in his path and picked it up with both hands, brandishing it.

Another scream pealed through the trees and sent Kevin off running again. Rustling leaves grew louder as he closed in on the shadowy forms writhing in the distance.

The hunter raised his blade high, the moonlight illuminating it like a beacon, as the woman struggled beneath his grip.

Kevin locked his gaze on the blade, raced towards it and swung blindly.

The tree branch cracked across the hunter's face. He toppled off his victim and squirmed across the forest floor.

"C'mon, let's go," Kevin ordered, grabbing hold of the woman's arm.

The two of them ran through the woods as Kevin looked over his shoulder and saw the impossible. The hunter jumped to his feet and scaled the nearest tree but... he couldn't have. *That didn't happen....*

"Shit," Kevin gasped. "He's up."

"He disabled my car," the woman cried. "We have to get out of here."

"This way," Kevin ushered her to the left. "We can use my jeep...it isn't far."

Tree branches crackled above.

Kevin pulled her one direction then another. "Wait," he panted but didn't want to stop running. "I thought...it was this way... where the hell is it?'

"Are you lost," the woman shouted.

"I'm not lost," Kevin snapped and stopped running. He searched around in every direction but the paths all looked the same. "I can't think with all this shit going on."

83

DARK THINGS II

"He's gonna catch us and cut us to pieces."

"Let me think for Christ's sakes."

Without a word Kevin grabbed hold of her and ran again, putting his free hand in front of him to feel his way through the woods. They worked their way around nature's obstacles until they stumbled into a ravine. Cold water soaked their feet.

"This isn't the right way," the woman cried. "There was no water. I know my truck isn't this way…this is the wrong way…" she ripped her arm out of Kevin's grip, sobs escaping her.

"Will you shut up," Kevin whispered. "You're gonna lead him right to us."

A rock skipped across the water and the pair froze.

A figure rushed from the shadows and barreled into Kevin. A scream pierced the night and Kevin felt the blade of the knife slash across his leg. Searing pain bit into him and he went down into the freezing water. The crooked outline of the hunter rose above him.

Kevin gasped as his entire body twitched with icy terror. Throbbing pain wracked his leg. He grabbed hold of it with one hand and raised his other in defense.

The knife slashed through the air but missed. Kevin looked up and caught sight of a rock colliding with the back of the hunter's head. The disheveled woman stood behind him, holding the rock for dear life.

The hunter fell face down in the water. Bubbles curled around his head as ripples formed.

"He's still not dead," she screamed, lifting the rock again.

"Stop," Kevin forced himself up and grabbed her arm again. "Let's just get the hell out of here."

They crossed the ravine and climbed to higher ground. Eventually they found a trail and followed it. Kevin didn't care where it went as long as it was away from the psychotic.

"I-I-need-to-r-rest," the woman panted.

"Okay, for a minute." Kevin saw a couple of huge boulders and ushered her behind them. "Well now I guess I owe you thanks for saving me from that psycho. Christ, what is that guy made of?"

"I didn't thank you the first time," she said.

"I know."

She began to cry.

"Listen, Miss?"

"My name is Sarah."

"Okay, Sarah, I'm Kevin. We're going to get out of here. We'll find the road and get the police."

"Really? I'll bet he knows these woods better than us."

"There are two of us. Strength in numbers right?"

"He's stronger than both of us. Ripped me right out of my truck. Busted the window with his hands."

"Anything else? Do you have to be so negative? Jesus, this night just keeps getting better."

"Don't talk to me that way. I didn't drag you into this."

"No, you didn't. I just couldn't…shit, I'm not exactly the heroic type."

"You are tonight."

He looked up and smiled. "I'll take that as a thank you."

She returned his smile.

"We should keep moving."

They made their way down the moonlit trail when a gutted rabbit appeared on the path. Its innards were strewn all over the ground. Kevin crinkled his nose and kept moving until discovering a fox a few feet away in the same condition as the rabbit.

He saw Sarah trembling again. Kevin eased her away from the animal. She'd been staring speechless at it, unmoving for too long.

Further away an enormous dead tree sprouted, its long, skeletal branches drooping before them as if in mourning. As they studied the grotesque display they noticed something within its branches—the head of a deer, a petrified tongue protruding from its mouth.

"This guy has some serious issues," Kevin said. "Got tired of gutting animals, moved on to humans."

"It's us." Sarah stared into the lifeless eyes of the buck.

DARK THINGS II

"That's us! That's what he's going to do to us!" She pointed at the head and started hyperventilating.

God, she's driving me crazy. Kevin pulled her from the tree. "Sarah, calm down. We have to keep it together if we want to get out of here."

"Don't you understand? We're not getting out." Sarah's eyes widened, her body undulated as her voice echoed. Kevin watched her derailing, panic sweeping through her, her movements erratic, her face red—

"Shut up!" Kevin slapped her thoughtlessly. "You're making us a target."

Her mouth gaped as tears streamed her cheeks.

"I'm sorry, I didn't mean to…"

"I needed it," Sarah murmured. "Let's get out of here."

They continued down the trail at full speed and finally spotted an incline cutting steeply into the darkness. A lone streetlight glowed in the distance and a smile curled across Kevin's face. He could see the outline of the road winding at the top.

"The road," Kevin beamed. "We're almost there." He tried to keep his voice low as he rushed towards the climb, dragging Sarah and himself through a sea of thorn patches, their faces lancing with scratches.

They fought their way to the road, scuttling across eroded earth, using moss-covered tree trunks for support. At last Kevin reached the road with Sarah behind him.

She looked around briefly, and Kevin noticed her eyes light up.

"I remember this," Sarah called. "I drove past here. My truck's this way." She pointed to the left.

"Awesome," Kevin panted.

Without another word Kevin pushed on, Sarah by his side, down the road until a strange sound paused them. A dark object whistled through the air and plopped at their feet. Sarah let out a horrific scream as the severed deer head stared up at them. Kevin felt his heartbeat ramp up suddenly and the slash in his leg blazed with pain.

Out of the nearest trees the hunter descended. He got into a crouched position and waved his serrated knife at them. Somehow, even in the dark, Kevin knew the freak was smiling.

"He's trying to bait us," Kevin whispered to Sarah.

"What do we do?"

"Run the other way."

"He'll just catch us. We should duck back into the woods…"

"I'm not losing the road again. This is it. It ends here."

"Kevin, thank you." Sarah turned to look at him. "You're a good man. God would be proud of you."

"It's not over yet, Sarah."

This is insane but I'm not letting him gut me like an animal. Kevin clenched his fists and rushed the hunter head on. The blade swung wide but Kevin hit the ground, appearing to trip over his own feet. He heard Sarah scream behind him. The hunter turned in distraction and Kevin seized the opportunity.

He leapt to his feet, dove into the hunter and the two went down, rolling across the road. Kevin felt immense pain bear down on his chest. He snatched gulps of air but felt his breathing grow difficult. Warm blood ran down his leg.

The hunter overpowered him and rolled on top. One arm clasped around Kevin's throat and the other raised the knife. Kevin watched shocked as an arm slid around the hunter's throat, stopping his deathblow. Sarah grabbed hold of him and jumped onto his back.

"Get off him, bastard!" Sarah screamed as the hunter struggled to his feet.

Scrambling to get up, Kevin wiped blood from his eyes and watched the hunter fling Sarah easily to the ground and drive the knife into her. She twisted as the blow rammed into her shoulder. She grimaced and screeched in agony. The hunter gave her a swift kick to the ribs for good measure.

Kevin seethed. He couldn't take anymore and raced towards them. The killer turned as Kevin's foot landed square in his gut. The kick sent the psycho backwards off his feet and onto the deer head,

DARK THINGS II

its antlers embedding into his back.

The hunter made no sound. No cry of pain. No screams. The knife plummeted from his hand as he struggled to free himself from the antlers. He wheezed and huffed rapidly as his attempts failed again and again.

Kevin picked up the knife and drove it into the prone killer's throat. A gurgle resounded and a stream of blood spattered Kevin's chest. He watched quietly as the hunter grasped weakly at the knife before his hands went limp. A moment later he stopped moving altogether.

"My God...my dear God..." Sarah cried, her tears coming in torrents. She made her way into Kevin's arms and the two embraced.

"C'mon," Kevin whispered. "Let's go find our cars."

Kevin let Sarah go to her car to check herself in the mirror. He checked her shoulder wound and managed to stop the bleeding. She smiled at him and ran her fingers across his cheeks.

"You don't know how grateful I am," she said. "I thought all the good men were gone. I prayed for just one *good* man to come into my life and God sent me you."

"Really Sarah, it was just luck. I..."

"No, you are a good man. Not a murderer or thief or an abomination." She leaned in to kiss him but Kevin stopped her with a gentle hand.

"Actually," he chuckled. "I'm a gay man."

Her eyes darkened. "No..." She reached for her glove compartment. "Then you *are* an abomination."

"Oh for Christ's sakes," he said. "Are you kidding me?"

"And a blasphemer. God came to me and gave me a mission to wipe the abominations from this world. Homosexuals are an abomination." She pulled a revolver from her glove compartment. "I was gonna start with my best friend, Tim. I was heading to his home before I was interrupted. I can no longer pretend to love him and his sickness, he's a filth upon our world. So instead, I will start with you, Kevin. My false savior." She pointed the gun at him.

Kevin ducked as the shot cracked over his head. He ran for

88

his jeep and climbed in. Sarah stepped into the road and aimed again, but her grip was weak and she faltered. The second shot shattered his passenger window.

He started his jeep and roared towards her and the SUV. Sarah attempted to lift her gun again but Kevin did not stop. He saw her eyes widen as a mask of terror twisted her face and drove into her, smashing her against the SUV and pushing it out of his way. The front end of his jeep crumpled but Kevin didn't care. He sped off without looking back.

"Christ, that's it! Tim and I are definitely over."

About the author:

John Grover is a dark fiction author residing in Massachusetts. He completed a creative writing course at Boston's Fisher College and is a member of the New England Horror Writers, a chapter of the Horror Writers Association. He is the author of several collections, including the recently released Feminine Wiles, sixteen tales of wicked women as well as various chapbooks, anthologies, and more. Please visit his website www.shadowtales.com for more information.

THE CHEVALIER SISTERS: A TALE OF VOODOO
by C.J. Sully

THE Louisiana forest was alive. Its rhythmic drumming pulse grew louder with each step and Thena Chevalier struggled to breathe.

Tha-thump, tha-thump, tha-thump, tha-thump...

Late autumn's cool, damp air stuck to her skin and she lifted her right "good" arm, to wipe her brow. Her left arm wasn't even much of an arm. It was more of gnarled stub, as if God had taken her clay form in the womb and pinched the limb off at the elbow. For grotesque balance, her right foot was clubbed and turned inward so that she walked with a constant limp. A slight hair-lip had kept her from being truly pretty in the face. Sometimes she stood in front of her vanity mirror with her Kashmir shawl draped over her deformed arm and held like a veil over her nose and mouth, thus revealing only her bright sea-green eyes and dark wavy hair. She pretended to be an Arabian dancer, nimble and desirable.

Dusa Chevalier didn't have to wear any veils. Her sister tore through the thick mist of the forest, letting wet branches slap the air after she brushed past them, not bothering to wait on the slow cripple that struggled so hard to keep up.

"Hurry, you're too slow," Dusa hissed over her shoulder.

Cobalt-eyed Dusa was 19, two years Thena's senior. All the men the Thena dreamed of courting, Dusa not only slept with, but broke their hearts when she discarded them like a spoiled child would her toys. She didn't care that she was practically a spinster. Father had given up on her. He only hoped, he often said as he put a bottle of gin to his lips, that she wouldn't ruin his name by getting illegitimately pregnant. Dusa's jet-black locks fell like an artist's brushstroke down her perfect pale shoulders. She never wore it up. Her lips stayed in a fixed, lusty pout that sometimes morphed into a wicked grin, especially when she was using the razor on Thena.

Thena was glad for tonight. Tonight she would most likely avoid Dusa's razor.

Dusa had started cutting Thena when Thena started menstruating. The midnight full-moon ritual was a secret between the two of them, the cuts being only on pieces of her flesh that could hide behind skirts or sleeves. Dusa originally had come up with the idea.

"There's magic in it," she'd said with a wink of her long-lashed eye.

She'd said that it would eventually make Thena beautiful. The appeal of being as gorgeous as her sister had been too strong for her to resist. After the first few times and seeing no results, Thena protested and started asking where Dusa had even heard of such magic. She asked her why she was doing it in the first place because Dusa didn't even believe in God or anything supernatural.

Dusa hadn't argued. She had continued the cutting, though getting a breathy, flushed look on her face each time the razor slid through the soft skin and Thena gasped. Thena never stopped her because she was afraid of what her sister might do in the cutting's stead. When she was bored, Dusa entertained herself by salting slugs and watching them writhe on hot rocks. She pulled the feathers out of live birds' wings. She slipped bits of poison into the servants' food that made them violently ill. Thena could survive a little cutting.

Tha-thump, tha-thump, tha-thump, tha-thump...

Thena didn't know, however, if foregoing the razor tonight was worth it, when the drum-pulse grew closer, and the flickering light of a fire glowed in a clearing less than twenty paces ahead.

Tonight was most definitely Dusa's idea, not hers; the girls having sneaked out of their plantation home after their father had gone to bed. Dusa had persuaded her to come by taking Thena's hands in hers, batting her long dark lashes, and being really *sweet,* as she sometimes was apt to do. Thena always had trouble resisting Dusa when she was like that. The dark beauty crawled inside of her and melted her heart with charm, making her forget all the hideous

DARK THINGS II

things she'd ever done. Thena knew it was manipulation. But despite that knowledge, Thena allowed herself to fall into the trap; they were, after all, sisters. And they did love each other, as sisters should. Love was complicated. A person loved the good and the bad in another if love was real. That was like Christ's love for all sinners. Everyone deserved forgiveness.

She didn't know how Dusa had heard of this private Voodoo dance and didn't ask. Occasionally the Voodoos would perform in the city for spectators to watch. But the private dances weren't talked about, other than in hushed tones. They did illegal things at the private dances, she'd heard. They took off their clothes and killed animals and got possessed by the Devil himself.

She hoped Dusa would be satisfied by a mere peek at the scene and then return home before Father woke up. But a grave feeling in her stomach told her that Dusa had more planned. Dusa did not fear the Voodoos like Thena did. She didn't believe in any of that "utter garbage," as she liked to call all things metaphysical. It hurt Thena the most when Dusa talked about their dead mother, and how she wasn't in a better place, but worm-food.

"Her body probably looks like Swiss cheese now with all the hungry grubby things eating through her," she liked to say.

The servants talked about Mrs. Chevalier from time to time. When Mother had Dusa, she was still young at heart and not ready for responsibility. She preferred to attend lavish parties with Father instead of hold her child. She would leave baby Dusa with her aunt who often drank so much wine while babysitting that she fell asleep, despite the wails of the baby in the crib. The servants weren't allowed to tend to the baby on any circumstance because Mother had not wanted her child to be "raised by wild Negroes." So Dusa had hardly been raised at all.

When Thena was born, it seemed her mother had had a change of heart and suddenly was ready to become a matron. Unlike with Dusa, she'd breast-fed Thena, rocked her to sleep, sang her lullabies. She'd had an especially soft spot in her heart for Thena, Father had said, because of Thena's deformities. She'd paid much more attention to her than Dusa, despite the elder child's exquisite charm and beauty.

Mother had grown violently sick when Thena was seven years old. She did not recover. Dusa had actually smiled that nightmarish evening when Father took them into a room and told them the grim news. Father ignored it. He retreated into his drinks, as always. Thena guessed the smile was a mask for her sorrow. But she wasn't sure.

Tha-thump, tha-thump, tha-thump, tha-thump...

Dusa stopped behind a large oak and leaned against it with her palms against the moss-laden trunk. Turning to her sister with a wild look in her eyes, she grinned.

"Look at them," she whispered. "They are completely gone." She tapped on her head and stuck her tongue out. "Crazy!"

Thena's body shook as she crunched leaves underfoot with every slight step, and she prayed that the Voodoos wouldn't hear her. But it was unlikely that they would, for they were entranced in their strange, wicked dance. Thena used the tree and Dusa to hide her as she peeked around both and beheld the likes of what she'd only before heard in stories.

There were a dozen or so dancers, all gyrating around a large black cauldron whose vapors smelled of salt and rot. There were only two males in the party, black; the rest were female, most of them black but some mulatto and white. They whirled around, their hair free, their loose dresses at differing stage of being shed. Their bare arms, backs, and breasts reminded Thena of those ancient Greek paintings of wild bacchanals.

The dancers threw what looked like frogs and snails and even a dead bloody chicken into the cauldron. They arched back their heads as they poured liquid spirits into their mouths and chanted something about "La Grand Zombi." One of the men pounded on a drum with his wide hands, sweat pouring down his face.

The other man, wearing a red loin cloth, grabbed something off the ground—it looked like a wooden coffin. A baby's coffin. Pounding his feet on the ground, shaking his hips and arching his back, he brought it to the leader of the Voodoo dance: the Queen.

Thena's mouth went dry. A light-skinned black woman stepped onto a crate, her long flowing blue dress undulating as she moved her lithe body like a snake. To call her beautiful would have been an understatement. She was stunning. Exotic. She was exactly as Thena imagined an ancient African queen would look. Her long brown hair fell loose, straight down her back. Gold hoop ear-rings adorned her ears. She poured a swig of spirits into her ruby-colored mouth, and then spat it out in a flume at a white woman dancing nearby. The white woman grinned elatedly as if she'd been honored, and she smeared the liquid over her face and down her bare shoulders.

Dusa shook her head and muttered, "If she'd done that to me, she'd be a dead Negro."

Thena made the sign of the cross, too terrified to move her legs and run away, though she could think of doing nothing else.

The Zombie chant continued, the man with the baby coffin opened its lid. He brought out a python and Thena gasped. He handed it to the Queen as the dancers reached a wild fervor, and the Queen, her green eyes shimmering like jewels in the night, brought the serpent's face closer and closer to lick her cheek.

That's when Dusa stepped out from behind the tree and yelled, "OH, STOP IT!"

And stop they did. Their faces all turned toward the voice that had interrupted them. Thena covered her mouth in terror and crouched down as best she could with her crippled leg, in the hopes that the tree would swallow her up and protect her from her sister's lunacy.

"Mary Beth," she said, cackling. "Look at you."

Thena peeked around the tree. That name belonged to one of Dusa's friends. Thena hadn't even recognized her.

"I can't believe *you*, of all people!" Dusa continued to the blonde, who looked down at the ground and brought her arms across her bare breasts and slightly turned away. "You told me you didn't believe in this rubbish."

Mary Beth continued to ignore her and stared instead at the

fire beneath the cauldron as if she were in a trance.

Scoffing, Dusa turned to the others. "And as for the rest of you...this is a bunch of nonsense. You have no so-called 'power.' It's make-believe, like faeries or *angels*. I'm not afraid of you. Soon nobody else will be. You should all go home."

The still dancers looked up at the Queen, who stared at Dusa not in ire, as Thena expected, but in dark amusement.

She never broke her gaze as she handed the snake back to the man, who placed it back in the coffin.

"Little girl," she said. "Why are you doing this?"

"Why not," Dusa said with a little shrug. "Because I like to do it. It doesn't bother me to live in a state of reality, and it doesn't bother me to point out other people's nonsensical beliefs."

"Are you so foolish as to be a non-believer?"

"Foolish?" Dusa put her hands on her hips and gave a delighted snicker. "This is all a spectacle, just as I thought. I wanted to see it for myself, and now I have, and now I'm going home to laugh about you some more and laugh at the people who fear you."

But it was the Queen who did the laughing. She put her hands on her hips and threw her head back. The sound of it—it was as if she had more than one voice. Thena struggled to breathe.

"No, child," the Queen said. She narrowed her emerald eyes and pointed a long finger at Dusa. "You will soon enough see the Power you blaspheme." Breathing in deeply, she grinned, and releasing that breath, a cold breeze swirled through the clearing. "Ah, yes. I see into your dreams. And so it will be. Yes. The angel of death. *He* will be coming for you."

Something in Dusa's demeanor twitched and for a moment, Thena thought she saw fear in her features. But that slight glimpse of apprehension was overshadowed by the other women in the group, whose bodies shivered and whose eyes were wide and doe-like, despite the alcohol they had consumed. Mary Beth glanced up from her stare at the fire. She met Dusa's eyes for a moment and shook her head.

"Whatever you say," Dusa said, smiling, total confidence

reappearing. "Mary Beth, let's get you out of here."

Mary Beth ignored her again, looking off into the forest this time.

Dusa sneered, clearly disappointed.

"Fine then!" As she turned to leave, she spat, "Let these Negros fuck you silly. Get with child. Destroy your life for nothing. You're going to owe me handsomely for not telling your father about this."

"Do not worry," the Queen said to Mary Beth. "Your father will not know." She turned to the drummer. "Play."

He hesitated, then slowly began to beat the instrument as before.

"PLAY," shouted the Queen, raising her arms to the skies. She let out a shriek and then a bizarre string of words in a language completely alien to Thena. She started turning in circles, laughing maniacally. It was time to leave, with or without Dusa.

Tha-thump, tha-thump, tha-thump, tha-thump...

The dancers seemed to ignore Dusa, who grabbed her sister by the shoulder, painfully yanking her up.

"Let's go," she said to Thena without looking at her. "This was a waste of my time."

Thena kept looking over her shoulder as they made their way out of the forest. Dusa strode gracefully. Thena stumbled. She, unlike her sister, expected the Voodoo men to follow and do violence to them both.

But when they reached the porch of their plantation and no Voodoos had attacked, she breathed a sigh of relief.

She looked back at the woods and the stars above. What normally would have comforted her about the sparkling night sky now reminded her of distant, foreboding fires, and eyes green like ancient jewels.

***

Thena couldn't sleep. She found Dusa in the kitchen, cutting into a previously untouched chocolate cake. Dusa served herself a large,

96

jagged piece and then sat down on one of the wooden stools around the island. She didn't offer Thena any, but Thena wouldn't have taken it anyway. She didn't know who made the cake or for what occasion, and taking a piece without asking would have been rude.

***

She stood watching her sister, whose face appeared quite serene in the light of her dim candle, considering what had just happened. The house was so quiet that she could hear each gentle tick of the grandfather clock in the living room. She should have been well into a deep sleep by now but she probably wouldn't get a single wink with the way her nerves were at present.

"Dusa," Thena asked in a small voice.

"What," Dusa asked with her mouth full.

"I…I'm going to bed. Are you going to be all right?"

"Hmm." Her eyes looked slightly glazed as they stared at her fork. "Yes, yes. Fine. See you in the morning."

Thena wiggled her tongue around in her dry mouth to form some moisture so that she might wet her parched lips. Only just now had her heart slowed down from its rapid pounding. Pounding just like the Voodoo drums.

"Sister," she said. "Aren't you at least a little afraid? The Voodoos have hurt people before. I've heard stories."

Dusa looked up at her, a lock of hair falling seductively over her heavy-lidded eye. "What, the stories of skinning live black cats with their teeth? Or maybe pricking dolls with pins and a person miles away feeling the stab? Or were you thinking of the reanimated corpses they bring from the grave?"

"I—"

"Or maybe you're thinking of Mrs. Maud's brother dying, what was his name, Louis, I think, something about living things crawling out of his mouth, or some ridiculousness." She made a sharp *tsk* with her tongue. "You can't believe the servant talk. Their brains aren't big enough to comprehend most things, so they make up stories to defend their confusion."

"B…but Louis was found dead! Face-down a…and blue, as if he'd suffocated, though there was nothing in his throat. Mrs. Maud said she saw the creatures coming out of him…saw him die!"

Thena never would forget how she'd overhead the head-slave, normally very poised and somber, nervously telling the other slaves about seeing her brother overtaken by a Voodoo hex in his own home, a hex which he'd virtually placed on himself by refusing to leave his wife for a Voodoo woman with whom he'd had a short affair. The married man had come to his senses. He'd told her he'd made a mistake, no harm intended, and wished to remain with his wife. But it wouldn't be that simple. The "mistake" had cost him his life.

"Sister, you are stupider than I thought," Dusa said. "You can't possibly believe in it. All the Voodoos do is dance and kill animals for show, and then they sneak poison into people's drinks. *That's* how their victims die. It's the only explanation. Mrs. Maud must have imagined the creatures. There's no magic to fear. In fact, there's *nothing* to fear in this world; I keep telling you that. Nothing exists that you can't see with your own eyes."

"Yes, but—"

"Has Mrs. Maud ever talked about the occurrence with you, personally? About what happened to her brother?"

"Well, no—"

"It's because she knows *we* are too sensible to believe in that Negro rot. That's why *they* serve *us*."

Thena stopped to study the ground. Could it be true? She, unlike her sister, always found the servants to be caring individuals and quite polite. They never cut her with razors or said nasty things about her mother. Still, most of them couldn't even read. Maybe Dusa had a point. Maybe they really were ignorant. But perhaps, if people like Dusa would give them the opportunity to learn… She'd never really thought about it until now, but that was an interesting notion. What if the Negros were given a fresh start, and could all go to school and wear fine clothes and own plantations and hire poor white *women* to take care of them? It would be a different world, indeed!

"If you're worried about the Voodoos poisoning me," said Dusa, "I'll have the servants taste my food before I eat it for a few weeks."

Thena fought hard not to roll her eyes. Who was she fooling? Dusa would never give the Negros a chance to learn. For that might mean losing control over people. And Dusa did love control.

"Yes," Thena said, more in response to her thoughts than to Dusa's statement. Then she had an idea. "But what about…"

She hesitated before she went on with her argument because she knew it could potentially spark Dusa's rage. Nervously, she grabbed hold of her left arm nub in her right hand, feeling the familiar wrinkled flesh, the bone that rudely ended where it should have continued into a normal forearm and hand.

"What about your angel of death dreams," she asked quietly.

Dusa's eyes shone with a storm of emotion.

When she had been younger, six or seven, Dusa had started to have nightmares that woke her in the night, screaming. They continued for several years. Each time one happened, Thena would come running from her bedroom next door at the sound of her sister's screams, and she would find Dusa sitting up in bed, her sheets soaked from sweat and urine, terrified that the angel of death was coming for her. His hooded shadow was all she'd seen, a shadow that materialized and had come off the wall; it'd stretched to the ceiling. He'd brandished such a terrible sword, but his wings alone, wings that spread the span of the entire room, had intimidated her into a frenzy.

Thena had calmed her down each time, holding her trembling sister, telling her that she was safe now, but that she should pray for understanding and make sure she was not tempting the Fates with her daily behavior. (She'd known this was the only time Dusa was vulnerable enough to elicit any remorse for her mean behavior during the day.) Dusa would nod, promise to change her ways, and then go back to sleep.

DARK THINGS II

But she never changed.

Dusa was 13 or 14 years old when she decided she would not believe in her angel of death dream any longer. Dusa had burst into Thena's bedroom on a Sunday morning and had woke her up only to boast of how she had defeated the dream by her decision not to believe in its power. She told Thena she accredited her previous "foolish" fear to superstition that she'd picked up from church and Mother and the slave's stories. She hadn't gone to church that day, nor any day after, and frequently told Thena that she shouldn't either. Thena continued to go anyway, and Dusa often quipped, "Suit yourself," when her rational talk didn't phase Thena's religious devotion.

In the darkened kitchen, Dusa took another slow bite of her chocolate cake and licked the icing off her lips as a mountain lion might lick its chops before pouncing on an antelope.

"Like I said," Dusa whispered, "it's all nonsense."

Thena cleared her throat, worried now that Dusa might not be alive in a few days. She would have to protect her sister, herself.

***

She waited under the covers of her four-post mahogany bed until she heard Dusa close her bedroom door. Then she sneaked across her hardwood floor, careful to avoid the beams she knew would creak, and silently emerged into the hall. Though Thena had been cursed with a marred physical appearance, she had excellent hearing and vision. Her eyes owned an almost catlike ability to see well in the dark. She lifted her clubbed foot and gently put it in front of her, then took a step with her good foot, then repeated until she'd made it down the full length of the Oriental carpet runner and reached the stairs. She briefly glanced down them, halfway expecting to see a black man in a red loin cloth with a snake over his shoulders. There was no man.

Crouching down, she looked back to the long hallway. It was clear also. Along the wall, adjacent to the top stair, was a loose board that blended in with the rest of the wall to anyone less observant.

C.J. SULLY

Thena had found it at the young age of three and had hid treasures, such as the rose Mrs. Maud had given her one day when she was sick, to a brass infant spoon she'd found on Royal Street, to an oval locket with her mother's picture inside. All of her mother's memorabilia stayed in this hiding place, for she feared what Dusa would do if she found them. She might destroy them or sell them for money.

She reached into the back of the dusty space and felt around until she found what she was looking for.

It was a tiny porcelain statue of St. Michael, the Archangel, and her mother's personal relic of "good juju." It had been her protection. She had given it to Thena when she'd grown so ill. She'd told Thena to keep it safe from destruction, that she might need it someday.

That day was now, she decided.

She didn't care if Dusa didn't believe in Voodoo. She didn't care that Dusa was not afraid. *She* was afraid. Though her sister had been cruel to her and made her feel as if she walked on pins and needles daily just to avoid her anger, she was still her sister. They were the same blood. They had lost the same mother, even if Dusa dealt with her death differently. It was very probably all a front, Thena thought, to look strong. Surely Dusa cared. Surely Dusa was redeemable. And surely, she didn't deserve to die a horrible Voodoo death.

She slid the board back over her hiding hole, and like a mouse, she crept back up the hall with the relic in her good hand.

Mother would have wanted her to do this. Mother had loved Dusa, despite Dusa's faults.

Thena listened at her sister's door until she heard the sound of heavy breathing. The young woman was deep in sleep. Thena opened the door and held her breath as she entered the room, crouched down by the bed, and hid St. Michael beneath the wooden frame.

She would have better dreams, knowing it was there, even if her sister didn't.

Or so she'd thought.

101

DARK THINGS II

Once in bed, she tossed and turned fitfully during the remaining hours of darkness, and woke often with a start, thinking she heard the distant beat of drums. Each time, she found it was only her hammering heart.

***

When she woke fully the next morning, her body feeling heavy and drugged from lack of solid sleep, she squinted as the sun beamed in on her, incriminatingly. And that's when she heard the screaming.

She quickly wrapped herself in her robe and hobbled down the stairs, expecting to see her sister dead on the front porch, where the shriek had come from. But Dusa was not there.

Gweneth, the servant that swept the porch every morning, stood right outside the door, having dropped her broom. She held one hand over her mouth, the other pointing to a small lump at the base of the steps. Two more servants, Rose and Thomas, had come to see what the commotion was about. Thena swallowed, her throat tight, as Thomas put his arms around Gweneth who seemed too shaken to stand anymore.

Thena slowly descended the steps and the lump came into focus.

"It's only a little bag," she said, attempting to comfort herself more than anyone.

"Don't, Miss," Rose shouted, holding out her arm to grab Thena before she touched it. "That be's a curse! Bad juju!"

"Oh, lawd, it's dem Hoodoos," Gweneth said between sobs. "They's come to hex us!"

"No, they haven't," Dusa said, appearing in the doorway. She hadn't bothered to put a robe on and the sheer material of her nightgown showed every sensual curve, from the swell of her breast and hips to the rumples of her pubic hair and pricks of her nipples.

She brushed past Thena and reached down to pick up the bag. Rose gasped, Gweneth fell deathly silent, and Thomas's lower lip trembled. Thena stood by as Dusa opened the little skin-colored cloth (was it real skin?) sac and poured the most vile contents into her left hand.

The putrid stench of pulverized manure threatened to make Thena vomit. Dusa scooted the dusty particles away from a dried toad and lizard, and, oh, no, it couldn't be—a human finger, the nail like yellowed bark, the skin like brown leather.

The Voodoos had placed it there sometime in the night. As a warning. Thena thanked God that she'd put the statue under Dusa's bed.

"Hmmm," Dusa said, smiling in her wicked way. "They'll have to do better than this."

She walked out barefooted to the outhouse that the slaves used and came back empty-handed. Then she went back inside the house and demanded her breakfast.

The three slaves seemed too petrified to move. Then Mrs. Maud strode out onto the porch, her long gray dress brushing the wooden floor. She stood, hands on her ample hips, her hair thrown up into a turban.

"Get back to work, all of you," she said.

"But," Rose stammered, "there was a—"

"I know what there was, I already heard. Now get inside and tend to the mistress."

Nodding, Rose went into the house, letting the screen door slam behind her. The noise made Gweneth jump.

"You two," Mrs. Maud said, "back to work now."

The older woman stayed so composed when the younger workers were so frayed. This was quite interesting, especially since Mrs. Maud was the one who had supposedly seen her brother come under a vicious Voodoo attack. Their eyes met, and Mrs. Maud nodded.

"Good mornin', Miss," she said. "I trust you slept well."

Thena only nodded back. Usually she was more talkative with Mrs. Maud, but this morning she had so many questions she wanted to ask that she found herself tongue tied. Flies began to gather on the ground where some of the manure had fallen. Their high-pitched *zzzz* barely registered in Thena's ears; all she heard was the memory of those wretched Voodoo drums.

"Anything I can do for you," Mrs. Maud asked.

Thena only shook her head. Mrs. Maud seemed too calm about the bad juju bag. Someone who believed in Voodoo with her whole heart would have been more frightened, surely. What if Dusa was right? What if Mrs. Maud had lied to the other Negroes about what had happened to her brother? But if that were so, then what could possibly be her motive for lying? Unless, of course, she had some reason to want her brother dead and had participated in his murder.

"Very well," Mrs. Maud said, excusing herself.

Thena shook her head. She was thinking too much. That's what happened when she didn't get enough sleep. She dismissed the whole scene from her head and decided to ponder on it later when she was more herself.

***

All through the day, Dusa cut little squares of her food on a plate and poured an inch or so of her drink into a cup for Thomas to taste-test before she ate. Thomas did so without a word, and luckily, he did not grow ill. Dusa carried a smug look on her face throughout the day. When their Father asked if either of them wanted to go into town, Dusa (who usually leapt at the chance and often went to town on her own) declined. Thena, who usually declined, did so also. She found it amazing that Father had not a clue that they had stolen away to the forest. Did he ever wake up to check on his daughters during the dead of night? Perhaps at one time, he did. Before Mother died. But now he seemed far more interested in Absinthe than in anxiety over his daughters' well-being. Thena loved him, regardless, and still enjoyed hearing him talk of local, state, and national news as they rode the carriage to and from church. He generally stayed sober on Sundays. But today was Wednesday. So he would make the rounds, checking the fields to make sure everyone was doing their job, and then it would be off to town for drinks and socializing.

Not minutes after he left was there a knock on the door. Thena was reading a book on Greek Mythology in the parlor, though the words swam on the page; she was so tired. The knock, however, jolted her, and she nearly knocked her cup of tea off the cherry wood end table. Voodoos probably wouldn't knock, yet her heart didn't slow its rapid pace until she saw Rose lead blonde-headed Mary Beth through the house and toward the stairs.

Thena only caught a glimpse of the young woman as she passed by, but what she saw made her head race with questions. Mary Beth was dressed in a fine gown of yellow chiffon, complete with matching hat. She carried a bouquet of irises, the scent of which left a trail of natural perfume. On her face she wore a nervous little smile that seemed forced.

Thena held her thumb in her book at the place she'd stopped reading.

She waited for Rose to descend the steps and disappear in the kitchen. Then she ascended the stairwell as quietly as possible. Pretending to adjust a painting on the wall, she listened as best she could, wishing Dusa had left the door cracked open at least a little. What she could hear was muffled, though she heard Mary Beth frantically say one sentence clearly as crystal.

"Please, I beg you not to tell my parents what you saw last night!"

Thena stared into the thick layers of oil paint that depicted a vase with roses lit by candlelight. She felt terribly sorry for Mary Beth, whose body she had seen far too much of last night. She could hardly get the image of her fire-lit bare breasts out of her mind.

Dusa's cocky voice was barely audible, but bits and pieces of what she said were clear:

"…don't believe in that…not scared of…such a fool…"

Then another full sentence from Mary Beth.

"But you don't know her, and if you don't apologize, you will *die!*"

"…don't care…no power…a complete ass…"

DARK THINGS II

Thena crept a little closer to the door, forgetting all about the painting. Pressing her ear to the wood, she heard Dusa's voice:

"Why don't you get down on your knees and kiss my bare feet, and then I might think about keeping your little secret."

There was a creak in the floorboard; Thena imagined Mary Beth to have taken a step back. Then another creak and shuffling of clothes. She strained to hear two faint kiss noises, barely audible, even for Thena's incredible hearing.

"Now, get out of here," Dusa said in that ugly tone that always made Thena's face flush in anger.

Thena scrambled to her room and made busy as if she were looking for something in her vanity. She heard Mary Beth's quick footsteps pad the carpet runner, then down the steps, and out the door, without so much as a goodbye.

"What are you doing," Dusa asked and Thena turned around.

Her sister stood leaning against the doorframe, her hair pulled back. She still hadn't gotten dressed and remained in her translucent night gown.

"Oh," Thena said, searching through her drawers, "I was looking for my perfume. Have you used it lately?"

"No. But you should find it because you smell like a fish. Honestly, I feel sorry for whatever man takes your virginity. He'll have to wear a pin to close his nose. You're not douching like I told you to."

The nerve of her! Of course she was keeping herself sanitary, though the douche was so dreadfully uncomfortable. She kept cleaner than Dusa did, Dusa with her many different nighttime visitors. Sometimes, early in the morning, the sour smell from Dusa's direction was so strong that Thena felt she would grow sick.

Stinging tears filled her eyes, and she continued her search through her drawer so Dusa wouldn't see. She discreetly sniffed the air, trying to pick up a trace of anything acrid, but didn't. Turning to tell Dusa that she must be mistaken, she found her sister already gone.

For a fleeting moment, Thena actually hoped that the Voodoos

106

had cursed her sister, and that the curse would be carried out that minute. Then guilt threatened to make her tears flow even more, so she put the entire conversation out of her mind and returned to her book downstairs.

***

Her eyes popped open around midnight, and she sat up in bed. She'd been at that level of half-sleep where her mind drifted and her body felt light yet she was aware of all sounds. When she swung her legs off the side of the bed, she hardly felt that she'd been dozing at all.

The night was chilly. One of the first cool fall evenings of the year. She fumbled with her slipper when it wouldn't slide easily onto her clubbed foot. For a moment she thought of lighting a fire, but compassion compelled her to check on her sister.

By now, she'd forgiven her for her earlier ugly behavior; however, she would not forget. Quietly she stole into Dusa's room and watched as her chest, covered by a thick quilt, rose and fell in deep slumber. Her face was turned to the side, dark locks draped across it and under the drawn-up blanket.

Careful not to step on any spots of floor that would creak, Thena lowered to her knees to check on the angel talisman she'd left the night before. It was still there, carefully hid in dark shadow and gripping its tiny, protective sword. As she leaned back, her nose tickled with dust. Then suddenly she froze.

It was the corner of what looked like a book, sticking out from in between Dusa's mattresses. Curiosity overcoming her, she pulled it out a few inches more to see the title, when she realized it was not a book, but a leather, gold-leaf journal with Dusa's name engraved on it.

Dusa had gotten it from one of her admirers one Christmas a couple of years ago, but she never spoke of writing in it. Thena itched to see what lay inside.

Dusa shifted on the bed above her, making Thena flush with adrenaline. She froze. She waited to hear the sleep in her sister's breathing. And when she heard a slight snore, she let out a silent sigh.

The journal was none of her business. She had no right to read it. She should leave it alone. She *would* leave it alone.

Stuffing down her piqued interest, she retreated back into her bedroom and listened as the grandfather clock struck each hour and wondered what sort of grotesqueries, like that horrid bag of dead oddities on the front porch, would appear tomorrow—and wondered whether or not she should fear them.

What she never did expect was the cat.

***

Hot tea was her salvation. The warmth dispersed the chill from her skin, and the caffeine kept her eyes open. While she made her way through the kitchen, bringing the warm rim of the cup to her lips, she wondered how long her body would go with inadequate sleep before it collapsed.

She stepped out onto the swept porch—no ugly Voodoo bags this morning, no shrieks of hysteria. Only the sharp smell of coming winter that teased her with memories of Christmas.

Mother always wore a red dress at Christmas.

Now, Thena did, in her stead.

Her mind drifted to thoughts of festive food, of good cheer, of presents.

Dusa's journal…

Thena shut her eyes, as if doing so might erase the memory of finding it.

What did Dusa write about?

Did she write of Thena?

Were there admonitions of grief? Pages of apologies she was too proud to voice to those she had wronged?

Thena squeezed her eyes shut tighter.

She focused on the cool air, the silence of the morning, and the warm vanilla vapors of her tea. She pushed the journal from her mind.

She opened them and saw the cat.

Its sleek black body stood poised under a great willow tree, like an ominous Egyptian god. There was nothing unusual about its size, yet Thena felt intimidated by its presence. Intimidation gave way to fright.

It wasn't until she noticed its eyes did she find the source of its sinister aura.

Blood.

Its eyes were two wide pools of blood.

She took a step back from the evil thing, too shocked to cry out.

It opened its mouth instead, and out came dozens upon dozens of buzzing flies.

She spun around, dropping her cup of tea. It shattered on the ground. She yanked at the front door with her good hand. It wouldn't budge. Stuck! She could hear the flies buzzing in a growing cloud that cast a shadow upon her like a pursuing hurricane.

"*Help*," she screamed and then turned around to see how close the horrible bugs were.

She saw nothing.

No shadow obstructing the light. No flies. No cat.

All gone.

She stared at the empty space and reached for the door handle. It turned this time, well-oiled, and the door opened without a problem.

She couldn't calculate how long she stood outside. Was her lack of sleep driving her crazy? She didn't have one of the maids clean up the shattered tea cup; she located the small hand-broom and erased all traces of her possible lunacy.

The house was quiet this morning. Apparently no-one had even heard her yell the word *help*. Had she imagined the whole thing?

She found herself standing in the doorway to her father's study.

DARK THINGS II

He sat at his cherry-wood desk, signing papers, gathering more papers into stacks, stuffing other papers into the trash. She watched him work, with him unaware, his mind in some far-off place that Thena probably never would go. The fireplace opposite his desk crackled in a gentle, warming rhythm.

Was he thinking of Mother?

Or was his entire existence found in the crystal glass he sipped from, the bourbon sucking away all traces of soul, leaving him with nothing but a cracking shell and a joke of an existence?

***

The rest of the day was long, dream-like, though Thena tried but was unable to nap. Dusa stayed away from her, not even saying two words.

***

Then it was night again.

Thena lie awake as was now the pattern. There was a slight scraping of wood against wood—the tale-tale sign that Dusa's bedroom window was being opened. Then whispering and a stifled giggle. Another "suitor" had come to visit. Thena thought of St. Michael, standing post beneath her sister's act of carnal passion. She thought of the journal being pressed by their rhythmic movements.

Where was the justice?

Where was the Voodoo?

Did any of it exist?

Where was Mother, now? Was she in heaven? Was she floating around the stars in some ethereal body, no longer sick from that terrible and sudden illness that had so shockingly taken her life?

Or was she gone, like Dusa so often said, her pale, decaying body merely food for the worms?

***

110

Thena knew what she had to do, but she was still afraid to do it.

Even as she approached the woman and delicately cleared her throat to get her attention, she fought her nerves and prayed she wouldn't back down.

"Mrs. Maud," she asked.

Mrs. Maud finished smoothing out Father's bed covers and straightened her back. She turned and met Thena's eyes.

"May I help you," she asked.

She wasn't smiling, but she wasn't frowning either. It was almost like she sensed what Thena was about to ask.

"May I ask you a question," Thena asked, hoping her voice didn't really sound as small as she thought it did.

"Of course."

"Your brother. Is it true, about the way he died, the Voodoo hex? Mrs. Maud, is Voodoo real?"

Mrs. Maud stared into her eyes for what seemed years, her deep brown orbs filled with secrets. She smelled of bleach and floor wax with a hint of sage.

"What do you think, Miss Thena," she asked.

"I don't know." Tears began to well, blurring her vision. "I just don't know about anything anymore. I'm so tired. I...I..."

"Shh, child," Mrs. Maud said, offering her handkerchief. "What's really bothering you?"

Thena pushed the door nearly shut, leaving it slightly ajar so she could hear if anyone came near.

"It's Dusa," she said in a hushed whisper, the tears flowing freely. "She doesn't believe in it, or anything! But that bag, and... and the cat, and the forest...and what about Mother? What about *her*?"

"Quiet, child," Mrs. Maud said, taking the young woman in a firm embrace. "Shh. What in the world is going on?"

"Please, there is too much to explain. I only want you to tell me what happened with your brother. What you really saw."

Mrs. Maud pulled back, holding Thena's shoulders at arm's

length. Her grip was firm.

"I saw my brother die, Miss Thena." She pressed her lips together. "He was hoodooed. End of story."

"Yes, but details! Do you know for certain that's what it was? Was there anything supernatural about his death? Anything that might prove there's something more—"

"May I help you, Miss Dusa," Mrs. Maud asked, looking over Thena towards the bedroom doorway.

Dusa glared at Thena, eying her tears like a predator.

"What's wrong with *you*," she asked.

"Why, Miss Thena hasn't been able to sleep very well these last few nights," Mrs. Maud said. "Not sure why. She came to me to see if I might have a brew to help her take a nap. Poor child. I've dealt with my own bouts of insomnia over my life, and it's no fun."

"Hmph," Dusa said, crossing her arms. "Just stop worrying about all the stupid things you're worried about and let yourself rest. Honestly, sister, you make yourself this way."

"Yes, I know," Thena said, her mind reeling. She'd lost her chance now. Dusa wasn't leaving. "What are your plans for the day?"

Dusa let out a long sigh. "Oh, I don't know. I may go into town to the perfumery." Her eyes darted back and forth between the two women, searching. "I need your help the dress I'd like to wear, Mrs. Maud. Come with me."

"Yes, Miss, as soon as I finish with your Father's room."

Dusa knew how to bully people, but when Mrs. Maud wanted to finish at task, she finished it. Still, Dusa had already won this game. She knew, somehow, that they were talking about her. How much of the conversation had she heard before she'd come into the room?

Thena excused herself and went to the kitchen to pour herself another cup of tea. She finished it at the counter next to the sink while staring blankly at the leaf-patterned wallpaper. How much had Dusa heard?

When she finished her drink, she walked out the kitchen door when Dusa grabbed her by the arm and yanked her into the hallway under the stairwell. Her nails dug into Thena's flesh.

"Whatever you're trying to do, don't go messing up our secret," she hissed. "Father can't know about our little trip the other night, or he might start paying attention to what we do. And then we'd have to be even more secretive, and that is a cramp to my style of living. I run this house. Do you hear me? And I run you."

Thena forced her lip not to quiver. The rage she felt was unbelievable. She wanted to rip her sister's hair out, tuft by tuft, and leave her in a bleeding heap on the floor. Their mother never would have let this happen.

"Let go of me," Thena said.

Dusa looked down at her grip, then shoved Thena against the wall. "You're a pathetic little nobody. You take my help and you spit it back at me. You'll never find a suitor if you don't start having adventures and start letting go of stupid things like church and befriending the servants. I had the time of my life last night with Jaque LaRue. All we need to do is get you a man to open up that flower"—she grabbed at Thena's crotch—"and you'll lighten up and be more fun to be around." Now she was smiling. "I'm sure I could find someone who would do it for us. And I might even be able to find someone not half-bad-looking. Trust me, it only hurts for a moment."

"I don't want it," Thena said, stepping backwards. "I don't want to use men, or to be with them, the way you do."

"Oh, yes, you do." Her eyes narrowed to slits. "You just don't know it."

"You're wrong."

"This week. I'll find someone. We'll sneak him in, and do you correctly, to make you a woman."

"No!"

"You need this, Thena. It's because I care about you. I want you to feel normal."

Thena knew, with every sickening caress her sister gave her deformed arm, that this was yet another game, meant for her twisted entertainment. She could only imagine what Dusa's mind was conjuring up right now, but it was going too far. If she brought someone to the house for Thena, Thena would start locking her bedroom windows and doors at night. And if she had to, she'd tell Father and make him do something about it. But for now, her best move was distraction.

"So what do you like about Jaque," she asked.

"Oh," Dusa's eyes lit up and she stopped her caresses. "For one, he's extremely well-endowed. I don't have to pretend like I can feel it with him. Plus, he's open to things in bed. He's talked of bringing in another man or woman."

Thena's mouth went dry. She wasn't sure she could handle knowing all that was going on next door. But as long as she wouldn't be involved, that was fine.

"Oh, so is he very handsome," Thena asked, glancing down the hallway, wishing she were in the garden, under the trellis, in the sun and out of this drafty hallway.

"*Very* handsome." Dusa gave a smug smile. "Very. In fact, I may stop by and see him when I go into town."

Her ruse had worked. Dusa would probably stay gone most of the day. Perfect.

"I'd better be on my way, sister, now that I think of it. Mrs. Maud is probably waiting for me in my room."

"Yes, probably."

"Well, I will see you later this evening!" She gave Thena a quick peck on the cheek and pranced down the hall like an innocent princess incapable of the sins she committed on a daily basis.

Thena waited until Dusa left the house. She watched with bloodshot eyes the carriage driver signal the horses to start their trek. They grew smaller and smaller as they traveled, and then turned a corner out of sight.

Now was the time…

***

With rash desire, Thena yanked back the covers from the side of Dusa's bed and pulled the journal out from between the mattresses.

She started at the first page, on her knees, her legs going numb, and read as much as she could in a half-hour span. She figured that would be long enough to allow herself to give into the illicit desire.

The clock struck 12:30 p.m., and she closed the book after finishing an entry Dusa had made two weeks ago.

She put the journal back in its place and arranged the covers as they had been.

The entries had been written with a careless hand, with ink blotches on the pages and sentences scratched out and words misspelled.

But there wasn't anything indicating any remorse, no great secrets that Thena didn't already know.

Dusa wrote mostly of her "suitors" and what they had done to pleasure her. It seemed a journal mostly devoted to her sexual exploits. But there were still several pages left unread. Nevertheless, she would read no more. She'd seen enough.

***

The day ticked by like a dream, and Thena spent it idly.

She ate dinner with her Father, neither one asking if they knew Dusa's whereabouts. Father read his newspaper. Thena stared into her soup. The tomato paste—it was the exact shade of the cat's eyes. Had she imaged all that?

Her mother had grown so thin in the end, so frail in such a short amount of time. Dusa had insisted on spoon-feeding her soup. Mother hadn't wanted to eat, yet Dusa continued to dip the spoon into the porcelain bowl and pour lukewarm portions into Mother's mouth. It was possibly the kindest thing Dusa had ever done. It was so out of place with the rest of her actions. Perhaps Thena had imagined that, too. Perhaps now her memories were beginning to become distorted.

DARK THINGS II

Dusa returned around 8 p.m. after dusk had fallen. She said a slurred "good evening" to Thena, but swiftly retreated to her bedroom, her breath reeking of whiskey and pungent herbs.

She'd sleep soundly tonight.

***

Thena sat in her bed after blowing out her candle. The winds outside grew strong with a brewing storm. The servants had already placed tarps over the gardens and prepared for a rough night.

At 11:00 p.m., Thena jumped.

Screeeeech!

Screeeeech!

Screeeeech!

The sound could have been a tree limb scraping Dusa's bedroom window, only there were no trees that close to the house.

One of Dusa's men might be outside. Only they never scraped the panes, and who would want to be out on such a nasty night as this?

Screeeeech!

In her mind's eye, Thena pictured hunch-backed green demons, fangs dripping with blood. Creatures having pulled themselves from the bowls of hell. Her breath caught in her throat. Was the Voodoo curse at hand? Did Dusa somehow find the statue of St. Michael and take it out of her room, thus leaving her unprotected?

Thena had to check. She had to.

Despite her efforts to keep the door from creaking, its dry hinges betrayed her, and she feared that she'd be discovered by not only her sister, but whatever hovered outside that window.

Screeeech!

The mauve curtains, their color faded even in the warm firelight, hid whatever it was that was making the noise.

Dusa didn't seem to hear any of it.

Thena checked under the bed. St. Michael remained in his place.

116

She crept closer to the window.

Holding her breath, she cast aside the drape to find…

Nothing.

The noise stopped.

She would not hyperventilate. She would remain calm. She had her mind. She was not losing it. She only needed to sleep.

And to finish reading Dusa's journal.

Dusa wouldn't wake up. She hadn't heard the scraping, so she wouldn't wake up now. Thena sat by the fireplace and scanned the remaining pages of her little diary. Her nightgown spread around her as she rested once again on her knees.

Several more entries about sex.

A short poem about herself and how she looked.

A paragraph about a necklace she'd located in town that she wanted.

Then Thena read the entry that would forever change her life.

We saw an actual voodoo dance tonite. Would you believe Thena came with me? She is so sukceptible to whatever I say sometimes I wish she would strike out at me and give me a fair challange. I still to this day do not know how mother favored her over me. She even believes the voodoo rubish and the church rubish and descretely tries to make no big occasion of her beliefs. I told her that Voodoos poison people to death…just like I had to do to rid myself of mother but Thena wouldnt understand if she knew that and might go to the police so she will simply have to stay ignorant. I will merely try as best I can to get her to see reality about other things though.

I digress. What I really wanted to write about was while we watched the negros dance like fools I saw none other than Mary Beth Dupont!!! Can you believe? I knew she was no virgin but

DARK THINGS II

Thena's hands began to shake.

The words on the page blurred.

Her eyes filled with hot, stinging tears.

The soup.

The way Dusa had spooned each bit of it into Mother's mouth during those last days.

Dusa? A murderess?

The boiling rage of an entire lifetime at last burst its dam of denial and welled up inside of Thena's breast. This could not be true. She would wake her sister—shake her violently, if need be—and demand to know that what she read was not true. She took a breath, wiped her tears, and looked up to the bed.

It was empty.

A hand darted from over Thena's shoulder and snatched the journal from her hold.

Thena nearly tottered over as she jumped to her feet. Dusa stood with her back to the fire. She held the journal in one hand and the statue of St. Michael in the other. A curious smile lined her face.

"Find anything worth publishing," Dusa asked.

Thena's tongue stuck to the roof of her mouth like an insect in tree sap.

"Writing never was an enjoyable activity for me," she said. "Reliving memories is, though. Don't you agree?"

The sap in Thena's mouth gave way just enough for her to say, "Tell me you didn't do it."

"Do what?"

With a force Thena thought incapable of her sister, Dusa threw the journal into the fire. The flames licked up the sides of the pages, curling them, charring them. Eliminating any evidence.

Thena couldn't believe this was happening.

"What about Mother," she cried.

"You're tired, sister. Delusional." Dusa looked down at the angel statue she cradled in her hand. "I suppose you put this under my bed to protect me. Well, sister, there's nothing to protect me from. And the sooner you know this, the sooner you'll accept that life does not go the way you want it to. People die, and deservedly so. And they don't live on after death."

She chuckled at the statue before thrusting it, too, into the fireplace.

"No," Thena shouted.

"Shut up." Dusa's face twisted into a witch's grimace. "It's time to shut up. Now, I know it's not a full moon, but perhaps it's time for us to use the razor."

She casually walked over to her nightstand and pulled that familiar broken piece of a sharp shaving razor from the drawer.

The look she gave Thena suggested that she might do more than make thin slits in her skin tonight.

"I want you to listen well," she said. "We can do this one of two ways. You can keep your mouth shut and pretend tonight never happened, or if you go running to Father, you might find yourself at the mercy of an accident. Are you listening?"

Thena would have been listening, and with fearful concentration, at any other time and place, but the fireplace had her whole attention.

The flames flashed from green to blue to purple to orange to red to green. The light dimmed and the flames shrunk until they disappeared into a black puff of smoke.

And the puff of smoke grew.

Dusa's smile vanished.

Distant laughter—the Queen's laughter—danced over the trees and through the night, a dark melodic taunt. Did Dusa hear that? Judging from the look on her face, she did.

The amount of smoke in the room swelled and lost its wispiness, turning liquid like floating ink until it stretched to the ceiling, taking the shape of—oh, oh, Dusa! The dream! The dream!

Thena's mouth gaped open, her eyes wide, a faint, terrified squeak escaping her throat.

The hooded being was from another world, a creature with wings and a terrible shadow sword. Dusa grabbed hold of Thena's bad arm. She trembled, her terror real, the gush of horrified tears streaming down as they once did long ago when she woke from her recurring nightmare.

A sound like the whipping gale of a hurricane filled with a thousand screaming souls nearly deafened Thena. The only other audible noise was Dusa's cries for mercy. But the winged shadow gave her none.

Thena shoved her sister from her and backed away.

As the shrieking gale reached a pitch so high it seemed to pulsate, the shadow plunged its black sword into Dusa's belly. Every inch of the shadow suck itself inside of Dusa through the wound, leaving her gagging, falling on all fours. She couldn't cough, couldn't make a sound. Her face turned blue.

Thena didn't try to help her.

Dusa's purple lips swelled, her hands clawing at her throat to get air. But it was only when the snakes and lizards and frogs began to slither out of her mouth in trails of mucus did Thena truly understand.

Dusa's body began to spasm and her eyes bulged out of her head. From her wide mouth there continued to spew a stream of vile black and brown life that slithered and crawled and hopped across the floor. She would not be alive much longer.

Thena let out a choked laugh, her tears soaking the front of her nightgown.

She laughed because her atheist sister had been wrong.

And because her sister had been wrong—because this realm of magical hell *did* exist—her mother was surely in heaven!

"Thena," said the voice of the Queen, trickling in like a seductive song through the window as Dusa's body twitched its last. "Thena, join us..."

Thena turned and walked to the window, entranced.

The laughing smile slipped from her face.

Suddenly, like magic, all the fear she held knotted in her breast for these people, these followers of Voodoo, melted into a strange, warm gratitude.

They had saved her.

C.J. SULLY

They had set her free.

Her eyes grew wide with knowing.

She could not stay here. Not anymore.

"Thena, come…"

Nodding, she grabbed the window with her good hand and flung it open with renewed vigor.

About the author:

C.J. Sully has a passionate love for all things New Orleans, including the exotic dark art of Voodoo. An aspiring fiction writer, she lives in Arlington, Texas, with her husband and weenie dog.

"—ROT—ROT—ROT—"
by A. J. French

"**LOOK** at the way he's standing," Jessy said. "Like he dropped a load in his pants or something."

Trance burst out laughing. "You ain't lying. Check this out."

He slued around his Wal-Mart-imprinted baseball cap so it faced front. Straightening his uniform, along with his nametag, he stepped into the toiletry aisle. The glare of the fluorescents accentuated his black skin, making it shine.

Grinning, he said, "Can I help you find anything, sir?"

The man in the aisle kept quiet. Jessy watched from behind, peeking out around a pile of cat food bags. Even at this distance, she could smell the man. She had half the mind to cover her nose. The store was located in a seedy part of town, so they frequently had homeless people and junkies wandering in, all with some brand of stink, but this fellow took the cake. He smelled like something gone bad, like something starting to . . .

—ROT—ROT—ROT—

"—ROT—ROT—ROT—" (something indecipherable here) *"—ROT—ROT—ROT—"*

"Excuse me," Trance said.

The man went silent immediately. Yet the echo of his voice seemed to linger in the air, to hover above the aisle like a flock of black birds. Trance glanced back at Jessy, twirling his finger by his head, mouthing the word *psycho*.

Jessy lifted her hands. *What do you want* me *to do about it?*

Trance turned back around, remarking audaciously, "Sir, if you're looking for the bathing products, you'll find them in aisle ten."

He had meant it to be funny, but Jessy wasn't laughing. *He can't take anything seriously,* she thought. *He acts like a grownup five-year-old sometimes.*

True, it had started out as a joke. But it didn't seem funny anymore. Not to Jessy. As soon as that man had started in with his *creepy* chattering, it stopped being funny.

"ROT—ROT—ROT—ROT—"

The man started up again, only now his misshapen body joined in, arms flailing from side to side, knees knocking, feet stamping. He wore a pair of grease-stained overalls with the left strap undone, so that it swung back and forth while he jerked about. His whole body appeared to sag, like the flesh was slipping off his bones; or like he was a bloated water balloon ready to pop, or an ice cube dissolving into a puddle.

Melting, she thought. *It's like he's melting.*

Trance started to laugh, but the man didn't seem to be aware of anything except the shelf of electric toothbrushes, at which he had stared for the past ten minutes. His long limbs and lanky torso whipped about. His sagging overalls puffed up, lending him the appearance of a thing being inflated—a blowup punching doll, perhaps.

Christ, that sound, that wretched horrible keening, what on earth is it?

"ROT—ROT—ROT—ROT—"

She could bear it for not a second longer. Leaving the sanctity of her cat food fortress, she approached Trance, who was now doubled over with laughter. She slugged him on the shoulder.

He immediately sobered. Standing up straight again, he said, "Yo, what'd you do that for, Jessy? You know I don't play when it comes to people hitting me." There was a tone of menace in his voice that had not been there before.

Good, she thought. *He can tap into that anger when he confronts the psycho.*

"Do something about him," she hissed. "It's not funny anymore, and we're going to get in trouble." She gestured at the group of customers who had stopped to witness the man's hysterics.

Trance registered this and suddenly gave a quick nod of his head, then walked over to the gyrating man.

DARK THINGS II

"ROT—ROT—ROT—ROT—" he was going berserk now, jumping and flinging and flying about like a crazed monkey, even reaching out to knock a few items off the shelves. They landed at his feet and he punted them away dramatically. One of the customers guffawed.

"Hey," Trance shouted, utilizing his big scary black man voice. "I will ask you nicely to pick those up, sir. Then I'm gonna ask you to leave. If you don't co-operate . . . " He punched his left palm like an outfielder awaiting the next pop fly.

The man ignored Trance completely, uttering his strange cry with more enthusiasm, even knocking more items off the shelves.

Trance shook his head, said, "Suit yourself," and lunged at him; an uproarious cheer came from the crowd (which was approaching twenty or thirty people).

Up until now the man had been sort of facing the display rack, so that his appearance was undetectable. But finally, with Trance closing in on him—and fast—he turned and continued his frenzied dance with his front toward Jessy. He was so repulsive that she nearly cried out in terror.

There was grease or dirt or blood or something covering his overalls and face. He wore a beard that was more foliage than facial hair, with leaves and twigs and weeds sticking in it. The horrible gleam in his eyes told of a special kind of madness, more lucid than the kind experienced by the crop of psychos who usually wandered into the store.

"ROT—ROT—ROT—ROT—" he screamed, as Trance ran up beside him, attempting to grab his shoulders.

That's when the man's demeanor changed. He stopped moving, stopped chattering. His mouth became a scowl. His eyes, fierce. He met his opponent with equal force and vigor, and they slammed into each other like two warring titans.

As they did, a strange thing happened. A horrible thing, tragic thing, unbelievable thing, which would be talked about in the store for years to come. Jessy would have to tell the police again and again just what happened, and even then they failed to believe her.

124

The customers watching would have to give their statements again and again, because nobody believed what they had to say.

It became one of those things like UFOs, or Bigfoot, or the disappearance of the Mayans. An unsolved mystery, an event nobody wanted to believe had happened. But it did happen. And there were dozens of people who witnessed it.

The man in the overalls suddenly liquefied as his body connected with Trance's. So instead of Trance connecting with substantial weight, it was like someone had doused him with a bucket of water.

He went sprawling to the floor with a cry, covered in the stuff—the soupy brown liquid that spontaneously appeared in place of the psychotic man. And now that the man was gone, only a fetid substance remained as proof of his existence.

Trance lay on the floor surrounded by an odious puddle, shrieking, writhing, clawing at his chest. The people in the crowd gasped. Jessy put a hand to her mouth.

"Oh God, Trance," she screamed, preparing to go to him. But before she took a step, the smell hit her. Something sweet and yet sickly, familiar and yet foreign, musky and immensely ripe. It swept through the customers, producing a wave of groans and complaints. Jessy heard retching sounds.

The stench was coming from the liquid, from that sticky stuff covering Trance. She didn't think she could get much closer without becoming ill.

Trance, meanwhile, was in unbearable pain. His cries rang out all over the store and more customers came by to watch.

Freeman, their boss, would be coming along at any moment, Jessy knew. And what would she do then?

Trance began to roll back and forth. "It burns," he yelled. "Mutherfu…it burns so bad, oh please God help me!"

"Oh Trance," Jessy whimpered.

His condition worsened. He began scratching at his arms, at his neck, at his cheeks. Blood seeped out as he broke through his skin.

DARK THINGS II

"It's eating me," he cried, and just then a great glob of flesh came away in his hands, revealing muscle tissue and bone. Everyone groaned, and Jessy felt her stomach turn. But Trance kept going, yielding multiple handfuls of skin, which he cradled in his palms like something treasured.

Suddenly he shot to his feet, the awful brown stuff dripping down from him, mixing with the skin and blood, and flaunting flashes of white bone, as he stood there in the aisle like a ghoul displaced from its cemetery.

Holding back his flaps of skin, Trance screamed and fled into the crowd, which parted to make way for him. Jessy was entranced by the trail of footprints he left behind—reddish, brown, awful things—because they remained on the tile floor long after Trance had disappeared from the building. In their own mocking way, the footprints wouldn't let her forget what had happened, or allow her to believe it was all a dream.

Sirens rang out; there were several minutes of utter chaos; but eventually, a flashing light appeared outside the windows. Help had arrived.

The police found Trance behind the store in the back parking lot, lying on the asphalt and sobbing in a pool of his own skin and blood. They crouched beside him and whispered words of comfort until the paramedics arrived.

He was loaded onto a gurney, wheeled into the back of the ambulance, and hooked up to a bunch of machines. The vehicle rolled away, and the emergency siren kicked on, heralding the ambulance's departure.

Trance started to make a very strange sound.

Benson, the paramedic nearest to Trance's head, leaned forward and tried to listen. "Quiet. I think he wants to tell us something."

"What," another paramedic asked.

Benson shook his head. "I dunno. But it sounds an awful lot like…"

"ROT—ROT—ROT—ROT—"

126

A.J. FRENCH

About the author:

A.J. French has appeared in Abandoned Towers, The Absent Willow Review, Down in the Dirt, Short Story.Me!, Black Lantern Publishing, Dark Gothic Resurrected, This Mutant Life, theDF_ underground, Fantastic Horror, Sex and Murder, Black Ink Horror, and Golden Visions Magazine. He also has stories in the following anthologies: Ruthless: An Extreme Horror Collection by Pill Hill Press with introduction by Bentley Little, Deep Space Terror, By Mind or Metal, Novus Creatura, and Pellucid Lunacy edited by Michael Bailey.

NOW PLAYING
by George Wilhite

GABE'S last clear memory was being quite drunk and a little stoned at the Halloween party, arguing with Randy and his jarhead buddies about the dangers of our country's imminent election of Ronald Reagan. Halloween, 1980, was a Friday night. Being Gabe's favorite holiday, he had anticipated a Friday Halloween since discovering the time sucking pastime known as partying. Now, that son of a bitch Reagan's bid for the White House being the following Tuesday had ruined everything. Gabe thought Reagan was nuts and would push the button for sure.

That night's ridiculous mixture of various types of alcohol mixed with some of the best pot imaginable caused him to black out. Then, about fifteen minutes ago, he woke up in a casket at the funeral home. "What kind of sick Halloween joke was that?" he thought, crawling out of the morbid wooden box. It was one of those expensive jobs, polished wood, shiny brass handles; probably weighed more than he did.

Sid came to mind. Sid's uncle was the undertaker in town. He must have devised this scheme, either for Gabe specifically or for whoever passed out first on Halloween. Just the kind of sick bastard to get off on that sort of thing.

Gabe sprung loose of the funeral home and just started walking with no particular destination in mind. He definitely felt like shit. Pain permeated his body and he tried to remember what the hell happened after he blacked out to mess him up this badly.

The worst aspect of his affliction was an intense burning in his gut. He felt severely nauseous but bizarrely enough, since he thought he could hurl any moment, Gabe felt incredibly hungry, as though he hadn't eaten in days.

Home was not far. Nothing was far away in this worthless Northern California town he could not wait to bust out of one day.

GEORGE WILHITE

Too bad all his spare time in the two years since high school had been wasted partying and slacking in just about every aspect of life. Gabe decided to just go home, hopefully not wake his parents, feed this hunger and pass out again on his own bed. Tomorrow, he would find out who played this joke on him and get his revenge.

Suddenly, he froze. His stomach exploded and heaved, and Gabe anticipated a load of vomit was coming. The revelation that followed was Gabe's first clue something odd was transpiring that night. Freaky Thing Number One. He had experienced the dry heaves before but as he retched and pushed his abdominal muscles, trying to vomit for relief, absolutely nothing came up. Not even saliva or bile. Nothing. It was as though his stomach was completely empty. Like when they prepare you for surgery.

"That's fucking nuts," Gabe exclaimed.

But then Freaky Thing Number Two transpired—he didn't say anything. He had thought "that's fucking nuts," but when he tried to say those words all that came out of his mouth was a series of incomprehensible mutters and groans.

Christ, Gabe thought. *I sound like fucking Boris Karloff in Frankenstein or something!*

Then, he tried speaking again. "Holy shit!" he could have sworn he was yelling, but again only the monster sounds came from his mouth.

This is a dream, he thought. Either that or I am fucking insane. The only possible third answer is someone gave me acid, shrooms, something I have never done before.

Then the fire in his gut returned but this time there was even a stronger sense of hunger than before, and along with this hunger came a tremendous rage, a bestial crazed adrenaline rush that lasted a few seconds and then subsided.

Shaking his head, even more sure some asshole had slipped him some kind of drug, in addition to the humiliation of putting him in that fucking casket, Gabe began walking again.

Then came Freaky Thing Number Three. He was putting one foot in front of the other, same as since the day he learned to walk

DARK THINGS II

as a toddler, but on this increasingly bizarre night he noticed his walk was off kilter. He was shambling slowly and was tilted to the right. The continued fire in his stomach preoccupying his mind had masked an equally strong pain in his hip which now became more apparent when he walked.

It feels dislocated or something, was Gabe thought, even though he had never experienced such an injury. He stopped and breathed deeply, taking in all the pains and mysteries of his body.

"Man, I am fucked up," he said, and again, only more grunting came out. In his frustration, he screamed into the darkness of the night and what came from his mouth was a surprisingly loud animalistic roar.

This sucks, he thought. *It has to be a dream!*

He scuffled forward again, wondering when he would finally wake up. The hunger within him grew deeply profound now, consuming his thoughts.

The same instinct that led him homeward caused him to pause in front of the Center Drive In. If Gabe had a second home this was the place. He and his buddies spent most of their spare time hanging out there. All his friends were old enough to attend any movie playing but too young to drink legally—another hypocritical US policy in their minds—we can be drafted and get our balls blown off in the next Vietnam but not buy a fucking beer—so, the drive-in was the perfect place to hang out, get drunk and watch all the B movies the walk ins rarely played.

The reason for the Center specifically was it almost always showed horror movies. 1980 had been a haven for horror flicks, a new one seemed to come out every two weeks, and the Center showed them all in double, sometimes triple features.

Gabe saw the marquee still read "Motel Hell" and "Halloween." Yep. The same double feature he just attended the night before the party. The newly released bit of grue teamed up with a classic from a couple years back.

He walked down the driveway towards the ticket booth. Maybe a little stroll through the joint would clear his head before going home. Once home, he would have to fake being straight if one or both of his parents were awake. He might as well be as close to straight as possible, get this drug someone clearly slipped him out of his system.

He was still trying to figure out why he still felt so much pain, and what was going on with the fire in his stomach. He way overdid it tonight. Tomorrow, he would probably hear all kinds of stories explaining the stupid stunts he pulled at the party once he blacked out.

As Gabe approached the ticket booth he encountered Freaky Thing Number Four—the booth was open for business. Then, he glanced over the fence and saw a film was projected onto the screen. What the fuck? He may have blacked out, but he remembered checking his watch at the party and noticing it was two fifteen A.M. and thinking it was a good thing he was off the next day. If he passed out sometime after that and then his friends played this prank on him, it should be approaching dawn of the next day.

The box office of the drive-in closed around nine or ten P.M.—basically once they started the second feature. The opening sequence of "Halloween" was playing on the screen so it was around closing time.

The moment this revelation struck him, the searing pain in his gut came back full force. The mystery of his painful empty stomach, his shambling walk and now the realization that more time had passed than he initially assumed—all these pieces of the puzzle must be related, he realized.

Here, so close to so many living human bodies, the full weight of Gabe's predicament crashed in on him for the first time. He experienced there, in the driveway, the phenomenon he would later name The Need.

Wandering alone, from funeral home to the drive-in, The Need had made itself slightly apparent, and Gabe had no reason to doubt he had emerged from that casket as anything but a confused severely hung over young man.

But when it sensed so many living humans in close range, The

DARK THINGS II

Need became manifest within Gabe. The Need was normal human hunger times a hundred. Gabe had never gone more than a couple of days without food, even if stricken with a stomach flu or food poisoning, so he did not know what starvation felt like first hand, but The Need seemed that way to him, a deep hunger that removed all reason from his mind, replacing it with a disturbingly simple animal-like agenda: to EAT—AND ONLY EAT—NOTHING ELSE MATTERED.

The Need filled Gabe with the intense adrenaline again and in mere seconds he found himself at the ticket booth. "I can't possibly move that quickly" the fading vestige of reason within him thought for a moment. Yet he had!

Reacting to the sudden movement she had barely perceived from the corner of her eye, the young woman saw Gabe before her. Her eyes wide, she opened her mouth to scream but his attack was so sudden that she did not have time to make a sound.

The Need gave him the strength and will sufficient to bash his first unfortunate victim's skull into the thick window of the booth. An instant later Gabe succumbed to The Need and ripped out her intestines and began feasting, feeding The Need, before she was even completely dead. She stared at him and tried to scream again, this time failing due to her own blood welling up in her mouth. By the time she was dead, Gabe had devoured most of the entrails that he could easily pull out of her and then he sucked at her brain as well.

As The Need subsided, Gabe's mind was whirling; this new changed nature at battle with the last remnants of his human thoughts. He looked at the defiled corpse of the woman sprawled on the floor below him, telling himself it was truly he that had done this to her. He tasted the putrid guts and blood in his mouth but the true horror came when he realized he was not revolted by this gory repast, but rather satiated. The hunger was gone, at least for the moment.

When will this nightmare end? He didn't think he was imaginative, or sick enough, to create this version of himself. But it

GEORGE WILHITE

had to be a dream, the fleeting part of him stated assertively, for it is simply impossible I am suddenly some kind of fucking cannibal.

A radio was on in the booth and as Gabe's mind fought to reason through the craziness of this night, he heard an announcer proclaiming that Ronald Reagan had indeed just been elected. That was the Fifth Freaky Thing of the evening—if this radio broadcast was not just another aspect of his elaborate hallucination, it was now November Fourth, the Tuesday after the party.

Fleeing the booth, the speed of his walk returned to the shuffle he had maintained before entering the drive-in. The Need had its own bizarre hunger that demanded respite but it was also clearly linked to his ability to move much faster and garnering the insane strength necessary to rip open a human body.

As Gabe pondered these changes it became apparent to him that the part of his nature feeding The Need was becoming dominant. As he reached the end of the driveway and entered the parking area of the drive-in he realized he was seeing the scene through a different set of eyes.

His fading memories told him that he was standing before a movie screen, projecting the first murder of Michael Meyers, the birth of a psycho, and that the cars that filled the lot likely held many friends and neighbors he knew well. But the dominant fixations of his newly transformed mind were breaking through all such civilized human thoughts and replacing them with more base thoughts: MORE MEAT and FEED. As those words screamed in his mind, his stomach raged again. So soon? He just killed that chick a few minutes ago.

The small rational part of him left guided him into the snack bar. He managed to make his way into the bathroom without being noticed. He really needed this. He had to see himself, and discover whether that would help him solve this mystery or not.

Remarkably, despite all the bladders full of beer that must be present outside, the bathroom was empty for the moment.

The instant Gabe saw his reflection in the mirror, all ambiguities that plagued him earlier dissipated. It was amazing how;

133

of all the senses, sight can often bring home the truth more than any other. He had been struggling all night to understand what was happening to him. Now, in his reflection, it was clear. The reason he shambled when he walked was his not just that his hip was out of place. The entire left side of his torso was oddly twisted in front of the right side, as though his entire spine was split in half. There was also a huge hole in his skull, exposing bone and brain. He was missing an eye. That confused him, for his vision didn't seem the least bit distorted.

I don't remember how it happened, he thought, but it's obviously true. I fucking died and now I'm—

A man about Gabe's age walked into the bathroom, interrupting his rational thought process again. It all happened much faster this time, the instructions ringing through his mind: Human meat—Attack—Feed and Satiate the Need. This time, however, the young man screamed and squealed like a stuck pig while Gabe feasted on his flesh, attracting the attention of the teenage boy manning the snack bar.

The door flew open and the boy screamed out the name Gabe was about to use for himself before he was interrupted: "Zombie! Holy shit! Fucking zombie!"

Unfortunately for the boy, those seconds he wasted standing there yelling was all the time Gabe needed to kill him as well and nobody else was in the snack bar anyway to hear his warnings.

As Gabe rushed out of the snack bar, the revelation of his predicament settling in now, he heard a radio from behind the counter. Initially, he paid little attention, assuming it was carrying more election results, but he heard something that caught his interest.

"If you just tuned in, there are reports from all over the country of the reanimation of the dead. The cause of this phenomenon is unknown, but it appears to be only infecting the unburied dead. There have been no reports of the dead rising from graves, only those who have not yet been buried…"

The voice trailed off or Gabe just stopped listening. Either way, he heard enough to know that his interpretation of the night's

"Freaky Events" was on target—the thing in the mirror—he, himself, was a zombie.

Funny, he didn't remember dying. It must have happened on Halloween, after the party; it seemed unlikely he would have lost days after that. Didn't matter now. He realized he was literally smelling the flesh outside, his mind, slowly turning from human to zombie, and The Need, could now discern between the scent of living human meat and the dead piles of flesh he created in the snack bar.

As he exited the building, he wondered if this phenomenon only affected those who were dead at a certain moment in time, or if his first three victims would now become zombies as well, shuffling around with their open wounds spilling out all over the place.

This was going to be quite a night.

Once outside, he greeted chaos.

There were half a dozen or so more zombies terrorizing kids in cars, pulling them out and feeding The Need.

Gabe looked at them, cocked his head curiously, seeing what it really looked like when a human was torn apart like that. All the horror movies he had seen did not compare to the terror of the genuine article. No matter how well one though they could act horrified, the screaming and squealing and loss of bodily functions that occurred when one of these victims was torn open was beyond his worst nightmares.

Such human thoughts were receding by the second, however, as the catalyst of his new changed nature worked its way through his system. It seemed stronger every time he fed. He walked into the parking area of the drive-in and allowed The Need to consume him. His instincts told him his key to survival was a purging of his humanity.

On the screen, Donald Pleasance foolishly left the nurse in the car and Michael Meyers kills her, steals the car and the terror begins anew.

Gabe squinted at the screen, noticing something wasn't quite right. There was something splattered all over the screen.

DARK THINGS II

No, he realized, it wasn't on the screen. Someone must have been slaughtered in the projection room and blood was splattered on the lens. Each scene projected above was now obscured by blood.

Gabe found that perversely funny. He tried to laugh but, like his attempts at speech, he roared instead. Each time he used his zombie vocal chords, this howl became louder and more primal. He was still vaguely aware of the irony of blood covering the scene of the movie before him, now introducing Jamie Lee Curtis and her friends. 'Hmmm, foreshadowing,' was the last human thought he had before he has raving again.

Within seconds, he had a woman on the ground, pounding her skull against one of the speaker poles to get to her brains.

"Gabe," he heard from somewhere behind him.

He sucked the brains out of the hole in the woman's skull as she kicked and screamed in her last moments of life.

"Fucking Hell! That's Gabe!" The voice came again from somewhere on the other side of his new existence.

"But he's dead," another voice exclaimed. A female.

"Duh. Ran his fucking car into a tree."

Finally, those words hit home. Gabe stopped feeding and turned around.

"So he's one of them," the girl said, wide-eyed at Gabe.

"Gabe…it's me," the boy said. "Zach."

Gabe flinched but his mind was still reeling back and forth between its human thought patterns, that wanted to remember these kids, and desired more knowledge of his death, and the new bestial patterns that only wanted to kill and eat.

Zach grabbed the girl's hand.

"Nancy," Gabe tried to say, remembering her name, but only another two syllable grunt came out. Those sounds, coupled with his overall hideous appearance, the blood and gore covering him, had the couple running in an instant. But they ran right into another pair of zombies directly behind them.

The scent from this new killing before him cleared Gabe's mind of any pity he had just felt for Zach and Nancy. Hesitation would not bode well for him. It was only a matter of time before lots of humans, armed with weapons, would hunt his new kind down. That was simple human nature. Kill first, ask questions later.

Gabe saw the carnage around him and wondered how long this would last. Who would win?

His argument with Sid, Randy and the others over Reagan flashed through his mind. Gabe was certain Reagan would start the Apocalypse.

Here we are tonight, he thought, laughing in his husky new monstrous fashion, scared out our wits by Michael Meyers and Ronald Reagan. One of them is gone when the last reel ends and the other may never make it into office anyway, now that this night has come.

That was one of the last rational thoughts Gabe would have as the madness of The Need grew stronger by the moment. He thought again about the cops and mercenaries probably on their way. His new animal nature needed to concentrate on these kinds of thoughts to survive.

As he left the drive-in and the few live humans left to his kindred spirits, he looked up at the screen once more.

Michael Meyers was driving down the street, stalking the girls he would kill later, one at a time. All but Jamie Lee, anyway. He had to remember there were plenty of clever ones like her that would find a way to destroy him. Tonight, being destroyed, dying a second time, sounded pretty good, but that would pass in time as the savage in him took control.

Gabe bid farewell to the drive-in and walked a few blocks to the entrance of the largest park in town without running into any trouble. There were sirens and flashing lights beginning to appear all over town but Gabe made it into the woods before the cavalry amassed in significant force. The park was one hundred and fifty acres of woods meandering around a large manmade lake. It had plenty of places to hide while this night played out.

Later that night, hiding in the woods, Gabe smelled and then saw a young woman his age, topless, running and screaming loudly.

DARK THINGS II

In that moment, he was not aroused by her large flapping breasts nor did he feel the slightest human connection towards her. When his zombie senses tracked her, all he sensed was MEAT.

The Need had won and his transformation was complete.

About the author:

George Wilhite has been an aficionado of the horror genre since his youth, discovering Poe and Lovecraft at an early age while also spending many summer nights at drive-in theaters watching the contemporary scene unfold. He is the author of the short fiction collection On the Verge of Madness and his work has also appeared in several magazines and anthologies, including Dark Recesses, Elements of Horror, Haunted, and I, Executioner, and in audio format on Well Told Tales podcast.

BUG BOY
by Matt Kurtz

BUG Boy's real name was Stanley. The residents of the small Texas town that he belonged to thought of him in two ways: the old folks thought he wasn't right in the head and the young ones thought he was creepy. But Stanley didn't care what either group thought because he didn't like people.

He liked bugs.

The insects weren't a surrogate for his childhood friendships. You don't collect friends only to torture them when you tire of their company—at least not if you're a functioning member of society. But then again, John Wayne Gacy was a functioning member of society.

***

With thumbs hooked tightly around the straps of his bulging knapsack, Stanley walked past the cemetery that kissed the property line of his house. There was another commotion going on within the rusted metal fence that surrounded the large lot. He stopped to get a better look, pushing his head between two iron rods of the fence, his large ears preventing his noggin from popping all the way through. In the distance, a small platoon of men armed with shovels surrounded a bulldozer that was digging up another grave.

There must have been more sink holes in the cemetery.

The settling of earth was normal for freshly-dug graves, but this was happening more frequently to the older ones. It got well beyond the point of the caretaker shoveling in additional dirt to make up the difference. These graves were sinking several feet into the earth—and steadily continuing their journey downward. The youngsters told stories to spook one another about the reason for the collapsing earth: the dead were clawing at the lids of their coffins,

139

making it through the splintered and rotting wood, only to have the six feet of earth from above cave in upon them. These zombies were tenacious, and it was only a matter of time before they crawled their way up through the freshly sifted earth to devour living flesh— starting with the children of the town as their appetizers.

But taking into account all the storms the area had been pounded with lately, the adults had a less fantastic and more practical theory: the oversaturated ground was finally dissolving a limestone bed located somewhere underneath the cemetery, causing one sink hole after another. The only problem with that theory was that every time an area of the collapsed earth was dug up, there was no limey muddy slop found underneath the coffin. Only loosely packed, dry earth.

The bulldozer still had a way to go before hitting the jackpot. Stanley didn't have time to wait since he couldn't be late again for school. As he went on his way he took comfort in knowing that at the rate the coffins were being dug up, he'd see a dead body sooner or later.

***

As dusk approached, Stanley sat on the grass in his backyard, shaking a glass jar above his head. The lot surrounding the backyard proper was wildly overgrown with brush and trees. It was this mini-forest that ran up to the cemetery's fence, providing a vast array of insect species, much to the delight of Stanley's eleven-year old heart.

Holding the jar between the setting sun and one squinted eye, he studied a slug recently found in a rotting log. Its slimy secretion looked funny on the glass when the sun shone through it. Stanley wanted more slime so he shook the jar rapidly. The slug slammed back and forth like a pinball at full tilt. When his scrawny arms started to burn from so much motion, Stanley stopped and held up the jar again.

After all that work, there wasn't much additional slime.

"Stupid," he huffed, the word whistling out from between

his huge buck teeth.

The slug bored him, which meant only one thing. Stanley reached into his open backpack and pulled out another metal lid—one without ventilation holes.

He switched the lids on the jar and set the container on the grass. Rolling over onto his stomach, he stared at the slug. It didn't move. Knowing it would take way too long to suffocate, he opted for his second means of disposal. He pulled out a magnifying glass and held it up to the sun. Crapola. It was almost dark and not nearly intense enough to incinerate anything.

Snatching up the jar, Stanley walked to the edge of the foliage. He searched around until he found his third and most thrilling method of disposal.

A mound of fire ants.

He kicked the pile with his shoe and stirred up hell. In a matter of seconds the ants were swarming the mound, looking like fiery snow on a television screen. Stanley unscrewed the jar, flipped it upside down, and shook the slug loose. It fell out, landing dead center on the swarming mass.

The ants were instantly upon the intruder that disturbed their nest, making it pay dearly. The slug moved *now*, wincing in agony as the ants stung, pinched, and tore.

Stanley smiled, grunting in exhilaration at the sacrifice he offered to the living fire.

A clicking noise, insect in nature, rose from the foliage a few yards in front of Stanley. By the time his head whipped in its direction the noise had already ceased. Stepping forward to investigate, Stanley's black, beady eyes shifted back and forth, scanning the bushes and trees.

The peach fuzz slowly prickled on the back of his neck at the odd sensation that he was being watched. A classmate hoping to play a trick on him? He smiled and welcomed it, knowing that they'd be sorry—just as they had in the past.

"STANLEY! DINNER TIME!!!" His mother's screech echoed in the distance of the front yard.

DARK THINGS II

Stanley continued his scan through the shadowy tree line, not even acknowledging his mother's call. She could wait. So could dinner.

"STANLEY!!!" The harpy shrieked in a tone that meant business.

Stanley didn't move. His black eyes, like beetle shells, continued to shift without blinking.

"Some other time...," he whispered and finished up in his head, *I'll get ya. I'll get ya real good.* He turned and headed toward the house.

From the dark brush, something large and ancient watched Stanley scoop up his knapsack and disappear into the back door of the house.

***

The next day in the school cafeteria, Billy Smithers was recounting a tale that his father (who was in charge of the investigation and excavation of the strange happenings in the local cemetery) had told him the previous night.

"And when they opened the coffin, there was Old Man Steele laying there with his arms folded neatly over his chest. He had worms danglin' out of his ears as a beetle popped out of his nose."

All the kids at the table let out a collective EEEEWWWWWWWW! This brought more children, curious about the commotion, over to Billy's table.

Stanley, who sat alone on the other side of the cafeteria, took enough notice to put down his liverwurst and pimento cheese sandwich.

"Oh, but that ain't nothing," Billy continued telling the growing crowd. "The old dude's suit was all moving around, like popcorn poppin' under tin foil. So, my dad took his shovel and knocked back his jacket to see what was causin' the movin'..."

The group leaned in. Loving every second of it, Billy had

142

MATT KURTZ

them waiting on his every word. "The jacket was pulled back and… his body was crawlin' with…" Billy scooped up his cold spaghetti and meat sauce with a plastic spoon and wiggled the hanging noodles back and forth "…huge maggots and worms!"

All the kids exclaimed in unison, EEEWWWWWWW! Some kids pushed their plates of pasta away in disgust. Billy had them exactly where he wanted and was about to continue when he noticed all eyes shift over his shoulder. Some kids slowly turned, going back to their lunches. Some looked down at their shoes and walked away. Billy thought it was probably Principal Natson about to warn him to stop with the spook stories. But when he turned around, it was Bug Boy he saw over his shoulder.

"Oh, hey Bug…" Billy croaked then cleared his throat. "Hey, Stanley."

"Were they crawling all over him and feasting on him?" Stanley asked in a flat whisper. "And how big *were* they?"

Billy gulped and dropped the pasta. He liked attention from the kids, but not from Stanley.

He had bullied Bug Boy once and almost got bit from the monstrous tarantula that had mysteriously appeared in his backpack after gym class. When he accused Stanley of the act to Principal Natson, a scorpion the size of a large crawfish crawled out of his backpack later at home. After that, Bug Boy wasn't just ignored, he was avoided. And not just by Billy, but all the kids.

"I asked how big they were." Stanley said, staring at Billy with his unblinking, black eyes.

"Ah…pretty big, Stanley. Pretty big," Billy replied, hoping that was the answer Bug Boy was looking for.

***

It *was* the perfect answer and it got Stanley's imagination reeling as he passed the cemetery on his way home from school. Wouldn't it be cool to have in his collection some bugs that fed on human flesh? It would be even cooler to bring something like that to the next Show

143

DARK THINGS II

'N Tell and watch his classmates squirm as they tried to figure out the mystery of *whose* flesh the bugs had consumed. Stanley couldn't help but snicker at the thought of making his entire class feel so uncomfortable with only a single bug.

***

Stanley heard the weird clicking noise again as he was watched a sacrificial grasshopper being torn apart by the ant mound in his backyard. He stepped into the weeds to start investigating.

Heading in its general direction, he saw the bushes move in the distance. By the time he sprinted over to them, there was nothing there.

Except for a large trail of slime.

Only something very big could leave a trail like that!

Shaking with excitement, Stanley followed the gooey trail around trees, over fallen logs, and through the brush. It brought him so deep into the woods that he lost sight of his house. The trail ended a few yards from the neighboring cemetery fence. It was there that he found a hole in the loose earth about two-feet by two-feet wide; the tall grass surrounding it was swirled and packed flat in a counter-clockwise direction. The slime went over the edge and down into the hole.

Stanley scuttled over to it and peered down the opening. It looked like it leveled off a few feet under the surface, heading directly into the cemetery.

Without hesitating, he jumped down into the pit, his feet sinking into the muddy mixture of slime and loose dirt. He crouched down to get a better look. Anyone else in their right mind would fear that whatever dug that hole might be waiting there, pissed off or hungry. But not Stanley. There was no fear, only excitement at where it might lead.

Frayed roots hung down on all sides of the tunnel, which faded to a wall of darkness. The slime trail started on the floor, then crept up the walls to the ceiling and back down again, repeating the

144

pattern as if whatever was doing the burrowing rotated 360 degrees like a drill.

Stanley had to see where it went. But first he needed a flashlight and his collection jars.

Climbing out, he looked back to where the underground passage led: directly *under* the cemetery! A crooked smile (unsheathing those crooked buck teeth) crept onto his face and kept growing until his nose wrinkled and his black eyes got beadier. By going into that hole he'd be the talk of the town. He was either going to have those bugs that dined on human flesh for Show 'N Tell or he was going to solve the town's mystery of what was causing the graves to sink.

And the answer was waiting at the end of a two-foot by two-foot hole.

***

Stanley finally heard his parents' footsteps in the hall trailing off toward their room. He had been dying for them to go to bed; the anticipation of his little adventure caused him to nibble on his lower lip to the point of nearly drawing blood. When he heard their door shut, he crawled out from under the covers fully clothed, slid on his shoes, then grabbed the flashlight and glass jar off his nightstand. He stared out into the dark woods from his open bedroom window. As the sheer curtains flapped around him from the incoming breeze, he bit down hard on his bottom lip. A salty, coppery taste filled his mouth, reassuring him that this was for real.

Then out the window Stanley went. Like pupae to imago, the metamorphosis from boy to town legend was underway.

***

He shone the flashlight into the hole, checked the perimeter around him one last time to make sure he wasn't followed, and dove right in. Within seconds, he was burrowing through the earth toward the graveyard. The passageway was tight, even for Stanley's scrawny frame. With the flashlight in one hand and the glass jar in the other, he grunted and snorted as he worked his way deeper and deeper. Much like the way a cat uses its whiskers, Stanley knew that if his bony shoulders could get through, the rest of him could. Continuing on through the cramped space, he prayed that the tunnel would widen soon. He wasn't pacing himself and was already getting tired. His heart raced at the realization that if he hit a dead end where he couldn't turn around or if it got much narrower, he might not have the energy to crawl backwards to get out of the tunnel.

He'd be stuck.

Suffocate.

NO!

This was all a test. A trial to see if he was worthy of the transformation. He'd make it to the other end. He just *had* to keep going forward.

After a few feet of mindless movement based solely upon instinct, the walls seemed to back away from him. Through the flashlight's beam he could make out that the tunnel was opening into a larger area. A welcoming breeze blew against his face, slicing the thickness of the hot air around him. When he finally reached the opening, he lunged forward, pushing out of the dirt tube. Like a baby being shot out of the womb, he landed with a hard *thud* onto the dirt floor and lay gasping for air. When the dust cleared and he was able to catch his breath, he scrambled to his knees, shining his light around.

He was in the hub of the underground system. Like a beating heart, its subterranean passageways acted as arteries flowing through Mother Earth in all directions. Numerous tunnels lined the walls, ceiling, and floor; some bigger and wider than others. Frayed roots hung and jetted out in all directions like an intricate pattern of veins.

He went to one of the tunnels and shone his light inside. It seemed to be blocked by an avalanche of rotting wood and dirt. Something metallic reflected in his light. Something gold...no... brass...a brass rod surrounded by ornate designs. Stanley was

146

curious how the tarnished brass got wedged in there. Then it hit him. His face scrunched up with a big smile, giving him a rat-like appearance in the gleam of the flashlight.

It was the brass handles on a crumbled and rotting coffin. Which meant that a little further beyond the coffin was a crumbled and rotting corpse. And within that corpse might be the plump and juicy bugs for Show 'N Tell. The coffins were probably sinking not from what the stupid townsfolk thought was some stupid dissolving limestone, but from whatever was digging these tunnels. Stanley shone the light around the cavern again and, for the first time in a long time, common sense prevailed. He was dealing with something much, much bigger than what he was used to. This thing was huge. Could probably gobble him up in one gulp. Maybe he should leave before—

No! Dang it! He *was* going to collect some bugs. He just had to do it quickly.

He unscrewed the lid of the mayonnaise jar and climbed into the tunnel to go root around in the rotting coffin.

A familiar clicking noise came from behind him.

Stanley froze for a moment, than scurried back out of the hole. His flashlight frantically searched around. The beam stopped in the corner of the cavern at a mound of loose earth. Stanley stepped forward, expecting to find a large hole beyond it. His beady eyes expanded (as best they could) and his brows shot upward.

It wasn't a hole. But a nest.

The mound was shallow in the center like an enormous bundt cake. Dead center was a mess of leaves and roots with five of the largest worms he'd ever seen resting on top—just like a cherry on a sundae. The worms were white, veiny, and glistening; each resembling (and the exact size of) a peeled banana.

Stanley stepped up to the nest to get a closer look with the flashlight. The worms squirmed and flopped away from the bright light, leaving a stringy trail of snot behind.

They were awesome. They were perfect.

Stanley grunted, bouncing from his excitement like a chimp

in heat. Though he didn't find these things feasting on human flesh, he'd embellish a little to his classmates.

Planting the flashlight in the soft earth so the beam shone into the nest, Stanley grabbed a stick and started pushing the worms into the jar. Four of them just barely fit. The sole remaining worm flopped back and forth, sensing its abandonment. Stanley screwed the lid on tight and turned back to the solitary worm in the nest. He placed the stick in the center of its squirming body.

He just had to see what it was made of.

Stanley jabbed downward. As the stick pierced its body, the worm twisted in agony. Stanley pushed harder. It let out a screeching noise and one end of it split open, revealing sharp mandibles. Stanley held it up to gawk over its pinching maw and revel in its agony. The shadow on the wall disguised the cruelty taking place, making it look as innocent as a camper blowing on his skewered hot dog fresh out of a campfire. But hot dogs don't scream out like this, unless microwaved for way, way too long.

Stanley couldn't believe the size of the thing's...*mouth*. A mouth that was full of sharp teeth just beyond flapping pinchers. A worm the size of a banana? And with teeth! The kids at Show 'N Tell were going to make lemonade in their pants for sure!

The jar in his hand vibrated. He held it up to the light and saw the four captive worms moving back and forth. They sensed the suffering of their sibling, flopping so hard against the glass in response that Stanley thought they might shatter the jar. The thing on the stick screeched louder, its agonizing cries echoing throughout the cavern.

Then, to Stanley's horror, from deep within one of the tunnels, something screeched in response. Something with a lot more bass and sounding a heck of a lot larger.

He threw the impaled worm on the ground and stomped it with his tennis shoe. When he still felt it moving under his sole, he pushed down hard, rotating his foot back and forth just like his grandpappy does to snuff out a cigarette. Clutching his worm-packed jar, Stanley snatched up the flashlight and backed away with a muddy mixture of blood and slime stuck to his shoe.

The ground began to rumble and a booming roar came from the opposite wall of tunnels.

Stanley ran to the opening that he thought he originally came from. He wasn't sure. But it didn't matter. There was no way he could get away crawling on his belly at a snail's pace from whatever was coming for him. He had to escape through a tunnel large enough for him to scurry on his hands and knees and just hope that it was the quickest way back to the surface—and one that didn't lead to a dead end.

The rumbling became heavier and a cloud of dust burped out from a hole directly over his shoulder.

Stanley jumped into the largest tunnel available and crawled as fast as he could. The worms in the jar flopped around, faster and faster. He thought about leaving them, which would free up a hand so he could move faster, but this find was too large to abandon. He was going to make it out of the labyrinth and take the worms with him.

He kicked up a cloud of dust behind him. If he stopped and the dust shifted, he'd choke on it for sure. He had to constantly be moving forward.

The trail snaked back and forth. He heard a deafening roar from only a few turns back. The worms in the jar screeched in response.

Mother was closing in.

He didn't look back and tried to move faster on legs and arms that were already burning. His left knee slid across the dirt and slammed against a rock, knocking him flat. The flashlight flew from his grasp. The beam spun and flipped, shining back on him like a spotlight. Stanley looked behind him and saw it illuminating the cloudy tunnel beyond his feet.

The dust shifted like a riptide, sucked back for a moment, then bellowed toward him. The force from something extremely large approaching pushed the air forward.

Flipping over onto his back to search for any immediate way

DARK THINGS II

out of the tunnel (and the oncoming juggernaut's way), Stanley saw the hole in the dirt ceiling. He reached up into it and felt quickly around. It was a large enough for him to hide in. He had no choice since the thing was almost upon him.

He grabbed the flashlight, jarring it against the wall in the process. The bulb flickered and went out. Before everything fell to darkness, Stanley saw two things that burned in his brain like a ghost image from a camera flash: the exact location of the hole above and an enormous open mouth with mandibles that filled the entire tunnel, approaching from around the corner by his feet, ready to swallow him whole.

Still clutching the jar and flashlight, he felt for the hole, lined up his path and pushed his body upward into it. Not taking into account how much headroom there was in his new found safe haven, his skull slammed into its hard, flat ceiling. A white-hot pain ricocheted around his brain causing his muscles to go limp for a second. The flashlight and jar fell to his side. Stanley pulled his feet safely through the hole then raised trembling hands to his aching head.

The rumbling below grew more intense.

The vibrations caused the jar to roll toward his feet. It came to a stop against something that sounded like wood. A tree root, perhaps?

The rumbling immediately halted and all was calm.

Stanley waited until the spinning stars in his head subsided, then flipped over in the tight quarters and felt above him, finding that he only had about a foot of headroom to deal with. It wasn't a way out but it was a good enough hiding place until the thing below moved on. He needed to find the flashlight to see exactly where he was and if it led to an alternate path.

He caught a whiff of a nauseating stench and figured he probably made fudge in his britches out of fear. His clothes were drenched in sweat so he couldn't tell if he had wet himself, too. Probably so. Didn't matter. When he got out of here, he'd just bury his clothes somewhere in the woods where nobody would find them

150

and sneak back naked into his bedroom while it was still dark.

He flipped over on his belly to search for the flashlight. His hands felt something soft that reminded him of his mama's bedspread. Then they felt something that was hard in some parts and squishy in others. He continued to feel around in the dark until he found the cold aluminum shaft of the flashlight.

The floor vibrated. Stanley froze.

A slow, steady, pulsing rhythm filled his ears.

Stanley waited another moment, then smacked the flashlight with his hand.

The bulb flickered and a grinning skull flashed in front of him.

Then it all went pitch black again.

In the dark, Stanley's beady eyes widened (as best they could) with horror. He smacked the bulb again in hopes that what he saw wasn't real. He jiggled the flashlight and gave it another whack.

The bulb shot on and illuminated his hiding space.

He was inside a coffin. Six feet under the ground.

The rotting, half-consumed occupant smiled back at him, welcoming his newfound bunkmate to stick around for a bit.

Stanley shrieked in horror as he realized that the hole he thought he crawled into for safety was actually the bottom of a rotting casket. He looked down at the opening that he made the mistake of crawling through, but saw that it was blocked by something—something resembling a slimy and veiny balloon. Stanley pushed on it to clear the hole but his hand slid off of the slick surface. He pushed harder, then pounded on it but to no avail. The balloon pulsated and a deafening roar from below shook the floor he laid upon.

The thing was blocking him in with its enormous body.

Stanley flailed around, his legs kicking within the cramped coffin. His fists pounded on the lid. His sweating increased. His eyes stung from the dust he stirred up. The deep breaths he took expanded his chest and made the walls of the casket tighten around him like a boa constrictor. The air felt thicker. Harder to take in. His lungs started to burn. His watering eyes, runny nose, and spittle became disgusting muddy streams that ran down his face. His pounding and kicking become more frantic. He was going to suffocate. He couldn't die like this!

His foot kicked out.

Shattered glass echoed in his ears.

Stanley shone the beam down to his feet.

The four worms were surrounded by the broken shards of the mayonnaise jar. They flipped over, facing Stanley in perfect unison. They screeched out. The booming response below rattled the coffin again, raining down a layer of dust and choking the air Stanley desperately needed to breathe. Like snakes ready to strike, they rose up.

Mandibles split apart. Rows of razor teeth gleamed in the light.

Stanley screamed right before they struck.

***

As the full moon shone overhead, Billy Smithers was cutting through the graveyard on his way home from a friend's house. Rapping a stick against each tombstone he passed, he froze when he heard the muffled, agonizing shrieks coming from below his feet. The ground he stood on shifted and dropped about six inches. Before the dust the earth had just farted upwards could settle, Billy ran out of the cemetery gates and down the farm road, squealing louder than a piglet separated from its mother's teat.

***

The next day the crew of workers, led by William Smithers Sr., dug up the grave that had sunk in the night before. Billy Jr. stood by his father's side and peered down into the six (and one half) foot hole in the ground. When the lid was lifted, the white velvet lining was wet with crimson. The half-eaten remains of Stanley Tiddych lay next to the rightful resident of the casket. The shattered jar with a Hellman's

152

MATT KURTZ

Mayonnaise lid lay at both their feet.

The workers were stumped at how the boy had got into a coffin that was buried under six feet of earth. It was like a magician trying to pull off some whacky trick that went horribly wrong. Though most of the men staring down at the double-occupied grave wouldn't admit it, they all shared a collective thought: *Yep, that boy was a strange one. Damaged goods and never right in the head to begin with. Guess the Lord finally took pity and showed His mercy. Mysterious ways, that's what this is.*

Billy Smithers, Jr. stared at his half eaten classmate and former school bully with a slightly different view. *Don't know how, but looks like the Bug Boy just got his butt exterminated,* he thought, and hid the smile that wanted to shine.

About the author:

Originally a part-time independent filmmaker and screenwriter, Matt Kurtz decided to narrow his creative energy to focus more on short stories and future novels. He has spent the last year feverishly pecking away on his computer in the vain attempt of getting as many pieces of fiction published before the Mayan Doomsday Prophecy of 2012 has a chance to occur. His fiction has appeared in SICK THINGS-EXTREME CREATURE HORROR, BLOODY CARNIVAL, MADNESS OF THE MIND, WERE-WHAT?, DARK THINGS, and an upcoming issue of NECROTIC TISSUE magazine.

DUMMIES
by Sean Graham

THE small infirmary was a barracks-style room with six beds running down each wall. Eight of the twelve beds were occupied by the sick and sedated; men, women and children wrapped in a thin layer of white gauze from head to toe. Nurse Rebecca walked down the center aisle, making the rounds, recording what she thought were the vitals of each patient, answering their drooling, limp faces with a bright smile. A constant buzz crackled over the intercom.

Patient five stirred, went rigid, her back arching towards the ceiling, and began to convulse violently. Rebecca ran to five's bedside and jammed a leather strap in her mouth. White foam seethed from between the leather and the patient's lips as she rocked upward and back down into the metal-framed bed, slamming it backwards into the wall.

"Dr. Watkins," Rebecca screamed. "It's five!" She had to sit on the writhing patient to keep her halfway still. The thin gauze peeled away, revealing scabbed and oozing welts. A man burst through the double doors at the far end and ran to patient five's bed as the raging body fell limp.

Watkins, who preferred to be called Dr. Watts, as in the measure of power, or Dr. Mega-Watts, as in a million units of power, pulled his nurse to her feet. "Well damn, lost another one. That's three this week." He shook his head. "Guess you better let the sheriff know we ain't gonna have enough for the barn raisin' next month."

"Wonderful," Nurse Rebecca said, rolling her eyes.

"I don't envy you, girl."

Rebecca left the makeshift hospital, which was more of a storage room for the ill; it used to be the general store before Milt opened up on Main Street and had been the old church before that.

154

SEAN GRAHAM

She straightened the crisp white smock and scratched at a yellow pus stain with her fingernail. The uniform made her feel proud. She was no nurse—no more than Watkins was a doctor; neither had finished the eighth grade—but the uniform made her feel like a nurse, made her feel important.

The Andersons were outside sitting on the porch drinking something with ice in it, probably lemonade, as Rebecca rounded the corner. A tall skinny man worked a push lawnmower, the manual kind without a motor. Its cylinder of spiraling blades whirled quietly as the man stared blankly at the lawn. Blades of grass stuck to his pockmark-riddled face. He wore a blue one-piece coverall that was filthy and stained with oil and grass and who knew what else. The crotch of his coveralls was wet and dark. Rebecca wrinkled her nose. Some people just don't know how to take care of their dummies.

"Hey there, Andersons," Rebecca said, waving. The elderly Mr. and Mrs. Anderson raised their glasses and smiled.

"Lose another one, Becka," Mrs. A asked.

"Yes. Wish me luck," Rebecca said, crossing her fingers. The Andersons smiled.

"We'll never get the barn raised at this rate," Rebecca heard Mr. A tell his wife of sixty years. Mrs. A nodded smugly. Rebecca ignored the exchange.

She walked down the street waving and greeting neighbors and lifetime friends. Two women, one skinny and one fat, worked at mending a picket fence. They moved in slow motion, deliberate and steady, their eyes looking simultaneously at the fence and a thousand miles beyond. Rebecca did not wave at them or acknowledge them in any way. There was no need.

A steady buzz emanated from a large bullhorn speaker mounted to a telephone pole at the intersection. Once it had been part of the tornado warning system, but not anymore.

Main Street was the only paved road in town. Shops lined it on either side. There was a barber, a women's clothes store, two cafes and a half dozen other storefronts, each of which sported an American flag hanging proudly from an angled pole. It wasn't a

DARK THINGS II

holiday; White Oak residents prided themselves on their patriotism. Once Rebecca heard one of the visitors call their town "quaint Main Street America." Rebecca had no idea what the woman was talking about, but thought the woman should know; she wore fancy sunglasses and a scarf, and those types knew stuff. That woman now shoveled pig crap up at the Franklins'. Beyond Main there was a scattering of homes and farms stretching out from town center where the two hundred residents of White Oak lived.

Rebecca looked in the window of the sheriff's office and town jail across the street. Deputy Larry was standing behind the front desk picking his teeth. Out front a work crew poured fresh asphalt and heat waves rose from the pitch mixture, making Larry look like he was dancing the hula. The crew moved slowly and methodically—pouring pitch, smoothing, tamping, pouring, smoothing, tamping. They didn't look up when Rebecca walked by them.

An angry buzzer sounded as she entered the sheriff's office, and Larry almost fell off his feet.

"Damn, girl, you'll give a man a heart attack," he said, trying not to look silly, but failing.

"I have to see Bobby...I mean the sheriff," Rebecca said.

Larry rolled his head dramatically. "Ahh, come on, girl, not again. Another one?"

She nodded.

"Hold on." And Larry left the front desk and disappeared down a wood-paneled hallway. She heard Larry say something and Bobby shout something horrible, something breakable smashed against something less breakable, and then Larry appeared in the hallway a second before Big Bobby Larson pushed past.

His gray sheriff's uniform stretched tight around his 350-pound frame. After years of trying, the shirt was forced to concede to physics and be content with never being tucked into the man's trousers; the belly was simply too damn big and fabric simply could not stretch that far. He wore a tight crew cut, and despite his perpetually flushed and fleshy cheeks he managed to maintain an

156

air of danger. He stopped behind the counter and stared at Rebecca.

"*Girl*," he said. "I thought you and Watts could handle this! What the hell is going on up there?" He slammed a meaty fist on the counter. "Couple of morons. I guess you don't like new barns. You don't like the quality of life we enjoy here, is that it?"

"I'm...I'm..." And Rebecca started to cry as she always did.

"Ehh..." The sheriff waved her off, but inside he was happy he had made her cry. "Larry, get Jesse's ass down to the county road with a couple of dummies and get that damn detour sign up..."—he glared at Rebecca—"...again."

"Yessir." Larry spoke it as one word and grabbed the telephone. Ten minutes later Jesse was behind the wheel of one of the only working vehicles in town with three men in blue coverall jumpsuits riding in the truck bed, towing an orange detour trailer, the kind shaped like a giant arrow with the lights that flashed in the direction you were supposed to take, except the lights didn't work anymore. Now it was just a giant orange arrow on wheels.

***

Right about now the two hundred dollars for a GPS navigation system he passed on at Mega-mart sounded like a pretty good deal. Mitch fought the huge paper map, trying to fold it into something manageable while still displaying the relevant section of the state.

If...if I am here and I need to be there... Mitch pointed to a large dot and traced backwards along a red line that diverged countless times until he reached the tiny piece of red line where he thought he was currently pulled over. He hadn't seen a sign or another driver in an hour, and the quality and size of the roads had steadily decreased in that time.

A right on 21. Looks like twenty or thirty miles then a left onto County Road 9110 and twenty miles back to the interstate. Mitch checked his watch; still had time to make the conference.

"Let's do this, Mulroney," he said to himself and tossed

the map into the backseat and pulled back onto the road. Zeppelin pumped from the stereo, and he tapped the steering wheel in time with the music. Endless flat fields rolled out to the horizon and the sun radiated unhindered by clouds. Despite his being lost, it really wasn't a bad day for a drive, and thirty minutes later he was turning onto 21.

Before he hit the 9110 intersection, however, a detour sign forced him to stop at a smaller T intersection. The giant orange arrow was pointing into the fields opposite the intersecting road. *Genius, guys...nice job.* He took a quick look at the map, couldn't find any evidence of the road he was being told to take. He could turn back and regroup or have faith in the geniuses who placed the detour sign.

Wasn't much to gain by turning around since he was lost back there too, so Mitch defied the arrow's guidance and turned left down the road instead of going into the fields. Like so many others in this back-country area of the state, this road had no signage, so Mitch was relying on the accuracy of future detour signs to place him back on 21, 9110, or even better, the interstate.

The road with no name quickly deteriorated, asphalt giving way to gravel, and within a few miles the gravel surrendered to hard-packed dirt. Mitch's economy rental screamed in agony, but its mercy cries fell on deaf ears; there was no going back, no relief, and the clock was ticking.

An hour later Mitch had traveled twenty miles, was fairly certain a tooth had rattled out of his head, and in his rearview there were red and blue flashers that had appeared from the ether. He looked, saw the 1970s cruiser and wondered what law he could have possibly broken on this road at 20 mph, and stopped the car. He would have pulled over, but the road was hardly wide enough for two cars as it was. The concept of a breakdown lane was laughable.

A door creaked and Mitch watched an officer step out. He wore pilot's sunglasses, had a serious comb-over and already had his nightstick in hand. The officer stepped up to Mitch's window, which was already rolled down. He bent and leaned way into the car, up to his waist, forcing Mitch to lean into the passenger side.

"You in a hurry," the officer asked. His name tag simply read "Larry" and his breath smelled like stale smoke. Mitch tried not to wince at the smell.

"Uh...not exactly, well yes, actually, but I was only going twenty miles an hour. The road conditions won't allow..."

"Now it's the road's fault, is that it," the officer snapped.

"Of course not, but..." He gestured towards the road as if looking at it would explain everything.

"Oh, of course? It's obvious, right? So now I'm stupid? I don't know a shitty road when I see one, is that it?" He backed out of the window. "Step out of the car, sir."

"What," Mitch said.

The officer brought the club down on the roof of the car hard. "Sir! Don't make me use this! Do not resist an officer of the law!"

Shit. Mitch eased the door open and stepped out. His cell phone was sitting on the passenger seat and he was struck with the desperate urge to call his wife. Officer Larry pressed him against the car and frisked him. He pulled out Mitch's wallet, tucked the five twenties Mitch was carrying into his breast pocket and scanned Mitch's driver's license.

"Mr. Mitch Mulroney. Triple M, I like that," Larry said. "Like the wrestler. I like wrestlers."

"I don't think it's an M."

"Shut your damn mouth!" The officer's eyes bulged as he screamed into Mitch's ear and hot spittle landed on Mitch's cheek. Mitch recoiled out of instinct and just a little eardrum pain. Larry chuckled. "Ah, fuck it; you're under arrest for being a dumb ass." And he bent Mitch's arm around, pinning him to the car, and Mitch heard the metallic ratcheting of cuffs and felt their pinch on his wrists.

"What are you talking about? What did I do?" Mitch said as he was shoved back to the cruiser. Larry said nothing and opened the door to the backseat and pushed Mitch inside. Only then did Mitch see that there was someone else in the cruiser sitting in the passenger

DARK THINGS II

seat. A man wearing headphones with greasy long hair rocked gently back and forth in the seat, eyes shut, apparently enthralled by the music in his ears. Pinkish pockmarks dotted his neck and the side of his face. Larry slid behind the wheel.

"Listen…" Mitch said.

"Shut your mouth, boy! If you say another word I'll brain you. Now shut-up!" Mitch did. He had no idea what was happening, but believed it was a real possibility that this man would kill or hurt him badly. This would all get sorted out back at the station, wherever the hell that was. The man in the passenger seat hadn't acknowledged them in any way or even opened his eyes.

They drove in silence and soon the wild fields became structured farmland and crops and a few rural buildings began popping up. People worked the crops by hand, picking and planting and digging. A large white barn appeared over the horizon and Mitch followed it with his eyes as they drove. The roof sagged and one wall was almost non-existent. Dozens of white boxes surrounded it like headstones in a graveyard. More people meandered among the boxes; some wore beekeepers' hoods and white coveralls, some did not. Tendrils of smoke drifted up from old coffee cans placed at the base of the boxes—hives, Mitch now realized—as the people opened them and extracted wooden combs of honey. The dense, brown jelly glistened in the sunlight.

The buildings increased and out of nowhere they were pulling into a town of some sort. A freshly painted sign welcomed them to White Oak. They drove down the central boulevard as the people of White Oak watched, jaws on the ground. He was probably the most exciting thing they had seen in months, years! They parked in front of the sheriff's office.

A little girl walked in front of them and their eyes met; she smiled at him. A man lurched behind her carrying several bags of groceries. He stared blankly at nothing, and Mitch had to blink when he realized the little girl was pulling the man along by a cord leash. Officer Larry got out and opened the back door. A steady buzzing sound filled the air, the perfect not-so-subtle background music for

160

this bizarre encounter. Part of his brain wondered if he was being filmed. If Allen Funt was going to appear at some point.

"Out," Larry said to Mitch.

"Got another one, Larry," an old man asked. He paused by the cruiser, staring at Mitch like he was a circus freak. Larry nodded.

"Officer, I want my phone call," Mitch said. He couldn't keep quiet. He needed to talk to his wife badly. Officer Larry whipped out the black club hanging from his belt and hammered Mitch across the temple. The world faded to black as the buzzing droned through Mitch's waning consciousness.

He woke with a throbbing headache to sounds of primal grunting that immediately invoked his survival instinct. The rational thought that was struggling to make its way to the surface of his gray matter was stopped hard by the brain's need to protect itself. He jumped to his feet and whirled, expecting to be attacked, but not really sure why or by what.

He was in a jail cell and alone. He turned and let out an audible sound of shock. The cell next to his, approximately ten feet by ten feet square, was jammed with people, all standing, shoulder to shoulder, pressed against the bars on all sides. They were filthy and pockmarked, and the smell of body odor and feces and urine filled his nostrils.

A buzzing sound played from an old radio sitting on a desk outside the cells. It was the same noise Mitch had heard outside before Deputy Dipshit whacked him. It made his eardrums itch and his brain vibrate. The people in the stuffed cell swayed slowly, silently to the rhythm with the ebbs and flows in the buzzing noise. They didn't seem to notice him, their conditions or each other. The primal sounds *were* coming from the cell, however.

Movement in the corner furthest from Mitch; two of the people, a man and a woman, had torn their clothes off and were ferociously copulating like dogs. Their eyes were locked in a faraway place, apparently no more conscious of their actions than they were of their surroundings. They swayed and thrust in time with the buzzing, their grunts and moans peaking with the rhythmic noise coming from the radio.

"Hey," Mitch shouted. "Hey!"

"They can't hear you," a voice from behind him. Mitch turned, and in the cell to his left sat another man. He was cleaning the sleep from his eyes. Two more men and a woman were asleep on the cell floor. None of the men was wearing a shirt, and Mitch realized his was gone as well.

"What the hell is this," Mitch said.

"Don't know really. They come and go. They don't tell us anything. We shouldn't be talking," he said.

"How long was I out?"

"A day, I guess. Stop talking."

"And you," Mitch persisted. The woman in the other cell squealed and her mate grunted.

The man turned and looked at some scratches on the wall. "Four days, I think."

The outer door to the jail opened and Larry walked in. The man ducked his head.

"Yo! Yo! Hey," Larry yelled and clapped his hands together loudly. Beyond the cells there was a window to the outside; a green water hose with a high-pressure nozzle on the end ran through it. Larry grabbed the nozzle and squeezed the handle. A narrow, high-powered stream of water shot out and ripped across the transfixed people in the cell. It parted the group like a laser beam and landed dead on the copulating duo. Larry directed it at their faces, and after a second they split and began swaying in time with the others, clothes still torn and lying on the ground.

"Damn animals," Larry muttered. "Five times a day I have to come in here for that shit."

Mitch pressed up against the front bars of his cell. "I want my phone call, you bastard!" Larry hit him with a blast of water and laughed.

"Stop your whining. It's almost over."

Sheriff Larson's belly entered the room, followed shortly by Sheriff Larson. He pointed at each of the men and women in the two cells, his lips moving as he did. "Four newbies. That should be enough for the new work crew, Larry." He said, smiling at Mitch, "Let's get'em going then."

"Yessir, boss." Larry left and a moment later returned with eight shambling men in coveralls. "Stick your arms out," he said to the imprisoned. The men and women in the opposite cell did as they were told, sticking their arms through the cell bars to be cuffed. Mitch saw fresh wounds all over their bodies, reminders of what disobedience got you here at White Oak. Larry cuffed them and they were escorted out by four of the men.

"You too, dumb ass," Larry said to Mitch.

"I will not," Mitch said, and he stepped back from the cell door and crossed his arms on his chest.

"Suit yourself." Larry opened the cell door, made a series of hand gestures and ushered the remaining four men into the cell. The beating was swift and severe. The men fell on Mitch like apes, pummeling him with flailing fists and arms until the darkness crept back into his vision and he was almost unconscious again. Unable to resist, Mitch was cuffed with ease and the four men carried him outside.

The bizarre caravan followed the same route Nurse Rebecca had taken days earlier back out of town and up the hill. At the Andersons' place they went straight towards the barn instead of right to the infirmary. People stopped to watch, smiles on their faces.

Larson brought up the rear, and when Watkins stopped to watch them pass he said, "Think you can keep them alive this time, Mega-Watts?"

"Sure thing, Sheriff," Mega-Watts said.

Then the buzzing sound from the bullhorn speakers stopped and eyes all around went wide. An "oh shit" expression manifested across the face of every White Oak citizen old enough to understand.

***

The tornado alert system was housed at the old White Oak city hall.

DARK THINGS II

Its copper tendrils spread out across town to over a dozen megaphone speakers and were intended to alert the citizenry of impending doom. It was kept in the basement—the basement that was currently being remodeled to accommodate the city's growing dummy supply. The jail was overcrowded, and you couldn't put dummies and newbies in the same cell; the damn dummies would incessantly hump the newbies to death. And it was becoming impossible to keep the dummies all in one area. The basement was being divided into two chambers—one for the boys and one for the girls, because a water hose just wasn't effective and they never stopped fornicating. Watts said it was something to do with a bee's natural survival instinct— reproduce or die—and a side effect caused by the large amounts of venom mixing with the human sex drive.

Everett, the carpenter, had no idea if this was true, but he knew they wanted the opposite sex more than a teenage boy did. He was working on the new basement framing when he ran out of electrical outlets and accidentally unplugged the tornado broadcast base station playing the looped track of recorded bee buzzing to make room for his circular saw. He immediately realized his mistake as the two dummies assisting him dropped their hammers and stared at him in bewilderment, their faraway gazes gone, replaced by a sharp focus.

***

Mitch hit the ground hard when the four men carrying him let go, and he instantly assumed the fetal position in preparation for the ensuing beating. The four men escorting the other prisoners stopped as well and looked at each other in confusion and then at Larry and the sheriff, the confusion replaced by hatred.

"Oh shit," Larry said and pulled his pistol. Sheriff Larson did the same, and the shooting began as more of the transfixed subjects awoke and began fleeing or attacking their handlers. The Andersons' lawn mower ran across the street screaming wildly and the sheriff dropped him with a single shot to the head.

164

Mitch gathered himself, took stock of the situation, was totally confused but recognized an opportunity when he saw it, and ran. The other four prisoners followed, hands cuffed behind them.

***

Everett had chosen these particular dummies for their size and strength, criteria he now regretted. The one Everett called Hoss lunged for his master, tackling him to the ground. He landed on top of Everett, and the forecast for the immediate future called for raining fists. The other dummy hightailed up the stairs and thankfully disappeared.

Unable to see through already swollen eyes and a fury of knuckles, Everett groped blindly for the saw, found it, pulled the trigger and slammed the machine into Hoss's head. The punches stopped instantly and blood spewed as Everett drew the saw across the raging dummy's forehead. Hoss went limp and Everett pushed him to the side and scrambled for the outlet, swapped plugs for the base station again and breathed for the first time in three minutes.

***

The bullhorns crackled and whined and the buzzing began again. Slowly the pockmarked slaves stiffened and began to sway to the droning rhythm. Larson fired two shots at the fleeing newbies, missing wildly, then realized he had tried to kill his investment and holstered the weapon.

"Get the hounds, Larry," Sheriff Larson shouted and brought the butt of his pistol down on the head of one of the dummies just for spite. Larry didn't answer; he sprinted the two blocks back to the jail, dodging chaos as he went. He ran past the cells into the small solitary chamber that used to be for holding violent prisoners before state officials could come and get them. Now it was used for something else. Larry opened the door gently.

Inside the small room were six lean and muscled men. Heads

shaved, wearing tattered jeans, they rocked rather than swayed to the angry buzzing that filled the room like a hurricane. Larry had to cup his ears the volume was so high.

In the corner of the room at the ceiling and on the floor were two televisions and a VCR. Playing in a continuous loop on both screens was a documentary film of bees defending their hive against wasps and ants and…humans. Frenzied bees covered the screen, swarming and impaling the interlopers. The men stared intensely at the screens, mouths foaming with pent-up rage. Hanging on the wall all around them were dozens of random garments. Larry grabbed Mitch's shirt from a hanger and pressed it to the face of the lead man and made several hand signs. The man inhaled deeply of Mitch's shirt, let out a bloodcurdling cry, and as one the men sprinted from the room.

***

Mitch's lungs were on fire. The gym membership that he paid for each month but never used was right up there with the GPS on his list of poor life decisions. He promised God that if he made it out of here alive he would stop his occasional smoking—and he probably meant it this time.

He ran down the street as a bullet whizzed by, slid behind a blue mailbox for cover, saw shadows from somewhere and decided to run again. To his right a short alley emptied into a freshly plowed crop field and beyond that, labyrinthine woods. To his left lay more of White Oak and White Oak inhabitants. He chose the woods and bolted from cover. As he broke from the alley he caught movement in his peripheral and saw the four others from the prison stumbling along his flank.

More movement now, faster and further back.

He risked a glance and saw six terrifying men following on their heels. These men were dirty like the others and unkempt, but there was no faraway glaze in their eyes. Their eyes were present and seething with anger.

SEAN GRAHAM

And they were fast. Very fast.

The woman, slower than the men, went down first. One of the runners tackled her from behind and Mitch had to turn away. Screams echoed as the others went down, and Mitch heard heavy breathing and felt the presence before he saw the shadow and he was down, driven into the ground face first.

The next thing Mitch saw was Deputy Larry standing over him, and then he was being dragged again. From an upside-down view he saw the other cuffed men being dragged at his side and the woman's lifeless body lying in a trough of tilled earth.

"That was a close one, eh boss," Larry said.

"Shut up, Larry," the sheriff said.

They dragged the three men up to the dilapidated barn and tied their feet with rope. The walls of the barn had fallen in several places, and the roof had multiple holes in it. Sunlight peppered the barn floor like Swiss cheese. Dr. Mega-Watts stepped in and poured thick syrup over their bodies until they were soaked, and then everyone left, closing the barn doors behind them.

"I don't think the barn is solid enough to hold in enough bees though, Sheriff. I'm glad we're building a new one," Watkins said.

"That's what you get for thinkin'," Sheriff Larson said. "Just don't let these ones die." And he walked off.

Nurse Rebecca began to spray the same sweet-smelling liquid into the air from a pump-action cylinder. Soon plump, fuzzy bees began to leave their box hives, and before too long the sky was full of the black and yellow insects. They followed the sweet smell into the barn in droves, and in seconds the screaming began. Larry and Mega-Watts watched through holes in the wall as the flying sacks of poison swarmed the men inside.

Mitch was completely covered in bees, bees upon bees in layers stinging and dying, leaving their entrails embedded in their prey. He tried to run, but the rope hobble prevented any real stride and he collapsed. The venom reacted with his nervous system, and Mitch could feel his body shutting down system by system until he was no longer able to move or cry out. The last thing that flashed

DARK THINGS II

across his mind was his wife's face smiling on their wedding day.

***

The Andersons sat on their porch drinking cold lemonade and watching their new dummy hard at work. Mitch swayed gently as he painted their fence in smooth, slow strokes. He was dully aware that he smelled bad and that he had urinated on himself again, but he didn't care. The sores that covered his body still oozed slightly and they itched maddeningly, but that was okay too. The sweet buzzing that filled his mind made everything okay.

About the author:
    Sean has several short stories slated for publication later this year by Wicked East Press, Sonar4, Blood Bound Books and Pill Hill Press (365 Days of Flash and Dark Things I) and others.

THE INTERVIEW NOBODY WANTS
by Scott M. Sandridge

"**BRAD,** I need you to do an interview." Sharon had her elbows on her desk with her hands clasped together and forefingers forming a steeple. Those pursed lips with her one brow up told me it was an offer I couldn't refuse.

"Sure," I said. "Who do you want me to interview?"

"Brian Basletum."

"Ok, who's he?"

"Don't know."

"What do you mean you don't know?"

"Exactly that. I don't know who he is." She leaned back in her black leather chair. I averted my eyes to the folder on her desk before she noticed me looking somewhere other than her face. She let out a sigh and said, "No one knows, really. No SS number, no employment records, no birth certificate, no one existing with that name at all. Hell, even his neighbors don't know who he is."

"A false identity with nothing faked to back it up? Maybe he's a writer. Could it be a pseudonym?"

"No one published by that pseudonym. And even if it were he would've had to give his real name to cash his checks. And guess what?"

I held my hand to my mouth as I stifled a cough. "No bank records. Nothing to trace the name to someone else. Maybe he's just some bum off the street playing a prank."

"A bum living in a multi-million dollar mansion in our local area? With the deed in his name?"

"But you said—."

"Yeah, so it's owned by someone who doesn't exist."

Now my interest was peaked. After popping a cough drop in

169

my mouth I asked, "A rich guy living in our small town that nobody knows anything about and who likely doesn't exist? What's up with that?"

"That's what I want you to find out. If anyone can worm it out of him, you can."

"One more question," I said, leaning forward. "If this guy for all intents and purposes doesn't exist, then how did you learn about him?"

She blinked twice, gave me her "don't be stupid" smile, and then said, "I didn't have to. He called me to set up the interview and asked specifically for you. His voice sounded familiar...yet strange."

For a moment I had this feeling that being a damn good reporter wasn't a good thing. Then the moment passed. "Great, when do I meet him?"

She pushed the folder toward me. "Tomorrow night at 11 P.M. at Basletum Mansion. The address is in the folder."

"Why a whole folder just for a name, phone number, and address?"

She shrugged. "Had to put something in his file. Didn't feel right keeping it empty."

I took the folder and rose from my chair, trying not to eye the cleavage threatening to burst out of her business suit. As I stepped toward the door she said, "One more thing: be careful on this one."

"Will do," I said. As I left her office I realized she had never told me to be careful before.

***

Basletum Mansion was small as far as mansions go, even for Sylvania Township. The granite walls gave it a medieval feel as did the Celtic symbols etched into the bronze gate. Missing bricks, cracks in the wall, and the stains on the gate made me wonder how anyone could be so indifferent about maintaining a structure of such artistry.

When I reached out of my car window and pushed the

intercom button, the gate opened without so much as a person on the other end asking me who I was. I thought about scrapping this whole interview, but something (curiosity, maybe?) compelled me to drive in. During the thirty seconds it took to pull up to the front door, I asked myself at least a dozen times why I was still here.

The mansion grounds were as run down as the wall and gate. All the plants in the garden were dead. I kept expecting a storm to pop up at any moment to illuminate the grounds with brief flashes of lightning that would make the white-walled mansion resemble a skull staring at me with mouth agape, but none of that happened. There were no clouds in the sky, and the wind was still. Silence pervaded everything. At least the lights were on, so I was thankful for that.

I walked up to the door and knocked. The door opened, and my eyes met the shoulders of a tall elderly man. His gaunt figure was wrapped in a black silk night robe and slippers. He smiled a thin smile that kept his lips pressed together, and said, "Bradley Stanton, I presume?"

"Uh, yes, are you Mr. Basletum?"

He gave a slow nod then welcomed me in. The interior of the mansion was much like the rest, minus the cobwebs. Though old and broken down, everything looked polished and clean. He led me through the main entry, down a hallway, then into his library. He offered me a seat then sat behind an oak desk, his elbows up and hands pressed together in a manner that reminded me of Sharon. He waited, saying nothing, merely looking at me with hawkish eyes and smiling—if you could call it a smile. Finally, I cleared my throat and said, "An air of mystery surrounds you, Mr. Basletum. How long have you—?"

"Bran," he said. "You can call me Bran."

"Bran? Isn't your name Brian?"

"Oh?" He waved one hand in a gesture of indifference. "Your editor must have misheard my name. Apologies."

"Certainly. How long have you lived here, Bran?"

"How long have you? This town, I mean."

DARK THINGS II

"Oh, 15 years now, and you," I said in between coughs. I hadn't smoked in a year, yet the cough remained. Maybe I should've seen a doctor about it, but it was just a lousy cough and office visits aren't cheap.

"Long enough. How long have you been a reporter, Brad?"

"About 10 years." I cleared my throat again, popped a cough drop. "So, what is it you do?"

"Do you like being a reporter?"

"Um, yes, of course. What...?"

"Do you not find it a headache sometimes?"

I forced a smile and said half-joking, "And here I thought I was supposed to interview you."

Bran's eyebrows arched up with surprise as his palms fell flat onto the desk. "Oh, dear me, I thought I had made it clear to your editor."

Well, that left my mind reeling. "Err, uh, made what clear, sir?"

His lips parted to reveal jagged yellow teeth, "I see now. I asked to see you for an interview, and given your profession she naturally assumed I meant for you to interview me."

Something in my head was blocking my ability of logical deduction; otherwise, I would not have responded with, "I don't see where you're going with this, sir."

That look of surprise, which now made my spine tingle, returned to his face. "No? Pity, I thought you were much brighter than that.

"Let me make this clearer then." He raised his hands back up and clasped them together under his chin, his head tilted slightly. "I did not call you here to interview me. It is I who wishes to interview you."

My pen and notebook fell to the floor. Somehow I managed to get my hands to stop shaking. I didn't know what it was that unnerved me. Maybe it was the shape of his shadow, but surely I had imagined that. "Interview me? W...what for?"

His yellow-toothed smile returned, and the light in the room flickered and dimmed. "For a job, of course. The last job you'll ever need."

I looked down at my notebook and pen. There wasn't much use in picking them back up, but the sight of them was far less unnerving than the old man's shadow. I recognized its shape, and the meaning of Bran Basletum's name became clear: *Bran, Bás, Letum*. Three words, each from a different language but with one meaning. Some part of my mind still refused to accept the facts in my presence—that small part of the mind that desperately wishes to remain sane.

Death hovered over me, no longer in the image of an old man, but in that fearsome visage all too recognizable. His cold, skeletal hands rested on my shoulders. His hollow voice chilled me deeper than any winter cold. "There are far too many people to keep track of anymore, and some have slipped my grasp and escaped their appointed hour. This is something I cannot allow. If you prove worthy, you will track these culprits down for me. For your service, you will be rewarded with power and an extended life that will not end until the contract is breached or a suitable replacement is found."

Somehow through my terror, I managed to stammer out, "A-and if I-I don't p-p-prove—?"

"Should you refuse or fail this interview," said Death, "then you will die at your appointed hour: tonight, at midnight."

I looked up at the grandfather clock next to the large window overlooking the dead garden. The copper on the clock's face reflected the pale moonlight in a way that made the clock appear like a sinister apparition waiting to devour me: an apparition that read 11:45. I coughed and felt something wet and sticky spray my hand. Blood.

I let out a deep shuddering breath and said, "Then let us begin."

"Excellent," said Death. "Now, I know what your record says, but I wish to hear from you, in your own words, exactly why you think you are the employee I'm looking for...."

DARK THINGS II

About the author:

Scott M. Sandridge learned how to write through hard work, trial-and-error, and the occasional writers' workshops. He is the author of over twenty published short stories, sixty reviews, and was the Managing Editor of the Christian Horror webzine, Fear and Trembling. His story, "Sleep Paralysis," was a top ten finisher in the 2008 Preditors & Editors Readers Poll for the category of Short Story—Horror. More information can be found at http://smsand. wordpress.com.

DELICIOUS MORSELS

by Piper Morgan

THAT thing was back again, staring at Kyle from inside the closet. For five days, he had asked his dad to find a door to replace the missing one, the one that was missing when they bought the house a few months ago. But that thought was pushed away now, because all he could think about, was how he was going to scream for help when his voice was trapped in his throat, or how he could maybe throw open the door and run down the hall. After all, the knob was less than a foot from the end of his bed. Taunting him, just like the thing in the closet.

Yeah, I can do that, his brain thought.

But his body had other ideas.

Terror gripped him so tight; he was surprised to hear his heart thumping in his ears. The pounding hurt so bad, he was sure it should have exploded by now.

When he first asked his dad for a new closet door, he laughed.

"Stop acting like a pussy," his dad's voice boomed in his head. "There's nothing in your closet. You need to man up."

But his dad was wrong. There *was* something in his closet, and Kyle was positive it was pure evil.

It first showed up a little over a week before. Through his hanging clothes and piles of dirty gym shoes, he saw it staring at him with deep garnet eyes and smiling with hundreds of teeth so sharp, they could easily gnaw through a two- by- four like it was cotton candy. And the thing's color, God...onyx so dark it made the depths of the ocean floor seem washed out with floodlights.

The air under the blankets was stifling, but he was too scared to move, petrified like a long dead tree.

Don't think of death, his brain said.

"Man up."

Kyle knew he had to get out. He willed his arms to slowly

move the cover from his eyes. They immediately darted to the open area of the closet even though he told himself not to look.

It was gone.

Now was his chance. He'd be able to sleep on the couch tonight, not terrified of opening his eyes, fearing he was being watched. Then he would deal with his dad's ridicule in the morning. Sure it would suck... but Kyle couldn't think of anything worse than the feeling he got knowing that thing was in his closet.

He threw back the comforter and scrambled across the bed. In his haste, his bare feet got tangled in the sheet momentarily.

And that was all it took.

From the corner of his eye, Kyle saw movement. In a split second, Mr. Black was back. He oozed from his space in the closet toward Kyle, hovered for a few seconds then melted to the carpeted floor and slipped under the bed.

Sweat broke out on Kyle's brow and a panic so horrible set in, he wet his shorts.

A slow rumble came from beneath him, and that's when he knew he'd never be able to man up. This would be worse than Mr. Black hiding in his closet.

***

It smiled with its mouth full of daggers and waited. Sometimes, it only waited a few months, sometimes it was years, but there were always others. And the waiting wasn't so bad. It could even deal with the cramped space and the horrid squealing and laughter, because, in the end, it was always rewarded with tender, delicious morsels.

***

"What do you think," Lynn asked, wrapping her arm around his waist as she stared at the house.

"That small bedroom gives me the creeps."

"If we fix the closet and paint the room, it'll be okay."

Jacob watched Lynn. This was what she wanted, and there was no way he would be able to change her mind so he sighed. "Okay Lynn. Go tell her we'll take it."

Her eyes twinkled and her face lit up as she squeezed his neck and squealed. "Oh, thank you!" She gave him a quick peck on the cheek before jogging over to the agent's car.

He looked at his daughter. "Mommy's crazy, honey, but we love her anyway, don't we?"

The little girl giggled as Jacob tickled her knee.

He turned to face the small ranch house. Even though the house itself was a nice buy and quaint, something just didn't seem right with it, especially the tiny bedroom on the back side, but he couldn't figure out what it was.

Lynn stood beside him again, Marti, their real estate agent for the past four months, following close behind.

"Congratulations," she said, offering her hand. "This is a perfect starter home."

Jacob nodded and looked at the older woman. "Are you sure there's nothing else you want to tell us about this place?"

A flicker of raw emotion ran over her face as she looked from him to his daughter. "No, nothing, other than the old water heater needing replaced. But as I told you, we'll get that taken care of."

***

Jacob stood in the doorway of the room, watching Lynn kiss the top of Aurora's honey colored hair as she put her in the mint green and white crib. The paint job and the sheer curtains that replaced the closet door did nothing to make him feel less uncomfortable in this room. He hated the thought of putting his only daughter in here, but he was tired of arguing with Lynn over it. They'd fought about it almost every night since they had moved in.

The tiny girl let out a sad cry as her mom started the mobile.

"I know, princess. New homes are always scary at first." She

DARK THINGS II

rubbed her daughter's shoulder. "Once you get used to all of the creaks and pops, it won't be so bad. Goodnight, sweetheart."

Jacob kissed her cheek and mouthed "sorry" to his daughter. "Love you, sweetie."

He left the room and Lynn closed the door as the child's tear filled eyes flickered to the open closet.

About the author:

Piper Morgan has been published in Strange, Weird, and Wonderful Magazine, Night Terrors An Anthology of Horror (Blood Bound Books), D.O. A., an upcoming anthology from Blood Bound Books, and will have stories appearing in Daily Flash 2011: 365 Days of Flash Fiction and Daily Flashes of Erotica 2011 (both from Pill Hill Press). You can catch her bitching and ranting at: http:// pipermorgan.blogspot.com or drop her a line at piperdmorgan@ gmail.com.

THE WELCOMING
by Shane McKenzie

PETER rocked himself in the corner of the dark room. He had no idea where he was or how he got there, having only awoken minutes before. His head still swam from whatever chemical he was forced to breathe, his only memory being the strong grip that took him from behind and the damp rag pressed to his face. He wiped the tears from his eyes and the mucus from his nose, and did his best not to look around the room in which he was held captive. The darkness hid his cellmates, but as his eyes adjusted, they began to take shape. The putrefied flesh melting off their bones, the expressions on their twisted faces. The sight of them gave him little hope for himself.

A limbless torso was propped against the far wall, its countenance one of pure terror and torment. Its dry, purple tongue hung from its blackened lips like a salted slug.

Peter hugged his knees and wept. He thought of his parents and how badly he yearned to be with them, to be engulfed in the safety of their embrace.

The only sound besides the beating of his own heart was the back and forth strides of heavy footsteps on the other side of the rusted, metal door. The footsteps stopped just outside the room, and as the door creaked open, Peter scurried across the gore covered floor to the furthest corner. Light spilled into the room and illuminated the carnage that surrounded him. He squeezed his eyes shut, murmuring to himself the lullaby his mother whispered to him every night.

"Hush little baby, don't say a word..."

Footsteps clopped across the floor. Peter held his knees and rocked, strings of saliva stretching from his face.

"And if that mockingbird don't sing..."

A fierce grip clamped his shoulder, pulling him to his feet and holding him there. He refused to look his captor in the eye, and concentrated on keeping his lids shut.

DARK THINGS II

"Good mornin', boy," the gruff voice said. "How you like your new room?"

Peter could only whimper at the sound of that voice. His body trembled uncontrollably.

"Look at me."

Peter refused to obey.

"Look at me, God damn it!"

The callused hand gripped Peter's face while the other pried at his eyelids. The serrated nails scraped the thin skin and his eyes burst open.

"Don't make me get rough with you, boy. There'll be plenty of that later," he said, releasing Peter's face and smiling, revealing black and yellow teeth.

"Why am I here?" Peter asked between sobs.

"Because I brought you here."

"P-please, I want to g-go home."

"You are home."

The man chuckled and began his retreat toward the door.

Peter collapsed against the wall and slid back down. He sobbed as he watched the man walk away. Just before reaching the door, the man bent down and grabbed something from the floor. He turned to face Peter once again.

"Hey, boy," the man said, that nefarious grin still plastered to his face.

He held a woman's decaying head like a bowling ball, his fingers pressed into her eyeholes. The greasy hair drooped over the gray face, bone shiny under the putrefied flesh. He grabbed the jaw and moved it up and down as he spoke.

"You behave yourself, now."

He rolled the head across the floor toward Peter, then left the room and slammed the door behind him. As the darkness engulfed the room again, Peter felt the weight of the head collide with his knees. He yelped and kicked it away, then pressed himself back into the corner.

As he began rocking himself again, repeating the lullaby

SHANE MCKENZIE

over and over, something jabbed at his leg. He reached down and wrapped his fingers around the object, bringing it to his lap for inspection. The bone was hard and smooth. He ran his finger across its edge until he reached the jagged end. It had been broken, and Peter touched the sharp points, staring toward the door.

A loud, gurgling scream erupted from outside of the room. A woman's scream. Peter didn't know there was anyone else in the house, and though he felt bad for her, it was better her than him. The sound of an electric drill tunneling through flesh was audible over the shrill screams. The man's gruff chuckle hovered over everything.

The sound of the drill stopped, but the woman's screaming only intensified. Peter squeezed the bone as heavy footsteps grew closer and closer. The woman's cries were mixed with sobs and pleading.

"Let me go, you fucking bastard!"

Peter jumped to his feet, the jagged bone shaking in his grasp. They were right outside the door now.

Peter's head jerked in all directions, looking for some kind of hiding place, but found nothing. He contemplated jamming his body behind the festering torso, but gagged at the thought. He faced the door and clenched his teeth.

The door swung open and slammed against the wall.

The man had his back to Peter, dragging the wriggling woman into the room. She wept and muttered incoherent words as her blood spilled to mix with the fluids on the floor.

"Shut your fucking mouth! I want you to meet someone," the man said.

Without much of a plan, Peter darted across the room and flung himself onto the man's back. The bone almost slipped from his hand as the man struggled beneath him.

He raised the crude weapon and buried it into the man's neck, who grunted and hissed as Peter pulled it out and twisted it back in.

They spun in place as the man tried reaching for the scrawny boy. Peter thrust the bone into the wound over and over, blood spurting into his face and stinging his eyes. The man collapsed to

181

DARK THINGS II

his knees and Peter jumped off, still holding the bone out in front of him.

"I'll get you," the man said as blood rushed from his neck and stained his shirt. "I'll gut you like a fish."

Peter screamed as the man fell flat on his face.

***

Clarence awoke with his face planted on the cold cement floor. He sat up and rubbed his callused hand across his weathered face. He groaned and massaged his neck. His hand came away full of blood, and the memory of the boy flooded his mind.

"Little motherfucker!"

The door stood open and bloody footprints tracked across his home to the front door. The woman lay in the same place, a pool of congealed blood surrounding her.

The boy was gone.

"Fuck!"

He stood up and slammed his fist into the wall.

Nobody escapes me.

He paced the room, kicking chunks of rotting meat into the air, cursing the boy. He walked back toward the woman and knelt down to face her.

"Where did he go, bitch?"

The woman stared blankly at the ceiling.

"Well, you ain't no good to me, are ya?"

He stood up and slammed his boot into her face. Teeth scattered across the floor like dice.

Clarence stomped across his living room and out into the warm night. The footprints led across his yard and into the woods, which meant the little bastard could be anywhere. Clarence didn't even know how long he'd been unconscious. If the boy had reached the town already, the cops would be huffing and puffing at his door in no time.

But what if he didn't make it there yet?

182

The boy wasn't from the town on the other side of the woods, but somewhere miles and miles away. Clarence was careful not to work too close to home. Though he'd had a slip up or two.

The little shit could still be lost in the woods.

Clarence ran to his shed behind his home and kicked the door in. His hatchet lay on the table where he'd left it; dried brain matter still clung to the metal. He trotted from the shed to the edge of the woods.

"Come out come out, wherever you are!" He cupped his hands around his mouth.

He launched himself into the woods, laughing and scraping his hatchet across the trees, leaving deep gouges in the bark. He called out to the boy, but the only sound was his own heavy breathing. Any trace of a footstep vanished a long way back, and Clarence aimlessly searched between the trees. He saw the town just beyond the tree line, the people scurrying this way and that.

The boy could be down there. Could be talkin' to police right now.

He reached back and tucked his hatchet under his belt, then covered it with his shirt tail. He couldn't risk going back home and waiting it out. He had to find the boy, one way or another.

He walked from the woods to the edge of town, smiling at passersby. He noticed some of the people stared at his neck with disgust, and he wiped away a handful of brown blood. The wound wouldn't stop seeping, and he swiped a hand across it every few seconds.

He passed the local meat market, a heavy set butcher chopping up bits of flesh. He stopped mid swing and looked toward Clarence as blood dripped from his hand and cleaver.

A burst of laughter made Clarence peel his gaze from the butcher to the stage across the street. A group of children were gathered around a shrunken, gray man putting on a puppet show. The puppets danced as he tugged on the strings. Clarence eyed the crowd of kids and made sure his escapee wasn't amongst them.

As he stood watching the show, he was bumped into from

behind.

"Excuse me."

An attractive woman nodded at him as she passed, shopping bags swinging at her sides.

"No problem at all," he said as that familiar rush took over his thoughts.

No! You have to find the boy!

He stared at the woman's swinging hips as she walked away. Her calf muscles bulged with every step. Clarence knew it wasn't smart, but he was powerless to resist the urge.

The boy could wait.

The woman turned a corner, cutting through an alley, and emerged into the neighborhood beyond. Clarence kept his pace with hers and tried to stay unnoticed.

She gingerly walked to a red brick house, paused at the front door to search through her purse, then pulled out a set of keys, unlocked the door, and stepped inside.

Clarence peered through the window. He pulled out his hatchet and twisted his hands over the handle.

She sat in a rocking chair, her bags emptied in front of her. She held two long needles and was working diligently at something as she rocked back and forth.

The front of Clarence's pants grew tighter as he watched. He grunted and licked his lips as he caressed the bulge, watching her every move.

It's showtime.

He circled the house and found the rear door swinging on its hinges. He gripped his hatchet tighter as he crept into the home.

The chair squeaked as the woman rocked herself, the only other sound was her angelic humming.

"Hmm hmmm hmm hmmm."

Clarence could smell her, his excitement like an enflamed zit ready to burst. He raised his hatchet high into the air and tiptoed closer to the rocking chair.

"Hmm hmmm hmm hmmm."

Clarence hesitated for a moment, listening to the melody of her humming with his rusty hatchet held high.

He swung down, lodging the metal deep into her skull. Her body jerked forward, the back of her head split open like a ripening melon. Clarence shuddered at the sight in front of him. He held himself steady as he quivered with orgasm.

"Oh, baby," he said as he wrapped his fingers around the handle of the protruding hatchet.

"Hmm hmmm hmm hmmm."

Clarence jumped backward and pulled the hatchet free as he stumbled away. The rocking chair continued to roll against the floor, the sound of scraping metal as the woman continued her knitting.

It's not possible.

Clarence bared his teeth and swung his hatchet with every ounce of strength he had, opening her neck like a bloody grin. He yanked it free and swung again. The head rolled to the floor with a thud.

"Hmm hmmm hmm hmmm."

Blood pumped from the stump of her neck and showered the body with gore. Yet the hands still worked, the chair still rocked.

Clarence dropped his weapon and backed away. He shook his head and mumbled to himself. "No...not possible..."

The chair came to a sudden halt as the body rose to its feet. The eyes of the head shone an eerie yellow as it stared up at him from the floor. A sickening smile spread across its face as the woman's body turned toward him. The hands held up the finished knitting project, the yarn soaked in blood. The words 'Welcome Home' embroidered on it.

"Welcome home, Clarence. How long we've been waiting."

"No!"

He backed away from the approaching blood-soaked body. It leaned over and scooped up the giggling head, then followed Clarence toward the back door.

"Where are you going, Clarence?"

"Stay away from me!"

DARK THINGS II

With a throat tearing scream, he ran from the home, glancing over his shoulder.

He didn't stop until he was back in town. People still crowded the street and there was no sign of the woman behind him.

But the people in the street stood still, every one of them staring at Clarence with those bright, yellow eyes. They grinned and exposed their rows of needle-like teeth.

"You hungry, Clarence?"

Clarence spun on his heels to face the gruff voice, which belonged to the butcher, who raised his dripping meat cleaver into the air and slammed it into his own belly. He pulled on the purple viscera and offered it to Clarence. His eyes shone, his shark grin splitting his face in two.

"Leave me alone," Clarence screamed. The townsfolk began to close in on him, all chanting his name. "All of you! S-stay away!"

Clarence pushed his way through the crowd, outstretched fingers scraping red lines on his skin. He ran toward the woods from which he came, giving slight pause as he passed the puppet stage. The children surrounded the puppeteer and pinned him to the ground. They tore at his flesh like a pack of rabid wolves. They fought over his innards like a game of tug-o-war. The puppeteer looked up at Clarence and smiled.

"Welcome home, Clarence."

Clarence ran toward the trees. The townsfolk came after him, calling his name, welcoming him. The children joined in on the pursuit with their slimy prizes still clutched in their hands. The puppeteer pulled his mangled body across the ground, leaving chunks of flesh in his wake.

"Come back, Clarence!"

Their eyes lit up the forest. Their terrible voices filled the air.

The sky became blood red with waves of flame rolling across it. Clarence stumbled and fell, his hands sinking into the ground beneath him. He stared in disgust at the rotting meat that replaced the soil. Maggots roiled and squirmed from the widening cracks in the fleshy ground. With a shriek, Clarence jumped to his feet and continued his escape.

His house came into view just over the horizon, and he pushed himself even harder. The creatures called to him.

He stumbled out of the woods and ran for his front door. He slammed it shut and turned the lock, then tore through the house, looking for anything heavy to stack against the door. He saw the things crawling from the woods through his window and hurried his pace.

"Clarence."

The voice startled him and he screamed as he spun to face it. The near-angelic voice came from the back room, the room where everything started.

The creatures began surrounding the house, calling for him. They scraped their long appendages across the windows as their eyes shone a sallow color into his home.

The voice called to him again from the back room, and he ignored the others to inspect. The drilled woman writhed on the floor, spitting blood from her mangled face. She abruptly sat up as Clarence approached and stared with her blinding eyes.

"Hello, Clarence. How I've missed you."

"I fucking killed you!"

Without hesitation, he ran toward her and kicked her under the chin. She slammed back to the ground and cackled. Clarence stomped his boot into her face, over and over, screaming all the while. She never stopped laughing even as her skull caved in.

A rustling sound surrounded him.

The floor was alive with movement. The scattered limbs and body parts writhed and wiggled like freshly cut worms. The limbless torso inched toward him like a caterpillar, waves of motion scooting it closer and closer.

"Clarence," it said. "I'm coming, Clarence."

Another body lay amongst the wriggling gore, and Clarence stared at it with a slack jaw.

"No, n-no way. Fucking impossible!"

He stared at his own dead face. A dark pool of congealed

DARK THINGS II

blood lay around the head, the neck wound crusted over. He turned to escape the horror but was stopped in his tracks.

The boy stood in the doorway. His razor teeth gleamed from between his lips as he smiled at Clarence.

"Welcome home, Clarence. You belong with us now. We have been waiting so very long."

"Please...no..."

"Welcome to eternity."

***

Peter pressed his face against the glass of the police car. He'd run straight into the woods when he escaped the house, and was thankful to find the town just on the other side. After telling the police everything, they made Peter get in the back of a patrol car and show them where the house was. They kept him waiting in the backseat and said that his parents had been called and were on their way. He sat in the car alone as the body parts were wheeled out of the house.

It seemed like it would never end. They just kept pulling more and more parts out, the smaller portions stuffed into plastic bags. The woman was pulled out on a stretcher, her pale arm hanging limply over the side.

Then Peter saw him. The bad man.

The coroner had placed a sheet over the body, but Peter knew it was him. He stared as the body was wheeled from the front door and across the yard. A red spot stained the sheet and Peter looked at his own shaking hands. Maroon bits of gore stained his fingers and knuckles, some of it embedded under his nails.

As the stretcher was wheeled out of sight, Peter clenched his fists and muttered to himself, "Burn in Hell."

About the author:

Shane McKenzie lives in Austin, TX with his wife and three dogs where he works for the police department. His work can be

188

SHANE MCKENZIE

found at Dark Recesses, Liquid Imagination, Screaming Dreams, Aphelion, and Blood Moon Rising to name a few. His first editing project, Ruthless: An Extreme Shock Horror Collection, with introduction by Bentley Little, can be found at Pillhillpress.com. He has work set to appear in the anthologies Elements of Horror, Letters from the Dead, DOA, Haunted, and Patented DNA.

DOUBT

by Matthue Roth

THE *thing in the back of his mind—*

Gabriel Bennett was not an impulsive man. He moved slowly, checking the ground before every step. He weighed decisions carefully, considering all possible outcomes rather than jumping to conclusions. He paid his bills the day he received them.

The thing that grew at him—

Gabriel couldn't shake the thought that something was happening to him. He was more observant than most. He heard the rumblings inside him, recognized them as something more than indigestion. (His food, like everything else, was meticulously selected: no beans, legumes, preservatives, or anything that might bring him gas.) He sat at home at night and, the way other people watched television, Gabriel watched the tremors of his skin: thought it was his own nerves trembling, but knew it was not.

The thing that kept him up at night—

He woke up early. He went to the doctor.

"Gabe, you can't keep coming here every time the wind blows you the wrong way," Dr. Roger told him. "I know we go back, but as your friend—as the guy who's always got your back in poker—this has got to stop."

While they'd been the best of friends for several years, going to baseball and the symphony together (Roger had even briefly dated Gabriel's sister), Gabriel had always thought of Roger foremost as his physician. Even while he'd been going to Dr. Furstman, before Dr. Furstman had kicked him out.

They met in university, where Gabriel was studying microbiology and Roger was fulfilling his pre-med requirements. He'd casually mentioned that he was going to be a doctor. "Oh, you'd be a good backup," said Gabriel, and it wasn't until weeks later, when the 3 A.M. calls started, that Roger had any idea why he'd said that.

Years later, they had not stopped.

"You've got to distract yourself," Roger told him. "Get out more. Go to a bar, have a couple of beers with friends. See a Broadway show. You have to start treating yourself right, Gabe."

"But I don't like any of that stuff," said Gabriel, probing his stomach with his finger.

"And that is why," said Roger. "You have to start doing it."

The thing that gnawed at him—

See, Gabriel knew he wasn't a hypochondriac. Hypochondriacs thought there was something wrong with them, but they could never figure out what it was.

Gabriel knew.

Last year, just before Dr. Furstman dismissed him, Gabriel had brought in records. Meticulously observed, dutifully recorded, he had over three hundred pages of notes from that week alone. Where the hernia grew. How often it throbbed, and for how long. The diameter of that hard spot near his stomach.

Dr. Furstman had taken one look at Gabriel's paperwork and said he was insane. Now, Gabriel knew better than to show anyone. His last visit with Dr. Roger was uneventful.

"It's your worrying, nothing but that," Roger told him. "That hernia's going to eat you alive if you're not careful."

"That's exactly what it is," Gabriel said. "Each time I think about it, I can feel it growing bigger inside me. When I ignore it, it goes away."

"So ignore it, then."

"That's the thing," said Gabriel, knowing it would sound crazy, but not caring. "It doesn't let me."

A week later, Roger was summoned to Gabriel's house by a police investigator. Roger was mournful, but unsurprised. This much worrying would kill anyone, sooner or later. It was just Gabriel's luck that his hernia happened this early in life.

"See, that's exactly what the boys in the morgue said," Inspector Nevins told him. "A hernia."

DARK THINGS II

"So what's wrong," asked Roger. "Why did you say you were suspecting foul play?"

"This isn't gonna be pleasant," the inspector warned, passing over a folder. "You might want to open it slowly."

Roger was a doctor. He saw disturbing things on a daily basis. Nothing, he thought, could rattle him—no bodily symptom, anyway.

But when he unsheathed it, he had to recoil. He reached for the trash can, retching.

"Yeah, the boys were pretty disturbed too," the inspector nodded. "Stomach physically ripped out like that—and from the inside, at that. Least that's what the morgue said. You got any idea what could do a thing like that?"

Roger took one more look at the photograph, gagged, and turned away.

"No," he said, "it was his hernia," and something deep in his stomach lurched, and then a throbbing.

About the author:

Matthue has published three novels and a memoir, most recently Losers (PUSH/Scholastic Books). He's also been published in anthologies by Scholastic, McSweeney's, and Soft Skull Press. Find him at www.matthue.com.

J.P. GILMAN

by Adam P. Lewis

"**HERE** you go young lady. This is J.P. Gilman's trailer," the security guard said. He tipped his hat and smiled. "Good luck!"

Carrie smiled. "Thank you."

The security guard walked away.

Carrie knocked on the trailer door with a flyer in her hand. It read: *Assistant Needed, Apply Today*, and heard a man bark in a coarse and annoyed voice through the door. "What the hell do you want?"

She bowed her head and raised her voice as she talked through the door. "I'm here about the assistant job." Her voice crackled from nerves.

Upon hearing Carrie's soft voice, J.P. Gilman, owner of Gilman's Freaks, hobbled to the window. He pulled back the curtain and peeked out. Upon seeing Carrie he smiled and licked his palms. He dragged his wet hands through his hair, trying to slick down the few strands atop his scalp to hide his balding spot.

Carrie's long blond hair, stout frame, and chubby body aroused him. She was just the way he liked his women, young with plenty of meat on their bones. His heart rate increased and his breathing quickened.

Gilman cleared his throat and opened the door. He asked in a gentle and warm tone, "What can I do for you, my dear?"

Carrie became sickened by the ammonia stench that swished past her face as the trailer door opened. The stench was so thick she could taste it upon her tongue. It reminded her of vomit and stale beer. She swallowed hard and held up the flyer. "I read your

193

advertisement. It mentions you're searching for an assistant for the rest of the summer."

Gilman licked his dry lips. The corner of his mouth curled up and his brow crinkled over his eyes. His voice rose in excitement. "I do...I do, welcome!" He shifted to the side with a hand stretched out, welcoming Carrie inside.

With caution, she stepped inside. Unsure of what to expect she cradled and comforted herself by clutching her left forearm and rubbing it. Gilman's appearance was complimented with the growing stench inside the trailer.

Gilman stood five foot tall and was extremely obese. His arms were matted over in thick, black hairs. Red and black acne scars pockmarked his face between dirt-filled wrinkles. His neck hid under a mass of hanging fat, which dangled like a necklace over his chest. Poking out from under a sweat-stained undershirt; his pimply stomach draped below his waistline. Tattered and stretched-out suspenders held up his oversized trousers that bunched up over his bare and dirt-stained feet. His toenails were yellow, cracked, and untrimmed.

"Sit down, *please*," he said, pushing dirty clothes off a wooden chair.

Upon seeing his hotdog-like fingers and calloused palms, the bitter taste of bile backed up into Carrie's mouth. She sat down and swallowed, forcing the bile back down into her esophagus.

She scanned the dim trailer.

Piles of dirty clothes littered the floor along with candy wrappers and Chinese takeout cartons. Dirty dishes covered in furry mold filled the sink and overflowed onto the counter tops. Flies and other winged insects buzzed about the trailer, feeding upon the rotting food and reproducing atop the filth. Convexed ceiling tiles were spotted in yellowish water stains from were rain leaked through the roof. The trailer walls were decorated with old carnival posters from around the country advertising Gilman's Freaks with bold lettering. Printed on the bottom of each, Carrie read the phrase, *Assistant Needed, Apply Today.*

ADAM P. LEWIS

Gilman plopped his large body down upon the tattered cushion of an office chair and cleared his throat. He hacked up phlegm and swallowed it. Then, "So you want to be part of my freak show? Why would a pretty young thing like you want to work around a bunch of freaks?"

She shrugged and squeaked out a nervous giggle. "Just thought it would be fun."

He smiled. "Well, you've come to the right place then. Working with freaks is very fun indeed!"

Holding her breath between short inhales in order to avoid smelling Gilman's suffocating sweat and urine stench, she asked, "Soooooo...what would I be doing?"

"Well, I need a girl to assist me during the show," he said, handing Carrie a piece of paper. "Here, read this as if you're trying to get the carnival goers to buy tickets."

She cleared her throat and began reading the paper. Her voice was low and lacked the excitement that boisterous Carnies exhibit.

Gilman interrupted and wiggled out of the chair to his feet, "No, no, no, no...read it like your life depended on it. Read it loud! Get the peoples' attentions that are walking around looking up at the rollercoaster, sniffing the fried bread dough in the air, and talking over bells ringing from the games. They have money in their pockets and there are tickets to be bought to see my show! Why waste good money trying to throw a ping pong ball into a fishbowl to win a goldfish? Those little suckers die within a week anyway. Get up on that chair and scream above the smells and noises of the carnival!"

Carrie understood and shook her head. She rose to her feet and stepped up onto the chair. She called out in an animated and entertaining voice, "Step right up ladies and gentleman and buy a ticket to see the show that guarantees bone-rattling chills! Those who buy tickets become ridden with nauseating shivers while viewing such acts as the Human Voodoo Doll, a woman that pierces her skin with skewers and swallows swords. Merman, the half man and half fish whose legs and feet are conjoined like a fishtail. Ms. Jiggles, the half-ton woman. Watch her eat your scraps of food chewed up

DARK THINGS II

by your very own teeth. But that's not all, folks. Step inside and be amused by Behemoth the Midget, the strongest dwarf alive, the Triangle twins, Siamese twins that dance and contort their bodies in various geometric formations. And Pickles, whose tattooed face resembles a clown. His grand finale will churn your stomachs worse than the loop-de-loops of a rollercoaster. Watch Pickles juggle cockroaches and eat them alive!"

Gilman rocked back and forth while wiggling his feet and clapping his hands together quick and loud. He yelled, "Bravo—bravo my dear. You showed excellent vocal tone and control and you were very convincing. My hero, P.T. Barnum would get a kick out of you. I just know he would. Did you know he got his start displaying freaks? I'm following in his footsteps, a mighty big shoe to fill!"

He snatched the paper from her hand and put his arm around her. He squeezed her tight as he pulled her shoulder into his chest. Carrie's face cringed in disgust.

He leaned toward her and whispered into her ear. "If I were walking by eating cotton candy or vinegar-seasoned fries, I think I'd stop and buy a ticket to see Gilman's Freaks. I'm not just saying that because I own the show. I am saying that because you'd make a great Carny!"

Carrie faked a smile and tried pulling away. "Thanks."

Gilman rubbed his chin and slowly nodded his head. "Yes, I do believe you have a future as a Carny.

Carrie felt his hot exhale tickle her ear and smelled his foul breath. It reminded her of a dead skunk lying on the side of the road during a hot August afternoon. She turned her head away and shifted her body towards the side of the chair. She could feel his body heat and heartbeat giggle through his fat and clothes. Gilman's body was overheated and his sweat seeped through Carrie's shirt and dampened her skin.

Carrie shifted her body again and asked, "What else would I be doing? Introducing the acts?"

Gilman laughed. "Oh no, that's my job. You would help me

196

out through other ways rather than just selling tickets."

"How would I do that?"

"Well, during the show I perform too. I'm one of the freaks," he said, smirking and rubbing his hands together.

She asked out of curiosity, "What's so freakish about you?"

Gilman stood, waddled across the trailer, and pulled out a large butcher knife out of the closet. "I work with very sharp objects!" He said, hissing in a low voice while smiling at his reflection on the knife blade.

Carrie faked a smile and tried to sound excited even though the sight of the knife made her feel uncomfortable. "Oh, you swallow swords?"

Gilman chuckled and pulled out a sharpening rod from a kitchen drawer. While sharpening the butcher knife he said, "Don't you remember? You read it in that paper I gave you; I already have a girl who swallows everything from swords to razorblades."

The metal slicing sound upon the sharpening rod pierced Carrie's ears, causing her to grit her teeth. Seeing the large knife waving back and forth unsettled her nerves. She breathed in deep and stuttered her exhale then gulped down a lump in the back of her throat.

"Ah, I think that is sharp enough!" Gilman said. Without winching, he plucked a curly strand of hair off his chest. He pulled his thumb and pointer fingers apart and dropped the hair on the knife blade. The hair split in two.

Carrie began fidgeting with the flyer in her hands as she watched the hair float to the trailer floor. Fright chilled her spine. Her legs wiggled and her lips quivered. She tried masking her jitters by asking Gilman another question, but her shaky voice hinted she was scared. "Wh-What do you do then?"

Gilman put down the butcher knife and picked up a rusty meat tenderizer. He held it under his nose and slowly inhaled the lingering scent of meat. His eyes closed as he savored the scent and smiled in pleasure. His voice turned guttural. "Me and my brother, we're a team act. We eat raw meat, the bloodier the better!"

DARK THINGS II

"Where is your brother now," Carrie asked, shaking.

"Oh, he's in his bedroom. He's resting up for our next show." Gilman laughed, pointing the tenderizer down the hallway.

He turned and slowly hobbled towards Carrie. His brow crinkled over his eyes and his delightful smile turned demonic as he licked the meat tenderizer before smacking his lips together. Under his heavy footfalls, which crumpled the trash under his feet, he let out a quiet moan of pleasure.

Disgusted, Carrie glanced away from him and glared over his shoulder into the closet. There she saw women's clothing on hangers. Dresses, blouses, and pants covered in red splatters and stains. She then remembered the words printed on the posters hanging on the wall, *Assistant Needed, Apply Today*, and glanced down at the flyer in her hand.

She looked up at Gilman and then at his hand that was stroking the head of the meat tenderizer like an old woman petting a cat. Her entire body began to shiver in fear as goose bumps prickled across her skin, standing up the hairs on her forearms and the nape of her neck. Frightened, she said, "I think I should go now. As fun as the job sounds, I don't I'm right for it."

She jumped up from the chair and kept eye contact with Gilman while backing away from him toward the exit. In doing so, she slipped on rotted pork-fried rice and tripped into and over the pile of clothes that once rested on the chair. She fell to the floor and braced her fall with her hands. Her palms landed upon a moist spot on the carpet. She turned over her hands and looked at her palms. They were covered in blood. Whimpering, she smeared her bloody hands across her pant legs and frantically crawled over the blood and trash-littered floor. Upon reaching the door, she stood and turned the door handle but it was locked.

She screamed, "Please, someone help me." She pinched the twist lock between her fingers, trying to unlock the door. But her blood-covered fingers slipped off the lock.

Gilman barked orders at Carrie as if she were an employee. "Get away from that door. Sit down!"

She looked over her shoulder at him and wiped her hands on the side of her hips. She begged, "Please, stay away from me."

Carrie's fumbled with the lock and at the exact second she unlocked the door, Gilman swung the meat tenderizer held over his head and struck it upon her temple.

The blow flung Carrie's head to the side and threw her off balance. She collapsed to the floor and rolled onto her side trying to push herself up onto her feet to escape. But the impact and sudden gush of blood pouring from her temple made her woozy. She collapsed to the floor again.

Gilman locked the door and raised the tenderizer to his tongue, licked off the blood, and swished it around his mouth. His eyes rolled into the back of his head as he savored the blood's salty taste. He smiled in satisfaction and put down the tenderizer. He picked up the butcher knife and stood over Carrie. Red droll dripped off his chin as he said in high spirits, "Congratulations my dear, you're hired!"

Carrie looked up through blurry eyes and saw the butcher knife thrusting down toward her chest. She screamed and put her arms up in defense hoping to block the merciless attack. Her muscles tightened and her heart rate increased as she anticipated the knife puncturing her flesh. She felt a hard wallop against her chest followed by the sounds of a loud thud and a gurgling moan and tiny popping sounds. She lay on the floor crying and begging for mercy until she realized she was unharmed.

She turned her head and saw Gilman lying on the floor with the knife snuggled halfway through his neck. A bubbling pool of blood burbled out from the entry wound as his lungs hissed with escaping air. His fingers, toes, and neck all twitched as his eyelids slowly fluttered closed.

She looked down at her chest and saw Gilman's leg strewn across it. She pushed them off, sat up, and backpedaled away from him like a crab scurrying away from a seagull. She cowered against the wall, crying with her knees pulled up to her chest. She scanned his body, making sure he wasn't alive. His chest didn't heave and wheeze as it had when he breathed nor did his fat giggle when his heart pumped. She saw tiny grains of pork-fried rice stuck to the bottoms of his blood-covered feet. Tangled around his left ankle were the very clothes that she tripped over when she stood and tried running away.

Carrie wiped her hands dry and opened the door. She staggered down the trailer steps and ran. She screamed over the bells and whistles of the games and rides and the joyous screams and laughter of the carnival goers, "Please, help me, please, somebody."

People turned and watched Carrie as she ran. Her clothes bloodied and her hair moist and clinging to her forehead and neck. Parents pulled their children close to their bodies, protecting them. Teenagers pointed and laughed. Venders and ride operators turned their backs on her, tending to their stalls as they continued to sell food and tickets as if nothing was out of the ordinary.

The security guard who showed Carrie to Gilman's trailer heard her cries for help. He didn't ignore them. He ran after her. "Stop, hold up there…what's the matter?"

Carrie turned. When her eyes met the guards and she fell to her knees in relief. She buried her face in her hands and wept, arching her back with each sob. Her crying turned intense, causing her to choke and cough as she tried catching her breath.

The guard squatted down in front of Carrie. "Slow your breathing down before you make yourself puke."

He put his hands on her shoulders but drew them away as he reacted to the moisture on her clothing. He turned over his hands. His palms were covered in blood. His eyes darted up and down Carrie's body. Her blood soaked clothes and perspiring body swept fear over his body. He hadn't seen anything like this at a carnival since a drunken patron fell out of the Ferris wheel bucket seat to his death.

"Holy smokes, what in tarnation happened to you?"

Carrie pointed back at the trailer. "He—he tried to…" Carrie started dry heaving. The images replaying inside Carrie's mind of Gilman's death sickened her.

The guard looked over his shoulder to Gilman's trailer. "J.P., do you mean J.P.?"

Carrie shook her head. "Yea."

The guard started shaking. "Dear God, what the hell happened in there?"

Carrie grabbed the guard by the forearms. She breathed deep and rambled. "He tried to kill me. He tried to butcher me for his act! He's dead. I think he's dead. He wasn't breathing. There was knife, a big knife. The knife was in his stuck in his throat. There was a meat tenderizer. He hit me. He hit me in the head with it."

She turned her head and showed the guard the bleeding welt upon her temple.

She shivered as she inhaled and exhaled, trying to control her nerves and thoughts. She continued rambling. "He stood over me with the knife. It was raised in the air. He started to chop at me with it. But, he fell. Slipped on garbage. He's dead. Yea, he's dead!" She smiled.

"Dead!" the guard said, surprised. His face drooped in sadness and his breathing quickened.

Carrie nodded and whispered, "He's dead."

He looked Carrie in the eyes. "Did you kill J.P.?"

She shook her head. "No. He fell on his knife. I swear I...I didn't touch him."

"Are you sure J.P. is dead?"

"Yes."

The guard stood up and grabbed Carrie's forearm. He yanked her up. "Come on, on your feet!"

"Where are you taking me?"

"Back to J.P.'s trailer to see if what you said was the God's honest truth!"

She resisted. She leaned back, pulling away from the guard with her weight. "Please, no. I'm not going back."

The guard grabbed her with both of his hands and tugged on her arm. He yanked her forward, causing her to stumble. "You're involved in a man's death. If what you said was or wasn't true then the police will want to talk to you, you'll have to be detained."

Carrie dropped to her knees. "Please, I'm begging you. Don't make me go back to him."

The guard tucked her hands under Carrie's armpits and dragged her toward the trailer. She kicked and screamed and dug her heals into the ground hoping to free herself.

The guard gritted his teeth and grunted as he lifted Carrie to her feet. He grabbed both sides of her face between his hands and said, "Christ, girl, cut the crap! If J.P. is dead then you have nothing to worry about. He isn't going to harm you."

He let go of her face and squeezed her left wrist in his hand. He dragged her to the trailer and climbed the steps. They stopped at the door.

The guard knocked and asked through the door, "Carnival security…you all right in there?"

Gilman didn't answer.

The guard knocked again, louder. "J.P…you okay?"

Still, Gilman didn't answer.

The guard twisted the doorknob and pushed open the door. He reached down to his utility belt and unlatched the flap that held his Maglite. He clicked it on and shined the bright beam of light at the far wall and dragged it across the floor to the sink and back to the door.

"Doesn't seem like J.P. is here, you sure that he's dead. Maybe you just confused yourself in all the commotion you've created."

"You brought me here earlier. Remember? You wished me good luck!"

The guard shook his head. "Yup, I think so."

Carrie pointed to the floor. "Right there, his body was right there!"

"Well there isn't anyone there anymore."

The guard shined the flashlight into Carrie's eyes. "You haven't been smoking weed or drinking have you because J.P. isn't lying dead on the floor or anyone else for that matter."

Carrie squinted and raised her free arm over her eyes, shielding them from the light. "What" Carried asked, "don't you believe me?"

The guard pushed the brim of his hat back and scratched his head with the end of the flashlight. "If there was a body I'd believe you." He shined the flashlight on the spot Carrie pointed to.

Her eyes widened. "I swear to you, he was right there!" She pointed to the floor.

The guard shook his head. "Well I don't know what to say now. There's only one way to find out. We've got to go inside."

"No. I'm not going back inside."

The guard grabbed Carrie's hand and dragged her inside. He growled, "I said let's go inside."

The guard pushed Carrie across the trailer, causing her to stumble over the trash. Her body banged into the wall. The guard shut and locked the door behind them. He kicked aside the garbage as he shined the flashlight back and forth, scanning for a signs that Gilman's body once laid on the floor, searching for blood, body tissue, anything. But the heaps of clothing and garbage and decaying food concealed any visible evidence.

He scratched his head again. "I don't know what to say. You sure you weren't in J.P.'s bedroom when all this happened? J.P. does have a way with women."

Carrie shuttered at the thought. "No, I never went into his bedroom. It all happened right here."

"His bedroom is right back there," the guard said, pointing the flashlight down the hallway. He grabbed Carrie's wrist again and led her toward Gilman's bedroom.

The hallway was littered with more garbage. Carrie could feel her shoes slide on moist areas on the carpet. The walls were decorated in more carnival posters. Carrie didn't read them. She already knew what was printed on them.

The stench became more suffocating as they neared Gilman's bedroom.

"J.P., you in there," The guard asked, knocking on the door

DARK THINGS II

with the end of the flashlight.

No one answered.

"He might be sleeping. He's got two more shows tonight." The guard knocked louder. "Hello, J.P.?"

Still no one answered.

Carrie said, "Maybe I was seeing things. Let's just go." She wanted out of the trailer. She turned and stepped away.

The guard grabbed the nape of Carrie's neck and squeezed. She looked at him from the corner of her eyes. The guard's face showed worry. "We're not leaving until we look into J.P.'s room. You said there was a bead body and we're going to find it."

The guard turned the doorknob. The paint along the doorframe stuck to the dark stain brushed into the door and made a cracking sound when it opened. The room was dark. The windows were closed as were the curtains. The air inside was thick and smelled like sewage. Both Carrie's and the guard's nostril burned as they inhaled. The guard pulled up his shirt collar, trying to filter the stench through his clothes.

He shined the flashlight around the room. The floors were covered in blood, bones, and various parts of human bodies in different stages of decay. The walls looked as though they were sweating as moisture crawled down the paint where it was absorbed by the thick-shagged carpet. In the middle of the room there was a bed covered with a plastic tarp. The dimples in the mattress held congealed pools of urine and black lumps of human excrement.

Carrie placed her hand over her mouth as her diaphragm squeezed and regurgitated her empty stomach. She gagged.

Coming from a corner behind the door, they heard a slurping sound and a heavy breathing. The guard slowly pushed open the door until the doorknob clanked into the wall. He raised the flashlight. The beam crawled along the floor, over garbage and body parts and then onto a large, moving mass of naked flesh.

The flesh was J.P. Gilman's act partner, his brother Jeb. He sat in a wheelchair. His body was just a torso with short pudgy arms and a large head whose jowls seemed to melt over his shoulders and down his chest and back. His stomach flopped over the wheelchair's armrests, hiding them under his skin. His breathing was high-pitched and crackled with each exhale. The left eye was infected with a sty that swelled up and hid the eyeball behind the eyelids.

In Jeb's hands, was J.P.'s decapitated head. It looked as though it were chewed off his shoulders. The end of J.P.'s earlobe disappeared inside Jeb's mouth. His teeth could be heard grinding and crackling the cartilage with each bite until the front of his neck expanded as he swallowed the bitten-off ear.

Carrie screamed. She turned to run but the door slammed shut before she could escape.

"Where do you think you're going," the guard asked in a low, monotone voice.

"What're you doing" Carrie cried, "please, let me go!

Tears welt up in the guards eyes. "J.P. is dead. There isn't anyone to look after and feed our brother Jeb no more except me."

Carrie whipped tears from her eyes and squinted at the nametag on the guard's left breast. It read, *Mitch Gilman Carnival Security Coordinator.*

Mitch's lower lip quivered. "You killed our brother!" He raised the flashlight over his head, holding it like a hammer.

Carrie cried, "I swear it was an accident!"

Carrie's back slid down the door as Mitch began bludgeoning her skull with his flashlight. The blub burst and died as he beat her. Minutes later, Carrie died too.

CUTTING CLASS
by Thomas A. Erb

RICKY Spelling stared out the window that overlooked the playground of Arcadia Falls' Middle school. The array of red, orange, and yellow leaves from the large rows of maple trees lined the small, but well used playground and created a cocoon for all the kids playing and running around below. The fall sun would have normally felt warm and comforting through the thick glass of the classroom's multi-paned windows. But today, it might as well have been another cold brick wall.

"So what are you gonna do," Ray asked.

"I don't know...yet," Ricky responded. His voice cracked and flitted into the humid air of Mrs. Dickson's classroom.

"You can't stay in here forever," The voice from behind him, woke him from his troubled haze.

"Yeah, those stupid jerks have been calling you names since kindergarten man," Dylan added.

"I know," Ricky said, pushing up his thick glasses, and continued to stare out the window.

"Come on, how many times do they have to smash your face into your locker before you do something," Ray added.

"Don't be such a wimp. It's only gym class. Don't let that piece of crap Mr. Brown make you his bitch," Ray shouted.

Ricky shifted on his thin, frail feet. He found his breathing difficult and it was getting worse by the day. He wheezed as he tried to draw in a deep breath. He snatched his inhaler from his pale blue shirt pocket and took a puff. He felt some relief.

"Ah, leave him alone guys. You know he can't do all the pushups and stuff that Mr. Brown wants him to do," Shelly pleaded

"Ah, the hell with that jerk," Ray jumped in. "If you don't

206

go Ricky, he will make your life miserable. You saw what he did to that Felton kid." Ray finished and Ricky watched Ray's reflection as it walked behind Mrs. Dickson's desk

"I know guys. I do the best I can every time but no matter what I do, it's never good enough for him," Ricky said and leaned his head against the window. The coolness felt good on his warm forehead. Soft flicks of rain began to splatter the glass and dark clouds replaced the sunny skies. Dark shadows replaced the warm beams of light and took over the classroom.

"Don't take his crap Ricky," Ray demanded.

Shelly stepped forward and placed a comforting hand on Ricky's frail shoulder. He couldn't feel her touch.

"That's easy for you to say Ray," Shelly said. "You can run the laps and do the pushups and stuff the way Mr. Brown wants you to. It comes pretty darn easy for you," She crossed her arms and finished with a pout.

"Yeah…so what," Ray shouted back. "If Ricky really got out there and tried, he could be just as good as everyone else. If not, well, then he shouldn't be out there."

"How much crap should he have to take Ray?" Shelly shouted and stepped forward into the classroom.

"What do you mean," Ray asked. Ricky watched him cross his arms and plunk down into Mrs. Dickson's cushioned chair.

"Come on, Ricky gets dressed for every class and does the best he can. But that doesn't matter. Everyone just stares and laughs at him and points. It's him and the other fat kids that Mr. Brown picks on for crying out loud." Shelly said. She slammed her hand on the desk and her face turned bright red.

"Well, Shelly's right Ray," Dylan said, then cowered and sunk into one of the desks in the front row.

The room seemed to darken and the shadows claimed all that was once light and filled the room with gray.

"All the more reason to tell that jerk gym teacher to pound rock salt and all the other idiots in your gym class, too, Ricky," Ray punched the large wooden desk and papers were sent flying to the cold gray tiled floor.

Ricky swallowed hard and turned his attention back out the window. This was an ongoing struggle in his life. He had no confidence. His dad was never around. He always had some fire department function to attend to or some bowling league that needed his attention. His mom always told him that it would be alright and everything would be okay. He never had the heart to tell her that she was wrong, that his life sucked, being the skinny kid and always sick. He was the one that everyone glared at and made cruel jokes about. He developed an effective defense system, but it wasn't perfect. Some days still came hard and crying on the bus on the way home wasn't an unfamiliar occurrence.

The silence was broken by a monotone voice that came from a small speaker hanging on the cement wall. Its static-filled words shattered the shadows and sent them retreating into the corners of Mrs. Dickson's room. Ricky cringed and slammed his eyes shut. He hoped the shadows wouldn't return ever again. But knew better.

"All students must report the gymnasium for the State's physical fitness tests. Mr. Brown is waiting for all to take the required test." The cold voice finished and hung in the air like a heavy summer haze.

The only sounds that could be heard in the sixth grade classroom was that of the rhythmic timing of the large numbered clock hanging on the pale green painted wall next to a long poster of the Presidents of the United States, the pounding slapping of the torrential rain battered the windows. But the overriding sound Ricky could hear was that of his racing heartbeat.

Ricky watched as Ray rose and walked over to him, put his arm around him, and leaned into his pale ear.

"Hey Rick, you remember when I brought my Dad's pistol into school a couple of weeks ago," Ray whispered low and Ricky caught the smile and wink Ray shot at Shelly. Ray pulled Ricky in closer. Shelly sneered at him. Ricky knew she didn't hear him.

"Yeah, I remember Ray, so what," Ricky's voice shook and caught in his throat. Ray was always pushing him to be stronger; to be a man and grow a pair. *Whatever that meant*, Ricky thought. No matter how hard he tried, he couldn't make Ray or their dad happy. He was always the scrawny baby and he would never be able to change their perception. He wanted to resist but that never worked. It always ended up with him getting his butt kicked and he became the entertainment at the family dinner table. So he caved like always and let Ray pull him closer-swallowing him up, and whispered into his ear.

"You know what Dad says Ricky; a man can only take so much and this dumb ass gym teacher has had his final joke on you bro," Ray said. And he could feel even more air come of his weak and tired lungs.

The dark clouds penetrated the classroom and large rain drops splattered against the windows and the shadows grew long and stretched out and created eerie shapes against the far wall. Ricky shivered as he felt the temperature in the room drop twenty degrees.

"I think you should just go to the gym Ricky, it's just easier that way." Dylan urged and Ricky watched him as he sank into one of the desks. His tone was one of defeat and desperation to Ricky's ears.

"Dylan's right. You know how Coach Brown can be. Just take the test and get it over with." Shelly's eyes dripped with soft tears as she too took a seat in one of the desks.

"The hell with that you guys. Brown's a dick and he will do nothin' but make Ricky cry. He will get him out there and have him demonstrate all of the tests, knowing that poor Ricky boy here, can barely change into his gym clothes, without being out of breath and he will laugh at him, and hell, they all will." Ricky tried to ignore Ray's harsh words but he couldn't deny what Ray was saying. He had always said the same thing. And the harder thing for Ricky to swallow was that no matter what, Ray was usually right.

"Come on now Ricky, are we gonna take this crap for the rest of your life or are you gonna be a man? Let's teach that piece of crud, who's the boss." Ray's shouting filled Ricky's head and he saw him reach into his jean jacket and pull out a snub nose .38

pistol. He smiled, as he shoved it into Ricky's quivering, sweat-covered hand.

"You don't have to hurt anyone Ricky, just scare the living crap out of them, that's all," Ray nodded and chuckled. Ricky grasped the walnut grip of the pistol.

Ricky heard Shelly and Dylan both jump from their desks.

"Don't listen to Ray, he's crazy! You can't bring a gun into school," Dylan pleaded. The tears streamed down like the pouring rain outside the window.

"It won't solve anything. It will only make us just as bad as Mr. Brown and all those other idiots that make fun of you," Shelly added. She tried to grab a hold of Ricky's arm, but Ricky pulled away as he slowly turned toward the doorway to the hall.

"Screw them Rick!" Ray shoved Shelly backwards and she disappeared, like a wisp of wind, into one of the desks. Ricky stopped in front of the closed door and stared at the window to the lit hallway. He felt Ray's cold grip on his shaking shoulders and stared into his wide eyes. The glint from the glass caught his reflection.

"I've had enough of the namby-pamby shit. There's been enough talk. Brown has had his day and now it's time for you to speak for all of those silently tortured kids, just like us." Blackness came pouring out of Ray's gritted teeth and the long, swirling tentacles of anger and hate slithered out and enveloped all within the classroom.

A loud, high-pitched wailing scream filled Ricky's ears and brought him to his knees and the stench of rotting flesh and brimstone filled the room. The windows crystallized and were covered with ice, as the temperature tanked to the low teens.

"Attention all staff...We are missing one student for the state exam." The blown speaker in Mrs. Dixon's room blared. *"Richard Spelling needs to report to the gymnasium immediately. All staff is to find him and escort him there safely."* The voice over the PA was as cold and vacant as the room Ricky found himself in.

"Don't do it Ricky, it's not right," Dylan begged, coughing from the black mist that filled the room. Ricky's tears were now as

THOMAS A. ERB

ebony as the swirling wisps that teased the white ceiling tiles high, above his spasm-filled body.

Ricky's head exploded into a million, shimmering shards of memories and dreams, of wishful thinking and excruciating flashes of agony and awareness. A swirling hurricane of pain and darkness engulfed him. His frail body dropped to the ground in its wake. He cried out for his mother and it was met with a sledgehammer of frozen blackness, which swallowed him whole. He wept black tears and his blood felt like it would freeze solid under his pale skin.

After a few long moments, Ricky stood up, wiped the black tears from his eyes and picked the revolver up and walked out of Mrs. Dixon's classroom. He left the door wide open. Small whips of dark, claw-like hands gripped the wooden door and slammed it shut behind him with a loud thunderous sound. The hallway was empty. The ghostly shapes thrashed and danced in the darkness as Ricky exited Mrs. Dixon's classroom.

No one followed him out.

No one was left behind.

The room stood silent and empty…the halls of Arcadia Fall's Middle School were filled with screaming children and then echoed with gun fire.

The weeping maple trees shed their leaves like falling tears that were lost in the raging rainstorm swallowing the dark school yard.

About the author:

Thomas A. Erb was born to create. His entire life has been filled with the pursuit of self-discovery through various artistic mediums. His themes range from exploring the hero within us all, to the inner struggles of our teen years and shackles that society clamps on certain "outsiders". It's this passionate path that Thomas digs deep into his written work. He helps pay the bills by freelance illustration and painting movable murals. He lives in upstate New York with his wife, Michelle, daughter; Talana and their two obnoxious dogs, Rask and Duchess. Wesbite: taerb.blogspot.com/ and email: thomasallenerb@gmail.com.

YESTERDAY'S SINS

by Joseph Mulak

RYAN'S hands were shaking as he reached to open the door leading into Shelley's Diner. He had no idea why he was so nervous, but there was a weird feeling in the pit of his stomach as he pulled the door open. He'd only had that same feeling once before, his wedding day.

As he yanked the door open, the aroma of hamburgers and fries wafted out. For a moment, the pleasant scent of cooked food made him forget his original purpose in coming, but then it all came flooding back.

He stood there a few moments, holding the door wide open as if letting someone else go in before him, but no one was there. When he realized what he was doing, he felt foolish and hoped no one had noticed.

Having never been to Shelley's before, Ryan had no idea how busy it would be. It was crowded, the din of customers making it hard to listen. Add that to the sound of food cooking on a grill from the kitchen, dishes clattering as busboys cleaned empty tables, and a bell notifying the waitresses that orders were up. Ryan never did like crowds, so his first instinct was to turn around and leave, but curiosity got the better of him. He needed to find out why he had been summoned.

Despite the racket and the large amount of patrons, Ryan was able to find Jerry with no trouble. He was, after all, a huge man. His beer gut had gotten even bigger since the last time Ryan had seen him and his bushy beard showed traces of gray that hadn't been there before. He had wild, unpredictable eyes, making him appear either slightly child-like or insane.

Just as he was walking over to the table, Jerry looked up and

212

grinned in recognition. He stood up to shake Ryan's hand.

"So good to see you, my friend," Jerry said in his deep, booming voice. His excitement didn't seem quite genuine.

"Yeah, it's been awhile."

"Almost fifteen years, I think."

"That long, eh?" Even as he spoke, Ryan's eyes were glued to the white collar that contrasted with an all-black outfit. At first he was taken aback, thinking that his friend had only called him after all these years to try and save his soul.

Jerry chuckled. "I see you noticed the collar."

"Yeah. Can't really say I'm too surprised, though. I mean, you were always the more religious one of the group."

"I prefer the term spiritual." He motioned to an empty chair. "Are you hungry?"

Ryan shook his head as he sat in the chair. "I thought priests weren't supposed to drink," he said, noticing a half-full bottle of Budweiser and two empties on the table.

The priest shrugged. "I don't see any harm in having a beer every now and then. Want one?"

Ryan shook his head and when the waitress came by to take his order, he asked for coffee. Once she left, Ryan turned his attention back to his old friend.

"So, what made you get in touch with me after all these years?""

"Cutting right to the chase, are we?" Jerry chuckled again, leaning in closer and lowering his voice. "I figured you should be the first to hear this since you were the only one I told I was going to do it."

"Do what?"

The priest had a smug look on his face. "Remember when we were kids and I told you something I always wanted to do?"

"Get laid?"

Jerry burst out with a laugh that seemed a bit much for such a poor joke. Ryan got the impression that he was merely being polite.

"No, the other thing. Come on, you have to remember. It's

213

something I promised I would do someday, no matter how long it took."

He searched his memory and managed to come up with a conversation the two of them had when they were younger, not even teenagers yet. He couldn't remember the entire conversation, but he knew it had something to do with angels.

"You don't mean...." Ryan trailed off. He couldn't even voice the idea. It was too absurd.

Jerry nodded. "Yep. I did it."

"You couldn't have. It's not even possible."

"It's possible. It took me ten years, but I finally found a way to do it."

"How?"

"I'll let you in on that little secret later on."

"Can I see it?"

The smug grin came back. "I was hoping you'd ask."

Both men quickly finished their drinks then left the restaurant.

***

Jerry's home looked like an apartment without a building attached to it. It looked tiny. The church seemed almost just as small. From the outside it looked like it might be able to fit a congregation of fifty people.

If that.

Ryan, not being religious, had no idea how the hierarchy of the priesthood worked. He never knew how one priest got the huge cathedrals with hundreds of parishioners, while others were stuck with these dinky little buildings not much bigger than a Vegas wedding chapel.

"Well, here we are," Jerry announced. "Welcome to my humble abode."

Ryan felt like saying, "You got the humble part right," but decided to keep the opinion to himself.

When they walked in, the house looked smaller on the inside than on the outside. The furniture made it look cramped, and Ryan had to maneuver around a bit to make his way through the living room.

"So, where is it?"

The large man let out another chuckle. "Impatient, aren't we?" He waited for a moment, as if expecting Ryan to answer. "Don't worry. It's downstairs."

As they walked, Ryan asked him, "Are you going to tell me how you caught it?"

"All in due time, my friend. All in due time."

Jerry opened a door in the kitchen that led to a set of stairs leading down into an unfinished basement.

"Unfortunately, the house is paid for by the diocese. They don't like to shell out for luxuries like comfort," Jerry explained. "Well, not when you're the priest of a very small parish." There was no laugh this time, so Ryan couldn't tell if he was being good-natured or if the statement was one of bitterness.

When he reached the bottom of the stairs, nothing could have prepared Ryan for what he was about to see. He hadn't actually thought that Jerry was serious. Being good-natured, Jerry also had a tendency to play practical jokes. Now that he was in the basement, he realized that his friend had not been joking at all.

The beast chained to the concrete wall had long, thin legs with feet that had three talon-like claws, its torso, while still skinny, also looked like it had some muscle tone. There were more claws on its hands that looked as though they could tear a person in half with only one swipe. Its face was almost oblong, and there were two long teeth protruding from its mouth that looked even sharper than its claws. Its entire body was a dull gray color, except for the bat-like wings which were more of a charcoal color.

"Beautiful, isn't it," Jerry remarked as he gazed up at figure before them.

"Beautiful? Are you kidding me? This thing looks like it belongs in a horror movie."

215

DARK THINGS II

"What did you expect? A halo and harp?"

"Well…yeah."

"Well, the Bible never does give an accurate description of what angels look like."

"Yeah, but still…" Ryan took a step toward it and as he did so the creature let out a loud screech, almost deafening him. When he looked over, he noticed the priest was covering his ears.

"What the hell was that?" Ryan asked once the sound had finally faded.

Jerry smiled. "If you liked that, you should hear it sing."

"It sings?"

"Beautifully. It's so magical; it almost puts me into a trance when I hear it."

"Does it do anything else?"

"Well, there is one thing…" Jerry trailed off and Ryan got the impression he was afraid of something. Regaining his composure, the priest continued, "But I'd rather you saw it for yourself."

Ryan was about to press the matter, then decided against it. Instead he asked, "How did you catch it?"

"The story of Elisha."

"Who the hell is Elisha?"

"A biblical prophet. There's a story when he and his servant were attacked by the Syrian army. The servant thought it was the two of them against the whole army, but Elisha prayed for God to reveal his angels and hundreds of angels appeared before the young man."

"I don't get it."

"The angels were invisible until Elisha prayed for them to be revealed to his servant. I also know everyone has a guardian angel that is with us at all times, protecting us. So, I prayed for mine to be revealed and there it was."

"And you caught it."

"It was quite a struggle, but I managed."

"So, now what?"

"What do you mean?"

216

"Well, you've caught this thing. Now what? Put it on display? Use it to become rich and famous?"

"I'm insulted you'd even imply that I would something like that."

"Then what's the point of all this?"

"Proof," Jerry told him. He still kept his eyes on the angel, as if even he couldn't believe he had caught this magnificent being. "Once I reveal this angel to the world, no one would be able to deny the existence of God. Everyone would have to believe. With this one creature, I can save the world."

Ryan felt the priest was deluding himself, but didn't want to stomp on his dream, or his "life's work" as Jerry had called it. "Wow. This is way too much for me to handle in one night."

"You're right. It's getting late. We should go to bed. Why don't you stay the night?"

"Oh, I don't want to impose."

What Ryan actually meant was he didn't think the house was big enough for two people, but he didn't want to offend Jerry.

"Oh, it's no imposition. I can take the couch, and you can have my room."

"Well, I'll stay, but I'll take the couch."

Jerry smiled once again. "Suit yourself."

***

While he slept, Ryan dreamed. Except, they weren't dreams so much as memories. The scene had happened almost ten years ago and he had almost forgotten it. He had tried so hard to forget it. But now, the small details came rushing back to him and he knew that everything he saw now was exactly as it happened.

Ryan found himself watching the scene, not from his own point of view, but that of an onlooker viewing the scene as if perched in the branch of a tree and could see a younger version of himself.

He saw this younger self crouched behind a shrub, watching Brad Denton as he worked. Ryan remembered how he had checked

217

DARK THINGS II

into the man, found out he worked for a landscaping company. After that, it was easy to figure out exactly where he was working.

Since all the other workers were at the front of the house, he felt sure no one would hear anything, since they were at the rear and far enough into the bush.

So all he had to do now was wait.

As he watched the scene unfold before him, he had to wonder what he'd been thinking. He looked at Brad, no shirt, hauling around armfuls of branches, carrying small logs over his shoulder. There didn't seem to be an ounce of fat anywhere on the man's body.

Then, he looked at himself. Years of abusing his body with tobacco, caffeine, alcohol and junk food had already begun to take its toll. Ryan was disgusted at how he had begun to age before his time. His hair was thinning and he had a spare tire that he kept promising himself to do something about, but never got around to actually doing anything.

Since he hadn't had the foresight to bring even so much as a pocketknife for a weapon, he was obviously outmatched. It almost made him cringe to realize how dumb he'd been.

It was that moment when the younger Ryan realized this and turned to make his way back to his car, still crouching to remain unseen. He didn't make it very far when his foot kicked something hard.

The older Ryan didn't have to wait to find out what it was he had kicked. He remembered exactly what it was.

A chainsaw.

Even now he wondered what would have happened if he had never bothered to pick it up. How would things be different if he had taken a slightly different route and had never happened upon it?

His hands shook as he reached down to pick up the saw. It was a smaller one, very light weight. Shaking it, he could hear the swishing of gasoline inside.

He made his way back to his original position behind the shrub and waited for his opportunity. As it turned out, luck was on his side again, as Brad appeared to be working late that day, most likely due to being behind in his work and wanting to catch up.

Dusk was settling when Brad had finally decided to quit for the day and walked toward the house. The shrub Ryan used as cover was directly off a trail, so he figured the target would most likely walk right past him on his way.

He'd been right. The younger man was walking toward him, his T-shirt slung over his shoulder and still wearing his work gloves.

The older Ryan wanted to yell at him, to warn him, but he discovered, as he already suspected, he had no control over the outcome. Things would play out exactly as they had before.

All he could do was watch himself lunge at Brad and yank on the ripcord at the same time. The roar of the tiny chainsaw was almost deafening. The motor itself wasn't loud. Ryan suspected it was simply his own imagination increasing the volume.

As he watched this, bits of another scene played through his mind. Sporadic images of Brad with Ryan's wife, Sandra, flashed before his eyes. He had walked in on them one day, and for a long time afterward was unable to get the image of Brad's face as he mounted the adulteress from behind out of his head.

Even though he had walked out of the room and never returned, never saw or spoke to his wife again, he harbored a hatred toward Brad unlike any he'd ever felt before. A hatred which had driven him to kill another human being.

Sandra's lover was obviously taken by surprise and had no time to react. By the time he realized what was happening, the saw was already digging its way through his skull.

He kept the chainsaw imbedded in Brad's head until the man fell to his knees. At that point, Ryan figured the only thing keeping Brad from falling over was the fact that he was holding him up with the chainsaw. He struggled to yank it out, using all his strength. Finally, he was able to jerk the saw free.

Once the chainsaw was removed, the body fell face first to the ground, convulsed for a moment or two, then remained perfectly

DARK THINGS II

still.

The first part of his plan complete, burying the body where it lay was the only thing left for him to do.

Since the job had not been completed, he figured the workers would have left their tools behind so they were ready to begin work immediately the next day. He found a shovel leaning up against the house, and he returned to where he had left the body and began to dig.

***

He woke from his dream, wondering what could have caused the memories to have come back to him so vividly after trying to ignore them for so long.

He got up from the couch and wandered into the kitchen to get a drink of water. The clock on the stove told him it was 3 am, and he could hear snoring coming from one of the rooms down the hall. Ryan assumed it was Jerry.

Another sound grabbed his attention. It was coming from below him. It sounded like singing.

Ryan walked about halfway down the steps and listened. From somewhere in the basement, came the most beautiful music he'd ever heard. An immediate calm came over him as he continued to get closer and listened to the entrancing sound.

The singing stopped before he reached the bottom of the steps. Since there was no one else in the basement, he figured it must have been the angel.

"You should hear it sing," Jerry had said.

He approached the creature who was now staring at Ryan, following his every move.

"I liked your singing."

The angel did not respond.

"Could you sing some more for me?"

Again, it showed no sign of understanding.

Both, creature and man, regarded each other for a long time.

220

Ryan, beginning to feel awkward, finally broke the silence.

"I had a dream, you know." He paced the room as he spoke, the angel following him with its eyes. "I have a feeling it had something to do with you. I mean, it had to. I haven't thought about that day in a long time. This can't be a coincidence."

He stopped pacing long enough to turn and face the creature for a moment. "What do you want from me?"

When it didn't respond, he continued walking.

Ryan let out a chuckle. "You know, this almost reminds me of one those cheesy movies of the week. This would be the part where I realize what I did was wrong and repent and everything's okay." He walked past a workbench and let his fingers run across the various tools laid out on the surface. When they touched a hatchet, he stopped to pick it up in his hands.

"Here's the problem," he said. "You can't exist."

The angel gave him a puzzled look, which was the first time it showed any sign it understood what he was saying.

"I spent my whole life believe there was nothing out there. Especially after I killed Brad. I mean, if there's no God, then I don't have to worry about it, right? But now," he walked toward the angel, hatchet in hand, "things have changed."

He stopped within a few feet of the creature. "I came so close to forgetting about Brad's death. Almost as if it never happened. It took me a long time to get rid of the guilt, and then you come along and bring it all back in the space of a few hours."

There was a short pause as he gazed at the beast one more time, noticing the puzzled look had been replaced by one of fear, as if it was reading his mind.

"But if you're dead," Ryan continued, "then you can't make me remember anymore." He raised the weapon above his head. "Please, don't take this personally. I just can't take the memories anymore. This is the only way I can move on."

He lunged, burying the hatchet in the angels head. A thick, white substance, almost slimy, squirted out, covering Ryan as the angel fell to the ground.

DARK THINGS II

Leaving the axe buried in the creature's skull, he turned to make his way back to the staircase, noticing an odor in the air that hadn't been there before. Sulfur? Brimstone? He couldn't be sure, but it was forgotten completely once a feeling of panic overwhelmed him. He knew he couldn't stay in this house. What would Jerry say when he found out Ryan had killed the angel?

But he didn't move. He stood there, staring down at the creature, instantly regretting what he'd done. He felt a tightness, almost squeezing sensation, in his chest making it difficult for him to breathe. His heart seemed to beat faster now. He attributed this to remorse.

He was distracted from these symptoms as the singing started once again, this time sounding as if choked by tears. Ryan hadn't taken his eyes off the creature, who still lay on the floor, unmoving.

He turned and saw another angel climbing the stairs. Where had that one come from? he wondered. He didn't have an answer, but it was obvious it was the second angel who sang as it wept, its voice fading as it climbed the steps and left the basement.

Something wrenched in Ryan's chest. The tightness he'd felt moments before had slowly expanded into pain, which seemed to be moving into his neck and shoulders.

He doubled over, holding his chest as the pain increased, eventually bringing him to his knees. He tried to call out, hoping Jerry would hear him, but he found he couldn't utter a sound as he fell to the floor completely, next to the lifeless body of the angel.

Jerry's words echoed in his mind about guardian angels. The priest had told him everyone had one. Jerry had also mentioned the one he'd caught was his own. Ryan briefly wondered what it meant for his friend now that he'd murdered it. Had he doomed the priest? He couldn't know for sure.

He forgot about it once he realized the one he saw leaving moments ago must have been...*Oh no,* Ryan thought as the realization took hold. *No, it's not possible.*

He didn't have time to let this new knowledge sink in, as he found himself slowly fading.

JOSEPH MULAK

He opened his eyes and saw he was no longer in Jerry's basement. Instead, he was in a room, which he instantly recognized as once being his bedroom. But that was a long time ago, back when he and Sandra had still been together.

At first he thought it might be another memory, but realized it was different. He wasn't viewing the scene from outside himself as before. He was in the room.

He didn't understand how he came to be in the house he once lived in. Since he hadn't spoken to Sandra in almost ten years, he couldn't be sure if even she still resided there.

He was interrupted by noises. He turned his head and saw Brad and Sandra on the bed, which confused him since he knew Brad had been dead for close to ten years.

Slowly, the familiarity of the scene dawned on him. This was exactly how it looked ten years ago when it had inadvertently walked in on them. The stench of sweat. Sandra on her knees, face buried in the mattress. Brad, behind her, too intent on his thrusting to notice anyone else in the room. The look of intense pleasure on Brad's face made Ryan want to vomit.

Ryan could stand nor more of this. He lunged for the door and pulled as hard as he could, only to find it locked. He kept pulling, though he knew it was useless, even putting his foot up on the wall to brace himself. The door wouldn't budge.

He banged on it as loud as he could, screaming until his throat hurt. No one came. And obviously, the lovers couldn't hear him since the noise he made didn't seem to faze them one bit.

Finally, exhausted, he turned and slunk down to the floor, back against the wall. He put his head in his hands, sobbing, as he realized what was happening.

He was trapped in this memory.

Something inside him—morbid curiosity, most likely—made him look up at the two lovers. He couldn't take his eyes off them, even though it caused him such emotional torment to watch, and the thought occurred to him that this might be an eternal punishment. This might be his hell.

DARK THINGS II

It might have been Ryan's imagination, but for a split second, he could have sworn Brad winked at him.

About the author:

Joseph Mulak is the author of several short stories, most of them in the horror genre. He lives in North Bay, Ontario with his four children and a dog named Tito, where he is currently at work on more stories, a YA novella and a novel. Visit him at josephmulak. wordpress.com.

PALE IN THE NIGHT
by Kurt M. Criscione

RETURNING to life was a pain in the ass. Sarah floated in the serene non-existence of purgatory, but harsh reality wanted her back, demanded to have her back. Resurrection was a real bitch.

It didn't happen all at once. The first sensation was pain, Sarah *felt* again, after the complete absence of all sensation it was cataclysmic. A sharp spike of pain pierced her skull. It stabbed through the right side of her body. Her back arched and she rolled over. The pain dulled and she sucked in a deep breath. She felt an itching across her flesh, drying blood and clinging dirt. She balled her fist and she felt sodden grit in her palm.

Her hearing returned, a slight ringing in her ears gave way to her own ragged breathing. As she sucked in another deep lungful of air she could smell again. A mixture of coppery blood, damp earth, and spoiled potatoes. It reminded her of a musty basement, like the root cellar of her grandfather's hunting property.

She tried to grab onto the thought, to any memory, but it dissolved in a new throb of pain through her skull. She reached toward her face, slowing her breathing, her fingers found sticky blood coating the right side of her face. She tasted more blood in her mouth and she spit on the floor. She pushed herself up on trembling arms and stifled a moan.

She could see the floor before her, she blinked, the motion making her feel sick and she steadied herself. The floor was loose earth, matted in the shape of her body and muddy from her blood. She choked on a sob and looked around the room, her gaze settled on an incongruity. A single red, high heeled shoe stood across the room.

She was having trouble determining distance and she craned

225

her neck to look up. A single bare bulb, barely brighter than a nightlight shimmered overhead, it cast the dim glow over what she could only consider a stall, or perhaps a cell.

Four-by-four posts were hammered into the floor and cheap sheets of plywood made up the perimeter of her cell. The door was a reinforced piece of plywood. She pushed on it with her foot and it flexed but didn't move otherwise. She heard the rattle of a chain. Tears sprang to her eyes.

She rolled to her back and slowly sat up. Nausea pulsed through her at the motion and her skull throbbed in time to her heart beat. She gingerly touched the right side of her head, a sob escaping her as she felt more blood and a soft sponginess. Her hands shook and she pulled her knees to her chest. She wept.

"We're dead. We're dead or we soon will be. We don't even remember. What don't we remember?" She talked to herself and rocked. The pain coming and going.

"Shut up! We're stronger than this do you want to be her?" Sarah blinked and turned toward the lone shoe. The high heel had a broken ankle strap and a darker splotch of red on its toe.

"Great now I'm arguing with myself. Hurt and insane, that's great. What the hell am I supposed to do?" Her voice was soft, a little girl's, the other voice was a hurt rasp, filled with anger.

"Get moving. Find Jason." Sarah blinked, memories surfacing from the murky depths, they came in a flash of lightening.

The inside of a tent and the soft caress of a flannel shirt on sweaty bare flesh, his smell still on the cloth and a tingle still on her skin. Jason. A rumble of thunder and a flash of lightening, a silhouette reflected on the canvas. Jason. Another flash of lightening and a looming shadow moving...converging...both shadows struggling...a scream, perhaps her own? The sound of canvas tearing...flaring pain. Oblivion.

She stopped rocking, the memory helped to center her. She still wore the flannel shirt, though now covered in mud and blood, was stiff where it had dried and clung to bare skin everywhere else. She had managed to get her boots on during the attack. A laugh

226

escaped her. Better had she found some shorts.

"Get moving girl." The gruff voice, again.

Sarah looked around the room and her eyes alit on a shallow gap beneath one of the plywood walls. She crawled toward the gap and began to claw at the earth with her bare fingers. The loose dirt gave way a mere six inches down to thicker clay. A sob wracked her shoulders and one of her nails tore free. She shrieked and leaned back, bile flooding her mouth, and her vision swam. Two deep steadying breaths later and her vision cleared.

A creek of floor boards cut her sobs. She clapped a hand over her mouth and stared up at the ceiling. Boards creaked again from somewhere within the house above. Had her captor heard her scream? Her breathing sped up and she looked for a weapon other than a sack of rotting potatoes. She saw the stiletto heel.

She snatched up the shoe and returned to digging into the clay—the sharp heel cutting deep furrows. She widened and deepened the whole beneath the wall. Limbs trembling and muscles in her neck burning she pushed her limbs to go faster.

A loud thud scared another scream from her. She bit her lip before it got too loud. She glanced back at the thick boards overhead. Light was piercing through the cracks between the boards, motes of dust dancing. The boards flexed. A door slammed, heavy footsteps, and the sound of something being dragged. The light disappeared as the shadow and its burden passed overhead and then trailed off deeper into the house.

She waited. Her thoughts a jumble, *Was Jason up there? Was that him being dragged? Where the hell was she?* She dove at the hole without further thought. Her shoulders were just slightly too wide and she had to twist and kick. She forced her left shoulder down against her breast with a grunt. Her shirt snagged and she grunted again and for the first time in her life she wished she had smaller breasts. The flannel tore and she slide forward. She freed her arm and clawed the ground ahead of her. She slid through the gap, tightening down again as she worked her hips through, she stretched as far forward as her battered body allowed.

DARK THINGS II

Her hand slopped into gooey warmth, sticky mud and something else, as she closed her eyes and pulled her feet through the gap and rolled over unto her back. She found herself in a much larger room; several forty watt bulbs hanging from bare wires at intervals across the room. More than half of them were burnt out but those that remained created pools of light.

The room was filled with evenly spaced high tables. She used one to slowly rise to her feet. Her legs trembled. Her right hand was covered in bloody mud to the wrist and she grimaced. She pushed back from the table and one of the hanging bulbs smacked into the side of her head. She reached up, felt the bulb and the switch beneath her finger, turning the light on without thinking. A pool of light surrounded her and she blinked hard, eyes dazzled.

They adjusted, her vision clearing the room into sharp focus. She screamed. It was a raw wail, a torrent of emotion that could not be stopped. The sound was echoing back on her by the time something snapped in her throat, the scream gasping off. She had found Jason and several others. She leaned against his table, her hand mired in his overrun blood.

Everywhere she looked she saw horror and blood. He was strapped down, nude, his chest cracked open. Flesh was flayed; muscles, nerves, and conduits all pulled off white bone. Her eyes flickered across his body and finally stopped on his face. His perfectly untouched face, clean and scrubbed, his eyes closed as if in slumber. His hair was combed, perfectly feathered over his right eye.

Her body began to tremble harder, the voices in her head were both silent. Black spots were overwhelming her vision again. A door slammed and feet hammered overhead. She blinked rapidly. *Had her scream summoned her tormentor?* Tears streamed down her face and she looked around for a hiding space. The room was all shadows and nooks; the tables covered in corpses at various states of decay and rusty bloodstains. Her gaze stopped on the back wall. It was covered in benches and tools, all sorts of tools. Hammers, axes, chisels, and saws. Augers and drills and garden implements. The only unifying theme was the rust of dried blood and the violence inherent in their design.

Incongruously, nestled among the bloody tools and debris, was a calendar. It was turned to last year, August 1984, a large breasted woman held up a power drill. A surge of anger stiffened her spine, the raspy voice returned.

"No further to go, Sarah. Only one way out." Feet hammered down stairs, drawing closer. She leapt forward, snatching an axe from the table and she moved toward the single door into the room. She slipped a knife into her belt as she passed Jason's table.

The footsteps stopped and she could hear chains rattling. She stepped up beside the door and grasped the axe tightly to her chest, breath ragged in her bloody throat.

Her captor grunted and slammed the flimsy door to her empty cell. The door beside her burst open, swinging toward her with brutal force. The dirt floor was uneven and stopped the door mere inches from slamming into her. He lunged into the room looking left and right. He was huge.

Back to her, he was a massive man, at least seven feet-tall, his bald head nearly touching the ceiling. He stepped out around the door and turned on her, so fast, so huge, he grinned. She gasped.

Taken as a whole he was a monster, but if one ignored his face, didn't look too close or maybe started at his feet, he looked a *Metal God.* He was one part Kiss, one part Judas Priest. Tank engineer boots with extra belts and four inch platforms added to his considerable bulk. He wore leather pants, his waist crisscrossed with chains and belts. A leather vest hung open revealing a chiseled body builder's physique. It might have been attractive save for the scars marring his flesh and its pale ashen hue.

Something was wrong with his left arm, the flesh of his shoulder was stretched, the muscles wrong, thick coils of scar tissue wrapped his shoulder and upper arm. It almost appeared as if his arm had been surgically reattached, Sarah wasn't certain doctors could do that. If he had bolts in his neck and green skin she would have thought he was Frankenstein.

DARK THINGS II

He had a baby face, smooth and lacking any hair, his eyes were washed out, almost colorless, pale. He saw her and his face broke into a grin. Sarah screamed when seeing that his mouth was filled with serrated, metal teeth. As he grinned, the sharp edges cut into his lips, blood ran from the corners of his mouth. His massive hands were covered in gore to the elbow and he wiped his chin, depositing more blood than he removed. His other hand wandered down to stroke a sudden massive hard-on; it swelled down his inner thigh.

She got the sense that he had stopped, to deliberately pose, that he enjoyed the attention, enjoyed her eyes on his body.

Sarah shrieked and charged. Pale looked startled, but still managed to turn aside as the axe swept the air and smashed into one of the tables. The blow jarred her, teeth clattering she swung again, over head. Pale sidestepped again, a dry laugh escaping his throat. The axe smashed into one of the rotting corpses on the table. Green flesh erupted, splattering like pudding, putrid bones collapsed and the blade caught in the corpse.

Pale stepped forward and grabbed the heft of the axe with one hand and slapped her in the chest with the other. The pain was instant and intense and she dropped to the floor clutching her left breast. Another soft chuckle and one of his massive paws grabbed her hair. He twisted his wrist, snarling the hair into a tight knot, and pulled her from the floor. Tears sprang to her eyes as her scalp burned.

Sarah kept her cool, and reached up to grab his wrist, and then pulled, trying to ease the torment of her scalp. With the other hand she reached down to her belt and found the handle of the hunting knife. She shrieked and stabbed the knife into his meaty forearm. The blade punched into his flesh, scraped across his ulna, and jammed its blunt back against the radial.

He immediately released her, staggered back with legs stiffened from shock, and tripped over a rusty tool box and slipped in the corpse ooze. She rose as he went down. She snatched a shovel from the ground as he sat, his steel teeth bared in an animal snarl.

She stepped forward and swung the shovel with everything she had left in her. The pan struck him flat in the face, a loud twang of metal striking metal, and the heft of the tool snapped with a dry crack. Her shoulder, wrenched from her burrowing, gave out. Her left arm, wracked with pins and needles, fell limp and useless to her side.

Pale dropped, laid-out cold, blood running from both nostrils and corners of his mouth. A tremble ran through her body and she turned toward the door. The vision in her right eye was fading in and out and the adrenaline rush had spiked the blood flow to her damaged skull. It felt as if it would split from all the pressure. The image of the open doorway shivered into two blurry openings and she stumbled toward freedom. With Jason dead and her captor down she only had one goal. She smacked into the door jam and took a few deep breaths, her vision cleared and the pressure in her head abated. She glanced back; Pale was still laid out, his leg shaking in some kind of fit.

A wide, sparsely lit hall ended in a wide set of stairs. The left side of the hall was lined with thin plywood doors, leading into the 'stalls'. The right side of the hall contained a single door, a slab of steel inset into concrete. She staggered like a drunk, her right hand touching the wall to keep her on course. She paused at the odd door, the cool metal hummed underneath her fingers. Beside the door was a keypad and above was a vent, it breathed cool air down on her and she shivered. The cold air was refreshing.

"Bitch!" His voice was cold, sepulchral. Sarah gasped and turned from the cool metal and looked back into the abattoir. Pale sat up and wiped the blood from his face with his hand. He rose to one knee, stopped to look at the knife jammed through his arm, pulled the blade free, and then tossed it aside.

Tears sprang to her already blurry eyes. The staircase swam and shimmered and she lurched toward salvation. She felt a surge as unknown reserves were tapped and she hit the stairs at a full run. Her hands clawing the way before her she slammed into the door at the top and it swung freely. The sound echoing through the sprawling house. His laughter followed her.

DARK THINGS II

The hallway was unlit though not completely dark. Light bled from other rooms from this floor and also above. She turned around and took in her four options rapidly; one door to the rear of the house, and two doors across from each other, right and left, into the wings of the house. But her vision was arrested by the massive double front doors.

She slammed the basement door closed and was glad to discover two small latches. She doubted they would contain the massive man, but she locked them anyway, and then limped toward the front door.

The door didn't even budge, not a rattle or flex, as she pulled on the handle and kicked the bottom plate. The knob twisted freely within her grasp but the door itself didn't move. Two dead bolts marred the center of the jam, requiring keys.

The basement door rattled and thrummed as Pale smashed into it. It held. She glared at the door, gave it a final kick, and then ducked into the door to her right. She stepped into the room on the right side of the house, at one time it was an ornate and stately sitting room. Two large dusty sofas faced one another under aging covers. A massive fireplace dominated one entire wall. Black soot discolored the once white walls. She tried to ignore the fire blackened skulls that grinned from the mantle and hearth.

She heard the splintering crack of wood giving away back in the hall. Her heart hammered in her chest. The calm overcame her as more adrenaline dumped from her new reserve. A high backed chair stood under a billowing shroud and she reached for it. It was sturdy, heavily carved mahogany, she staggered under the weight—more dragging than carrying the chair back into the foyer.

Pale's arm had reached through a hole in the door; he was blindly working the latches. The lock tripped and the door creaked open and he came through in all his gory metal god glory. He even paused for effect, a 'look at me' gesture. She looked and willing life back into her numb left arm, hefting the chair with all her might. Pale sighed, the chair took him full in the chest and he dropped back down the stairs with a grunt and a scream. His great mass broke several of the risers, the cacophony of noises continued for what seemed like minutes. Though Sarah knew it was her addled mind that contributed to the slow motion effect of the fall.

Sarah stood, tension ebbing and flowing throughout her body. She turned and wandered back into the sitting room. She stood staring at the shrouded furniture and willed her mind to think, to function. One of the sheets moved in a soft ruffle and she tensed again. She relaxed as another current of air moved the blanket.

Picture windows dominated the front wall of the house, rotting curtains hung in thick, layered, sheets. They eddied with the breeze and she felt hope re-ignite. She practically leapt across the room; grabbing handfuls of the aging fabric she tore the curtains right from the wall. It was damp, musty, and heavy; once she started pulling the whole wall came apart. The fabric tore, the hangers pulled from the wall, the entire mass came tumbling down and she danced back.

The windows were painted into the frame, numerous layers of peeling lead paint, making them completely immobile. She cursed and screamed as she heaved her body against the sash. The window wouldn't budge. A single broken pane blew cool air into her face, mocking her with its freedom. Her left arm was once again going numb, losing strength. It wasn't properly seated in the socket and the exertion was making her nauseous, pain lanced her side. The front yard was overgrown and hidden behind layers of trees. Set well back from any visible road she could see hills in the distance. A far-off pair of headlights were weaving along the hill. They appeared to be heading toward the trees, possibly a road that would wind past the house.

Desperation surged through her, she needed to get out of the house, make it too those trees before that car came and went. She surveyed the room and stopped on a low coffee table. Its surface was scarred from mistreatment. It looked like someone had been using it for a chopping block. But that just meant it was all the more sturdy. Sarah grabbed the edges of the table and pulled, her back strained from the effort. The table had to be made from solid oak.

DARK THINGS II

She dragged it a few inches along the floor, but otherwise made no progress. It was too heavy and she was far too damaged.

Gasping for air, she looked around the room for a better tool, she shuddered as her eyes rolled over the carnage in the hearth, but she forced herself to look. Among the charred and blackened bones she spied the handle of the poker. The hearth was huge, fully six feet wide and almost as tall. She could have stepped inside, and if not to hurt, she could have climbed the massive chimney to freedom. The tools for the fire place were even more robust than standard: massive tongs, retaining chains, and a poker that was just over six feet long.

It was more a pole arm than a fireplace tool, half its length was forged steel the rest was stout oak shaft, and the hooks on the end looked more like a pick then a poker. She leveled it like a spear, hooking the heft into her armpit. She gripped with both hands, the left still ineffectual. She charged the window and steel tip popped through one of the panes without resistance; she reversed, pulling the hooked tool back through the window. The hooks caught on the muntin and transoms of the next panes and the whole center of the window shattered.

Using the bar, she cleared the entire sash, and with barely a thought, she leapt through the window and into the scraggly grass beyond. She dropped the pick and cleared most of the broken glass. She laid on the grass breathing deeply, giddy waves of emotion fluttering in her belly. Back in the house she could hear furniture splintering. Why couldn't the bastard just stay down?

She rolled over and prepared for his appearance. He loomed into the window, a snarl twisting his already ugly features into something more bestial. Splinters of wood marred the side of his face and his left forearm.

Sarah acted; her hand closed around the heft of the poker. She stood, lunging off her legs, and thrust the poker out ahead of her. The blunted tip caught him below his right clavicle and punched into his chest, into the thick meat of his upper pectoral. He grunted, gnashed his serrated teeth together, tearing his lips and mouth to bloody meat. She pushed until the hooks stopped any further penetration. She released her grip and staggered, tripped, and rolled away from the window.

He tore the poker from his chest with a howl. He coughed blood and disappeared back into the room. A second howl of pain and anger.

Sarah blinked and then pushed back to her feet. She turned to run, her brain fixating on the head lights on the road, sheer determination to get to help, to get away. She made three shaky steps and then halted. A sleek black car sat idling in the drive way. The headlights dazzled her. The well dressed man stood beside the open driver's side door, starring at her. At least she thought she felt his eyes upon her. It was hard to tell, he was a silhouette in a suit of black. Only the glint of blue lenses on his eyes denoted the direction of his gaze, his head cocked to side.

Sarah took a few tentative steps toward the figure and a smile broke out across his face. It stopped her cold. It stretched his face, wider than normal, sinister, all teeth. She shivered, a whimper worked through her throat, her brain misfired and for a second she saw a purple haze around the stranger, swirling and filled with a crackle of black lightening. Then the door to the house banged open and she turned.

Pale roared, the poker in one hand and a massive cleaver in the other. Thick syrupy blood oozed from the wound on his shoulder. His roar was all sound and emotion, no words. Sarah shrieked and would have curled up then and there, but suddenly the stranger was standing before her. He wrapped an arm about her shoulders.

"Pale! Enough. Clean up this mess, get that window boarded and take care of those wounds. We'll talk later," all delivered in a clipped British tone.

Sarah shuddered again. She pulled away from the supportive arm and looked at the stranger. Now that he wasn't standing behind the headlights of the car she could see him better. He looked like no one special. He was tall and in decent shape, his gray suit was impeccably tailored. Wide at the shoulders, narrowing down his body to the highly polished, pointed toes of his shoes. He wore a gray

DARK THINGS II

vest, a black shirt and a black tie. His hair was perfectly combed and probably held in place with half a can of Aqua Net. He was clean shaven and his eyes were hidden behind blue glasses. His mouth was wide, as the door to the house slammed behind Pale's retreating back, it began to quirk. The corners of his mouth twitching into a smile, it was as if he was fighting that massive, unsettling, grin.

"You've had a very trying time, my dear. It's remarkable that you made it this far on your own. I don't know if that's a fault in my design or if you're simply that lucky. From the looks of you I doubt you'll survive the night. Shame really, the boy is going to be a pain. This does present certain problems; it will hasten my time line, but over all this might be beneficial." He paced around her as he talked. Half of what he was saying seemed to be directed more to him or the air. He paused to prod her and she grimaced as pain raced through her arm.

"Right, well, no use wondering about what should or could be, here we go. If you follow the driveway to the end and take a left on the road it will lead you to the hills. If you have the fortitude you can walk the seven miles into town. Tell them of the horrors in the hills, of the Pale man and his gardens of corpses…err…did you see the gardens? No matter. You may survive if they get you to the hospital. That's a fair chance, no? Now if you're really brazen you could take a right and head down the road until it becomes a dirt track. After a mile there is a fence, it becomes a state park, only three miles in is a Ranger station. Much closer but no road going directly to it…and there's always the chance that Pale slipped out and slaughtered the entire station. You have to play the odds. Now lass, remember the Pale man in the hills has come to kill, again. Exciting times, I hope that history remembers you." He leaned in close and kissed the top of her head, she shuddered and staggered away from him. The grin stretched across his face, perfectly white and perhaps a little too sharp, his teeth shone in the lamp light.

He chuckled as she shook her head, trying to clear the visions, they kept coming and going. She staggered away from the strange man, waiting for him to snatch her and drag her back into the house. But all he did was watch her, then he reached into the car and shut off the engine. She staggered another twenty-yards before turning to look back again. He waved to her and she broke into a trot. A second wind…hell a fourth or fifth wind in all reality struck her and she broke through the trees and unto the road.

She looked left and then right. The vision in her right eye occluded again, a vision of men in uniforms crucified to a burning watch tower assaulted her. She turned left and began to walk down the road. Seven miles to town, left right left…the pale man was killing in the hills.

Left, right, left…seven miles.

About the author:

Kurt M Criscione has written and told stories since he was a small child. In the past three years he's become serious about getting published and no longer doing it "just for himself". He writes genre blending stories usually Horror and Fantasy, occasionally the Dark Space Opera. He's starting to make a splash with his Dark Fantasy Anti-Heros Keegan and Slater.

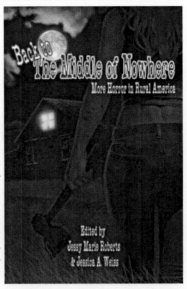

THE PLACE TO GO FOR ZOMBIE AND APOCALYPTIC FICTION

LIVING DEAD PRESS

WHERE THE DEAD WALK

www.livingdeadpress.com

Breinigsville, PA USA
25 October 2010
247988BV00002B/1/P